PRAISE FOR

THE

Pretty CROOKED

SERIES

· ·

"Fans of mystery and suspense will enjoy the fast-paced style of the Pretty Crooked series. Readers who enjoyed Ally Carter's Heist Society and love romantic tension will relish this second entry and look forward to the conclusion in the last book."
—*VOYA*

"A pretty twisted, modern-day Robin Hood story."
—Melissa de la Cruz, *New York Times* bestselling author of the Blue Bloods series

"Filled with mystery, high-tension heists, and flirting with an enigmatic bad boy, Pretty Crooked kept me hooked right up to the action-packed ending."
—Tera Lynn Childs, author of the Oh. My. Gods., Forgive My Fins, and Sweet Venom series

"Tantalizing. For fans of Sara Shepard's Pretty Little Liars books."
—ALA *Booklist*

BOOKS BY ELISA LUDWIG

PRETTY CROOKED
PRETTY SLY
PRETTY WANTED

Pretty
SLY

Elisa Ludwig

KATHERINE TEGEN BOOKS
An Imprint of HarperCollins Publishers

Library of Congress Cataloging-in-Publication Data
Ludwig, Elisa.
  Pretty sly / Elisa Ludwig. — 1st ed.
      p. cm.
  Sequel to: Pretty crooked.
  Summary: Fifteen-year-old Willa takes to the road with
Aidan in a stolen car after her artist mother disappears,
heading for the Santa Barbara, California, hotel from which
her mother sent an email, but soon they are the targets of a
nationwide manhunt.
  ISBN 978-0-06-206610-7 (pbk.)
  [1. Fugitives from justice—Fiction. 2. Missing persons—
Fiction. 3. Crime—Fiction. 4. Identity—Fiction. 5. Mothers
and daughters—Fiction. 6. California—Fiction.] I. Title.
PZ7.L9762Ps 2013   2012008898
[Fic]—dc23   CIP
                                                   AC

Typography by Joel Tippie and Laura Lyn DiSiena
15 16 17 18 19   PC/RRDH   10 9 8 7 6 5 4 3 2 1

First paperback edition, 2015

TO MY FAMILY–who taught me what love and protection are all about.

PROLOGUE

"JUST GO!" AIDAN yelled.

There wasn't time to sort it out. I had to jump. The man was right behind us now, yelling. Aidan was depending on me, and we were in this together. I inhaled big gulps of air like I was about to dive underwater. Counted *one, two, three* . . .

As my feet left the wooden planks, cold air rushed around my face, so sharp it was almost a burning sensation. My arms flapped uselessly at my sides. I wasn't flying. I was falling.

On the way down there was nothing but nothing. Air. A painful silence. For minutes, it seemed.

Then my feet jammed hard, and I landed in a heavy squat, snow crunching all around my sneakers, my bones thrumming from the impact.

Three seconds later, Aidan fell beside me, flinging bits of crystalline ice.

We looked at each other and then up.

The man had disappeared somewhere inside the house. He was coming down or calling the cops. He could report us. He probably would report us. My heart was in my throat, hard and whole as a jawbreaker.

Okay, so this break-in had been a bad idea. Aidan was right. We'd pushed our luck a little too far. If only—

Don't think.

Aidan was on his feet. I got up, too. And we ran like hell.

On the other side of the building was our stolen car, but we both knew it was too risky to go that way. We didn't need to say it out loud. In all the days we'd been on the road together we developed a silent language. We had to head for the trees, even though it was impossible to gauge how deep they were or what lay beyond them.

Aidan was like a lightning bolt, several paces ahead, the reflective strip on his bag catching the bright white around us. He turned around and urged me on. It frustrated me that he was naturally faster. I pushed as hard as I could to keep up with him. My ankle was sore from the fall and the pain rang out with every step, but I couldn't pay attention to that now.

Our rhythm was steady for a few moments: the sound of our shoes swallowed up in the blue holes of the snow, punctuated by the bag flapping on my back and my own heavy breathing.

Keep going, Willa.

The cold air raged through my lungs. Gravity had us racing down the slope of a hill, legs rubber-banding our bodies onward into the thicket of pale-barked branches. The last bit of daylight was sputtering out in purple splashes on the sky but the world bleached out to a blur between my now-frozen eyelashes.

In the distance I heard the sound of a car starting. And was that a siren, too? Maybe I was imagining the siren part.

The déjà vu hit then, so powerful I almost lost my balance: I'd been here before, and not just in my head. The night I broke into Kellie's house. Chased by cops. Busted.

I couldn't do that again. I *wouldn't*.

Please, I thought. *Just let us get out of here.*

I closed my eyes as I wished and kept running, foolishly. I knew I could trip on the twigs scattered over the snowy ground or run into a tree, but I had to play by the wishing rules.

Never mind that I'd broken every other rule in the book. I probably didn't deserve to get out of this.

"Willa!"

I opened my eyes and saw what Aidan was pointing to, lights and flashes of blue glass ahead.

Through the trees, a tall building loomed in front of us, its wings like open arms welcoming us back to civilization. Groups of tourists hovered on the sidewalk around it. Stateline, Nevada's casinos and hotels. Surely we could get lost in a crowd like this.

It was our light at the end of the tunnel. Our neon, blinking light. Maybe my wish was going to come true after all. Maybe I really was lucky.

We just. Had. To run. A little farther.

Soon, we'd be on blacktop again. I sped up, anticipating its hard support.

My legs were caked in snow. I could see us mirrored in the side of the enormous building, our bodies dark and distorted, emerging from the woods like figures from a nightmare. But this wasn't a nightmare. This was our life. Our life on the lam.

ONE

THE SAFE WAS empty.

As in vacant. Cleaned out. Filled with nothing.

My fists opened and closed at my sides. Shock blotted out the rest of the room, the wreckage of my mom's closet, even Aidan standing next to me.

"The money's gone," I said out loud finally, the words at once both obvious and foreign on my tongue. I was referring to my mom's painting fortune, the money we were supposed to be living on, and though Aidan probably had no idea what I was talking about specifically, he could see that in the most general terms this was all very, very bad.

I could only stare into the flat silver void of the open metal box, as if by staring I might psychically fill it back up, the green bills in their neat little rubber-banded stacks, flying in reverse through the room and landing in soft thumps. As if I could go back in time to a moment where the money, as far as I knew, was still in the safe.

And why stop there, really? While I was at it, I would've liked to unsee all of the chaos of my ransacked house. Fling my mom's clothes onto their hangers, her scarves and underwear and socks swishing into place in closed-up drawers, send the sheets sailing to the ceiling so they could land on the bed, flat and even and unwrinkled. The downy snow of feathers on the carpet floating up and into the mattress slits, which would knit themselves back together seamlessly. The shattered bits of the ceramic lamp reassembling into wholeness.

Then my room: My books filing one by one in an airborne arc onto the shelves. The tangled heap of clothing and makeup and shoes on the floor unknotting and separating into the carefully organized arrangement I'd once maintained. The spilled nail polish whirring a pink stream into its little bottle.

Us too. Aidan and me scrambling backward, sucked down the hallway, the expressions of surprise at each new bit of destruction falling off our faces like discarded masks. Our cries of dismay garbling demonically into our throats. The breath refilling our lungs. The front door swinging open and pulling us back out into the Arizona dusk.

Aidan and me, kissing, just outside the house. That's where I'd have to stop.

Our first kiss. His arms encircling me. The herbal smell of his soap. His fingers threading through my hair.

That one perfect meeting of our lips and breath and skin.

Sure, there were lots of moments leading up to the kiss that I would've liked to forget. Glimpsing the flannel-shirted intruder dashing out my back door. The two of us chasing him across town in Aidan's car, to no avail. Me returning, dejected, to see what had become of my house, certain that this had been all my fault. My comeuppance for messing with the Glitterati. Hell, I'd erase the last three months if I could.

But not if it meant losing those crazy perfect few seconds of Aidan bounding up the driveway. Coming back for me. The sudden thrashing of my heart as he neared. The unexpected warmth of his mouth. No one ever forgot their first kiss, did they?

And he was still *here*. Only now he was looking at me with a furrowed brow.

"I don't know, Willa," Aidan said softly. "This doesn't look like the work of the Glitterati."

His voice, deep and buttery, broke through my thoughts, and I reluctantly tumbled back to the present moment. The one where nothing was making sense. The one where my house was wrecked, the money was gone, and my only theory about who was behind this was full of holes.

"No," I said. "It really doesn't."

I paced around the shredded remains of my mom's room as we tried to talk it through. This was Wednesday evening of what was officially already the longest day of my life. The longest week, if you—*shudder*—counted back to my nights in juvie. It seemed impossible that only hours ago Aidan and I had met up at the animal shelter where we were both doing community service. We'd of course had no idea when Aidan dropped me off that we'd find the house like this, or go on a car chase, or any of the rest of it.

"I could imagine Nikki or Kellie hiring someone to come in and mess stuff up, mess with your head, but I don't think they'd go this far," Aidan said, still puzzling it out. "Why would they break into your mother's safe?"

I had no good answer. He knew Nikki and Kellie and Cherise, aka the Glitterati, better than I. He'd been going to school with them forever. For a short time, when I first started Valley Prep in the fall, I'd been part of the clique. Before I'd started stealing from Nikki and Kellie. (Yes, it sounds bad, I know. But I was trying to help the girls they were bullying. Anyway, I'd gotten busted breaking into Kellie's house, and that's what landed me in juvie.)

"Nikki and Kellie don't need the money, that's for sure," I said, gnawing on my thumb. And while they were willing to go illegal in all the usual teenage ways—drinking, smoking pot—I couldn't imagine them risking their trust-fund futures to take money they didn't need. Even if it meant getting back at me for what I'd done. But if it wasn't them, then who?

Maybe I had other enemies. Cherise, my supposed best friend, had disowned me when she found out I'd been stealing from the others. The entire population of Paradise Valley knew about my thieving. It had been on TV, in the papers. (The whole serial-theft thing had really made a splash, which goes to show you that these rich towns are kind of lacking in the news department.) So it could have been anyone, really.

Something else was bothering me. I walked back into the closet and knelt down for another look. It was empty, yes, but unharmed. The lock on the safe hadn't been picked or burned out or busted in any way.

How could that be? I drew in a breath and felt my heart pulse through it.

"It was opened by the combination," I said.

Aidan folded his arms across his chest. "So Plaid Shirt had to have known it."

"Only my mom had it, though. Unless . . ."

. . . They'd found it somewhere else. With a start, I dashed down the hall to my mom's office-slash-painting-studio-slash-inner-sanctum. The one room we hadn't checked out yet.

Plaid Shirt had been in here, too. It was obvious from the computer monitor that was smashed and the hard drive that looked like it had been hit repeatedly with a hammer. The file cabinets were open, though they were still mostly empty from the other day when I'd watched my mom destroy old papers in a shredding binge. Sickened, I went to the closet where she kept her paintings and slid open the louvered doors.

Empty.

Aidan came to stand next to me.

"They took her paintings, too," I said.

He pinched his chin. "Anyone you know that would be after her art? I'm sure that's the kind of question a cop would ask."

"They could be worth a lot of money, but I don't know who would know that," I said. My mom had supposedly sold some of her work at auction, which was how we could afford this fancy place, the exclusive zip code, the elite school. The thing was, I was pretty sure she'd lied about selling those paintings—just a few days ago I found all of them in that closet. And if *that* was the case, then I had no idea where that money actually came from.

"Collector? Art thief? Whoever he was, he knew what he was looking for," Aidan said.

We walked back through the house into the kitchen and I tried to see it through a thief's eyes. (Maybe not so much of a stretch.) Full shelves of dishes and glasses had been tossed and trampled. Some of the cabinet doors were hanging off their hinges. He'd even unloaded our refrigerator. Which was just tacky, in my opinion.

"He must have," I said. "I just don't know why he had to pulverize every last piece of tableware."

All I knew for sure was that the first beautiful house

we'd ever lived in was ruined.

But it was almost like all the destruction, all the wreckage around the house was some kind of subterfuge to distract us from the robbery. Like he'd wanted it to look like it was sabotage. I had to admit that it was a pretty smart approach—one that I wish I'd thought of in my own thieving days. Whoever Mr. Plaid Shirt was, he was good. A pro.

"He wanted to scare you."

He'd been watching us. A wave of dizziness hit, and I felt behind me for the stable support of the wall. I could no longer look at the situation like a fellow thief. I could only see it as a victim. This wasn't just a prank by some kid. This was a criminal in another league of criminals. If scaring me was what he wanted, he'd accomplished his mission. And whatever this thing was, it was much bigger than I'd thought.

TWO

WE HAD TO call someone. I knew that much. Someone who could help us.

I was on the floor and desperately rifling through the pile of broken stuff, looking for the cordless phone. My hands shook, panic rattling my movements.

Then I remembered.

My mom had disconnected our landline and cell phones after the local media firestorm when I was arrested. With all the reporters camped outside our house, she'd been freaked out about our privacy, and now that someone had actually broken in, I could understand why.

"Can I have your phone?" I asked Aidan.

But he didn't move a muscle. "Are you sure about this? I don't know if the police are going to take either of us seriously, considering we both have records."

Never mind that I still had no idea what was on

Aidan's record or why he'd recently gotten kicked out of Prep. I remembered the way the cops had treated me the night they took me in. Not the most sympathetic bunch. And my mom might not appreciate the possibility of us landing on the nightly news again. Why couldn't I be a normal citizen with a normal break-in to report? I would've given anything to be normal just then.

One thing I knew: Cops or no cops, she was going to lose it when she got home. Things were already rough between us. My run-in with the law, the call from the police station in the middle of the night, and the legal fees that followed were not exactly good for mother-daughter bonding.

But it was more than that. Ever since we moved to Paradise Valley, she'd been acting moody and reclusive, coming and going at odd hours. There was the lie about the paintings. And other things, too. She'd claimed to be volunteering at an art center and a food co-op but the stories didn't add up. I even followed her one day after school, only to discover that she was meeting some guy in a Target parking lot. At first I thought she was having an affair but now I was pretty certain this guy was an FBI agent named Jeremy Corbin. Because he'd been here, too. After the intruder. He'd left his card for me on the doorstep.

Corbin.

I reached into my pocket and pulled out the card to reread the note scrawled on the back in blue ink.

Willa, I know you're in trouble. And I can help you.
Call me if you need anything. JC

How had he known? Was he psychic? It was eerie, almost. Could this theft have something to do with my mom, something more personal?

"We could call this guy," I said, handing Aidan the card.

Aidan turned it over in his hand and squinted. "Who is he?"

"An FBI agent. He left it here—today, before we came back."

"That's weird," Aidan said. "Like, *after* the house had been broken into?"

I nodded. "He knows my mom. It sounds like he knows what happened here. Maybe he saw something."

"I just don't get it," Aidan said, handing the card back. "Why would FBI just be hanging around?"

I shrugged, doubt weighing on me.

It *was* strange. What if my mom wouldn't want me to call him? I still didn't understand their relationship.

Ugh. How was I supposed to know the best way to handle this situation? I was fifteen years old. I didn't know how to drive yet. "Maybe we should wait until she gets home."

"That sounds like a good idea. She might have more information. If she does know this guy."

"She definitely does," I said, remembering a recent

night in a restaurant when Corbin had been lingering around our table. Later, he'd tried to talk to my mom and she'd blown him off, not wanting to acknowledge him for some reason. "I've seen them together."

The corners of Aidan's mouth turned down with intrigue. "Interesting."

Yeah, it was "interesting" all right. My whole life had gotten really "interesting," but I was pretty sure it wasn't something to be proud of.

"So we'll wait, then?"

"I guess so," I allowed. All in all, it seemed like the wisest decision. "She should be back any minute now. But if you need to leave . . ."

He put his hand on my shoulder and gave me that twinkly-eyed, lethally charming look I'd come to associate with Aidan Murphy eye contact. "What kind of guy do you think I am, Willa? Do you think I'd really just leave you in the middle of all this?"

"It's not about what kind of guy I think you are," I said. Though I had to admit that at this point I understood way more about Aidan's lips than I did his inner psyche. Of course, I hoped to get to know both. "I don't want you to feel like you have to take care of me."

"I know I don't. You seem perfectly fine on your own. I just happen to enjoy a good mystery—and, you know, hanging out in wrecked houses. This is a particularly fine example."

I smiled for the first time in what felt like hours.

"Well, my wrecked house is flattered."

"I knew it would be."

We went back into the living room. I looked at the couch where my mom and I used to curl up with our old wool afghan that had followed us through all of our moves—twelve in my fifteen years. We'd watch movies and have pj's-till-five Sundays.

The couch was upended and torn apart. Aidan helped me set the furniture upright and rearrange the cushions so we could sit. I was tempted to clean the rest of the house but I'd seen enough TV shows to worry about disturbing the crime scene.

I folded my legs underneath me. "So we're thinking this whole thing was about the art, with no connection to me?"

Something about that just didn't sit right. It seemed like too much of a coincidence. Here I was, a known and convicted burglar, and then my house, which was very nice but unremarkable in a town of ten-million-dollar-plus megamansions, was targeted for robbery? My mom was talented but she was no Banksy. I wished Cherise were still talking to me, because she was a dedicated reader of crime books and she would certainly have a few ideas.

"Maybe yes and maybe no," Aidan said. "The thing is, random robberies rarely happen in Paradise Valley. I mean, we've got one of the lowest crime rates in the state. That's what they kept saying on the news when you . . . well, when your thing happened. 'The most robberies the town had seen in decades.' That's why you were such a big deal."

"Maybe I started a trend," I said mournfully.

"You never know," he said with half a grin. "You definitely had people talking about all your Sly Fox maneuvers. Dodging security cameras, hopping gates, picking locks. Stealing from the rich and giving to the poor. Not the most original scheme, maybe, but it had a certain populist appeal."

"So says the son of the billionaire CEO," I retorted.

"Hey, I'm down with the people. Anyway, my point is, these things have a way of taking on a life of their own."

"That's what I'm afraid of. That it's my fault." I sighed. I knew what I'd done was wrong. I'd been sentenced, I was starting my community service and probation, and I was ready to move on. Start over fresh.

And now this. We were tangled up with the law again, somehow. It just didn't make sense, though. Why had Corbin been here? And how did my mom know him?

But it would all be explained when she got home, wouldn't it? "What time is it, anyway?"

"Eight," he said, pulling out his Droid to check.

"How long have we been here?"

"Two hours, maybe?"

Two hours? How had that much time passed?

Where the hell was my mom, and when would she be coming back? Then, another thought: What if she'd been here when the break-in happened?

A sickening feeling settled over my skin like a cold sweat.

"Are you okay, Willa? You look pale."

I could barely speak. "Your phone."

This time he handed it over right away. "Are you calling the cops?"

"No." With shaking hands, I logged into my Gmail account. I hadn't checked it since we'd gotten home—I'd been too overwhelmed to even think about it.

As the page loaded, I saw I had twelve new messages in my in-box—I quickly scanned the list of names. It looked like there was some brand-new hate mail from Nikki and Kellie.

Fantastic. I deleted their messages without reading and continued scrolling down.

From: Joanne Fox

"There's an email from my mom," I murmured. I clicked on the message—sent at 4:47 P.M., with the subject line *Letting You Know.*

Dear Willa,
By the time you read this, I'll be long gone, and I wish I could explain why. But trust me when I say that you're much better off not knowing the details. The only thing I can tell you is that I have to leave. I really have no choice.

I'm sure you might find it hard to believe right now, but you are the most important person in the world to me. Leaving you behind is the hardest thing I've ever done, but I hope that once things are sorted out, I can come back for you and make it up to you.

I've tried to plan for this moment the best I could. I left you something at 3829 Chandler Ranch Road Unit 87. The key is under the agave plant in our front yard—you may have to dig a little. That should help you at least financially for a while. In the meantime, please stay with Cherise. I know her family will take good care of you. If anyone asks, I'm on an artist residency in Japan.

Don't call the cops—that will only make it harder for both of us. And please, please, please do *not* come looking for me. I'll be in touch when I can.

I love you.

Fingers cold, mouth dry, I handed Aidan the Droid. "She's gone."

"What do you mean, 'gone'?" He jiggled the phone in his hand.

"Read it." I gnawed on my thumb, watching him as his eyes tracked over the screen.

He frowned, closing his hand over it, and looked up.

"Whoa. This is really weird, Willa. Do you think it has something to do with the break-in? Do you think she was *kidnapped*?"

As the visual of my mom being tied up and taken away by some dangerous people flashed across my mind, hot acid rose in the back of my throat; my whole body shuddered. It was too awful.

"I really don't know," I gulped, trying to force down some air. "But we need to find that key."

Twenty minutes later we were in front of the house kneeling on the gravel beneath the two giant agave plants. These were the same plants Aidan had once nearly hit with his car, back when I'd first moved to town and he'd driven me home from school. I remember being flummoxed by his very special combination of sexiness and arrogance, coupled with the reckless driving.

But that all seemed like eons ago, now that we were using my mom's garden spade to dig up the landscaping in some sort of screwed-up version of a treasure hunt.

Well, Aidan was doing the digging and I was doing the encouraging. A small mound of gravel had already piled up beside him.

A gecko skittered between the rocks a couple of feet from us. The palm tree in front of my house swayed gently in the breeze, dry fronds rattling. Your typical night in the paradise of Paradise Valley, Arizona. *Some paradise.*

"I don't think I see anything. Are you sure this is right?"

Since this was the first I'd ever heard of my mom burying anything in the yard, I was not clear on this point. It was also nighttime and hard to see exactly what we were doing or what we were looking for.

"These are the only agave plants we have. Here, let me," I said, moving closer. We didn't have time for questions. We just had to find it.

I knelt down and sank my hand into the hole, which was surprisingly cool. As I worked my way deeper, densely packed sand passed through my wiggling fingers. Then my thumb brushed against a smooth and slippery surface.

"Wait, I feel something," I said, my breath quickening.

With the help of my other hand, I worked to loosen the object from the surrounding dirt. As I brought it up, I saw it was a red satin envelope, like the kind jewelers use to package earrings. I recognized it immediately. My mom had given me a necklace in this very same bag. I was wearing it now, as I did every day. It was a cloisonné bird pendant that she had gotten from her mom, the grandmother I'd never met.

I opened up the envelope. Inside was a small steel key and a plastic access card, a pink ribbon holding them together. This was it!

"Let's look up that address," I said, sliding the key

onto my keychain. "I think it's in Scottsdale."

"Now?" Aidan asked, incredulous. "It's kind of late and dark. What if the place is closed?"

"Then we break in if we have to. Aidan, I can't wait until tomorrow." My voice was firm but my insides were shaking. "I need to understand what's going on and there's no way I'll be able to sleep tonight."

"And I guess you need me to drive?"

I did. My beloved vintage bike had blown out during the chase from the cops the night I broke into Kellie's house—it was now probably police property. Losing it was just another kind of punishment, another reminder that I'd really messed up. Yet again, I wished I could undo all that I had done. Maybe my mom would still be here.

He nodded. "Okay, okay. We'll go now. But maybe we should call someone to come with us."

I shook my head. Was he crazy? We'd both just read the email. "No way. My mom doesn't want anyone to know what's going on."

"Well, *I* know," he said. "Somehow I don't think she meant for that to happen."

"Right, but that was only because you were here with me." *And because I trust you.*

Well, that's what I should have said, but I was too distracted by worry. Besides, we'd only just crossed the line from flirt buddies to something else. That something else was still undefined, for the moment.

"We could call that Agent Corbin," he suggested.

"No," I said, vehement. "The cops are out of the equation now. She said so. We're on our own. And I thought you were anticops."

Aidan looked at me with concern, his face falling out of its usual sardonic angles. "Yeah, well, that was before your mom skipped town. I just have a weird feeling about this. Someone could be waiting. Someone shady."

His words washed over me. Was the email a fake? A forgery? It was possible but I doubted it. The language sounded just like my mom. Someone could have forced her. . . .

Yes, there were plenty of terrible scenarios we could conjure up, but I couldn't allow myself to go there. If my mom was in trouble, I needed to help, and right now this key and this address were the only things connecting me to her. I couldn't let her down—not now. I'd disappointed her enough already.

I tried to push past him back into the house. "Then I'm going to have to take my chances and go myself."

But Aidan stood close, his chest squared off as if to block me. "I can't let you go alone."

"Well, then, I need you to promise me that you won't tell anyone—not about any of this." I paused and tried to take a softer approach. "You're helping me out here, and I do appreciate it, but I need to make the rules."

He shrugged his arms open. "You know how I feel about rules."

"Seriously, Aidan."

"I'm being serious. I'm also trying to be responsible, for once. We're in this together now."

Together. Before I could say anything else, before I could make him repeat the promise, I was caught in his arms, pressed against him. I could feel the muscles of his chest, the wiry strength of his shoulders. I felt the urgency of the moment coursing through me, and underneath that, his warmth.

I did feel safe, almost. And I also felt the sheer thrill of being so close to him. *Aidan. Aidan. Aidan.* I doodled his name on the notebook of my mind.

We unfolded ourselves from the hug. He kissed me softly on the mouth. It was different from before, somehow. Quieter. More nourishing, maybe. But just as good.

I went back into the house to get my bag. Aidan said he was going to wait outside and text home to say he'd be late. I ran my hands through my hair and splashed some cold water on my face. Then I grabbed a can of pepper spray my mom had bought me at the hardware store.

"We're single ladies," she'd said at the time. "We need to watch out for ourselves."

Outside, Aidan was waiting for me in the driver's seat of his Mercedes—I could make out the dark shape of his profile from a distance, his head bowed over his phone. I shut the door to my house, locked it, and headed down the path to the driveway. As I walked, the cool metal of the pepper-spray canister shook in my jeans pocket. My mom had always wanted me to be prepared for dangerous situations, but somehow I wasn't sure if what was happening right now was the kind of thing she'd had in mind.

THREE

I WAS RIGHT—THE WeStore facility was in a forgotten corner of Scottsdale, a good ten-minute drive from my house. I'd been to this particular area of town before, back when I'd brought some stolen goods to hock at the Finer Things Pawnshop.

It wasn't pretty—certainly nothing like where we lived, where every house, tree, and desert vista seemed to have been conjured up by an interior decorator to the universe. This was the area of town you only knew about if you needed quick money, or a gun—maybe even drugs.

As we pulled up to the security gate in front of the WeStore complex, I caught myself instinctively checking out the locks. Tre, my friend and tutor in all things larcenous, had shown me how to break into gated communities and disarm systems, among other skills. But there was no hacking, reprogramming, or code-breaking necessary now. My mom had kindly seen to that. Aidan simply rolled down his window and held up the access card to the digital reader. A little red light flashed and the gate swung open. Totally legit and supereasy.

So why was my heart racing?

We drove on in through the entry, and up a long driveway lit by towering street lamps. At the end were rows and rows and rows of identical concrete sheds with orange-painted roll-down doors.

Maybe it was my recent visit to juvie hall, but to me they looked like jail cells, each block labeled with a letter. The buildings were surrounded by asphalt, a big sea of a parking lot, which was empty but for a few cars.

I tensed. "This place is creepy."

"Well, normally people come here in the daylight," Aidan muttered. "Now which way?"

I ignored his crack and squinted into the dark outside of the car. "That sign over there says Units 70–90. Aisle G."

Aidan pulled up in front of the block and parked. Before he turned off the car I noted that the dashboard clock glowed nine P.M. The endless day kept going.

Without the music from his stereo and without the gentle hum of the Mercedes's engine, the quiet felt violent and sudden.

"Guess we should actually go in, huh?" I said, unbuckling my seat belt. I slung my bag over my shoulder and closed the passenger-side door. We walked toward aisle G. Sensing us, a light mounted on the corner of the building snapped on with a buzz. It was supposed to be comforting, but I felt caught in the spotlight, like a movie convict escaping prison.

Aidan's hand encircled mine, and we fell into step. The soft pressure of his fingers sent another kind of shiver through me. Was this what it was like to have a boyfriend? Nothing about my life felt remotely normal so it was hard to judge.

As we walked along the row of doors, each identical and closed off to the world, I imagined what was inside the little chambers: possessions that were too important to throw out but too difficult to hold on to, or things the owners wanted to hide away. Some of these units looked abandoned. Maybe the people had meant to come back but never had the chance. Maybe they'd even died.

I stared at my shadow looming in front of me, long and thin like a bony finger. The sound of our footsteps ricocheted on the concrete. Every so often a light overhead buzzed on, while another switched off.

Then I remembered a cop show I'd seen about a serial killer who kept his victims trapped inside a storage unit for days, starving and torturing them before he actually murdered them.

That was all I needed. Dismembered bodies to think about.

"It's the last one on the left, I think," Aidan said.

I nodded, letting go of his hand and pushing in front of him, wanting to seem braver and more in charge than

I felt. This was *my* scary storage unit, after all. As a criminal in training, faking it had become my MO, and it served me well every time I needed to pull off another theft with a fresh set of challenges.

And we had the key, right? This was legal. So it should have been no big deal.

No big deal, a voice in my head repeated, a mantra as much as an affirmation.

"Hey," a deep voice boomed behind us. In the next five seconds, a million images ran through my mind, several of them involving chloroform-soaked rags and the backs of retrofitted vans.

Panicked, I grabbed at Aidan's shirt as I turned around.

Then I saw it was only Tre emerging from the shadowy night. He was wearing a baseball cap and jogging to catch us. "Scared you, didn't I?"

He twitched his hands in my face like a zombie, teasing. I clutched at my own chest now, trying to hold my heart in the place where all the bad action-movie clichés had jolted it. "Sheesus! Yes. Yes, you did. What are you doing here?"

"I got a text from this dude." He pointed a thumb in Aidan's direction. "Something about needing backup."

Aidan and Tre exchanged some kind of secret handshake, or so it seemed to me. "Glad you made it. But we could've done without the dramatic entrance."

I glared at Aidan. He'd texted Tre? So he'd deliberately

gone behind my back after I asked him not to.

"That's funny because I told him we didn't need help," I said, scowling.

"Look, Willa, I'm sorry," Aidan said, shrugging and not sounding terribly sorry. "But I told you I didn't want us to get hurt. And I felt like if anyone would know what to do, it would be Tre."

"You know, because of my vast experience with the criminal underworld," Tre said, stitching up his eyebrows. Under the brim of his hat, his broad, square face relaxed into a playful smile.

I looked from Tre to Aidan and back again. "That's not really the point. What did he tell you, Tre?" I had to know how much Aidan had shared.

"Just that someone did a job on your house and your mom bounced."

So everything, basically. I shook my head. "This was supposed to be a secret. My mom's safety could be at stake."

"Hey, we're all on your side," Tre said, patting my back. "Don't you trust me, Willa?"

Tre had always been there for me, even when everyone else at Prep decided I was trash. And he'd always been honest with me, too, telling me straight up, when he found out how I was really using his lessons, that he thought what I was doing was wrong. I *did* trust Tre, and I respected him. It was Aidan I wondered about now.

I put an arm around Tre—his height and my lack

thereof meant it landed on his waist. "Yeah, I trust you."

I could feel Aidan looking back at me and I refused to make eye contact. Did he think I was some little kid? Did he think I needed him to make decisions for me? That wasn't cool.

"And this guy"—Tre flicked his chin in Aidan's direction—"he was just worried."

I was sheltered now by Tre's body. I peered around his chest at Aidan, who batted his eyelashes at me and tented his fingers together like a choirboy.

It was classic Aidan. Working the charm angle. He had me. He knew he did. All I had to do was think of earlier—the driveway, the lawn . . .

"C'mon, Willz," Tre said. "Don't be mad. We just want to help Sly Fox out. We want to be part of the dream team."

I still cringed a little when I heard the nickname the press had given me. "Yeah, okay, you two. I get it. Let's move on."

"So should we do this thing?" Tre asked.

I nodded. Aidan turned back to the unit and hunched over to unhook the padlock. Then he pulled open the metal gate, which rolled up noisily, its echoing rumble like an approaching train.

Inside, another sensor-rigged light flicked on, cold, blue, and harsh in the cement-floored room. Aidan cocked his head at us, then inched his way in. We followed, moving tentatively. No one wanted to say anything, but I think we were all half-expecting to get jumped. Maybe Aidan had been right to tell Tre after all—not that I would ever let him have the satisfaction of knowing that.

Fortunately, there were no signs of human life. The room felt cool and smelled like musty paper. It was surprisingly big, about twenty feet by twenty feet, with several cardboard cartons, some old furniture, and trash bags full of stuff. And I'd had no idea that my mom even kept a storage locker.

Clearly, she wasn't totally honest with me about lots of things.

"So what are we looking for?" Aidan asked, squeezing himself between boxes.

I scanned the room. "Money, I think. Just don't ask me where."

I made my way down an aisle of boxes. Well, at least it all looked fairly normal, this secret enclave of my mother's. Enough junk to justify paying for the place, but not enough to qualify for a reality show about hoarding, thankfully.

Tre held up a key. "May I?"

"Be my guest," I said, and watched as he slit open the tape on a box and began rifling through the contents.

Aidan went to work on another pile of boxes. I made my way toward the back of the unit, trying to scope everything out before I formally started my search. I felt like I should be able to home in on what I was looking for, like a heat-sensing satellite, but that was probably ridiculous. I had no such powers. And whatever it was could be anywhere.

In the farthest right corner, there were a few grungy kitchen chairs I recognized from our last house in Colorado, and a large wooden trunk. Behind that, leaned up against the wall, were dozens of large flat rectangles, wrapped in black plastic.

Her paintings! So they hadn't been stolen after all? She must have moved them here herself.

I quickly ripped off the plastic and started flipping through the stack, feeling nostalgia wash over me like a warm summer rain. Each image was familiar, even though I'd probably never seen them all together like this.

My mom had faithfully captured every place we'd ever lived—and we'd covered quite a lot of the West Coast, moving twelve times in the last fifteen years.

Her style was abstract, yet she was always able to catch something important and essential about each landscape she painted. There were the huge open plains threaded with orange and blue that could only be the Sonoran Desert of Paradise Valley; a series of forests, inspired by our time in Washington State; a vast man-made lake I remembered visiting one summer in New Mexico.

Maybe she'd lied about her amazing art career and hadn't actually ever sold anything, but there was no denying the fact that she really was an artist. You couldn't just fake images like these. No matter what else you were trying to fake.

I felt a twinge in my chest. Sadness that my mom had hidden so much from me. Had she thought I wouldn't understand, whatever it was? Regret, too, that I'd let her down, maybe when she needed me the most.

"Find anything, Willa?" Tre called out to me.

"Not yet," I said. "I mean, not what we're looking for."

I chewed on my bottom lip and kept studying the paintings as if they were maps, in search of more information. As far as I could tell, all of the pieces that had been stored in the closet at home were here, and it was safe to say she'd moved them here herself.

Unless someone else had access to this place. Someone who could be watching me right now.

Shadows flickered in my peripheral vision. I turned around and kept going in a full three-sixty.

Nothing. I was getting carried away again.

I took a deep breath and tried to exhale my way through the sense of unease as I went back to the paintings.

There was a half-finished piece I remembered watching her work on back in her studio at the house. Then two others that also seemed to be works in progress. The very last painting in the stack was a large canvas, probably sixty inches square, much bigger than the rest of them. I pulled it away from the wall and held it up by its wooden stretcher frame to examine it.

Oddly, I didn't recognize the image. As far as I knew,

I'd never seen this painting on her easel. Of course, she'd done most of her work when I was at school, but she usually shared it with me at some point, especially when she was excited.

I noticed, too, that it was unsigned. And the paint just seemed to run off the bottom edge, as though the canvas had been moved in a hurry. I pushed my finger against the surface, and the paint smudged ever so slightly. Maybe this had been the last thing she'd done before she'd left.

"There's nothing in those boxes back there except a bunch of books and magazines," Aidan called, pointing a thumb over his shoulder. Then, in a few long strides, he was beside me, looking at the art. "What's this?"

"A painting. Can you take a photo of it?"

"Sure. But why?"

"I don't know," I said. I wasn't able to articulate what I was thinking. "Can you just do it?"

He got out his phone and snapped the picture from a few angles.

As he turned the canvas over to slide it back onto the stack, my eye caught on a flash of white.

"Wait!" I yelled. "Don't put that away yet."

Tucked into a corner of the wooden frame was an envelope. On which, I could see as I pulled it out, my name was written in blue ink.

It was heavy in my hand and I ripped it open quickly, running my finger under the envelope's crease. I reached in and pulled out a rubber-banded fold of hundred-dollar bills.

"Cashish." Aidan whistled. "Must be ten grand, at least."

He was right—it was a substantial amount; I could tell by the weight. I held it in my palm for a minute. I felt funny counting it right there, so I put the wad back into the envelope and slipped it into my bag.

Don't ask me why, but we tried to put everything back the way we found it. Maybe we were all just a little unnerved by the stillness of the place, the loneliness of it. All I knew was that I wanted it to be right when my mom came back.

The more I thought about it, the more I felt she couldn't have been kidnapped. She'd had the time to leave the money and the key for me, and there was no way she would've known to do that. But the fact that the painting was unfinished told me she must have left quickly, maybe more quickly than she expected to.

And the money in the safe? This money had to have come from that. So maybe she took that, too. But why was the house wrecked? What was that guy looking for?

I replayed the events of the past few days in my head. She'd come home late the other night, late enough to be morning, acting odd. She'd told me that she loved me, that she'd always wanted the best for me. She'd hugged me tight. Had she known, then, that she was leaving? She must have.

Well, I couldn't just let her go like that.

We closed the metal door and locked it up again.

"So, Willa, where are you headed now? Need a ride or anything?" Tre asked as we walked back down the aisle to the parking lot.

"Actually, I was just going to go home."

"But you can't stay there, can you?" Aidan said. "I mean, after everything that happened today?"

He was right. At the moment, my house seemed just as spooky as the storage facility. "My mom told me to go stay at Cherise's for the time being, but we're not exactly on speaking terms right now. I'm not about to show up at her door in my pajamas."

I thought wistfully of my former best friend. Nothing sounded better than hanging out in her room, listening to records as she shared her latest DJ finds.

"I could sneak you into my guesthouse," Aidan said. "I mean, if you wanted . . ."

Spending the night? At Aidan's? The offer was beyond tempting. "I need to go to school tomorrow. Could you drop me off in the morning?"

Aidan looked away. "Eh, I'm not really supposed to be on campus. Not after what happened." He meant, not after he'd been kicked out. "But I could get my dad's driver, maybe . . ."

"You can stay at my house if you want," Tre offered. "I'm going to school tomorrow, so I can take you. We have an extra room, and my parents won't mind. My dad's away now, anyway, for a game in Houston." Tre's dad was the coach for the Phoenix Suns.

I closed my eyes, exhausted suddenly by the options, by the plans, by all that had happened and all that still lay ahead. "Yeah, okay," I said, grateful for the offer. "That would be nice, Tre. Really nice."

"Cool," Aidan said, and I could tell he was a little hurt.

We'd been through a lot together in the last twenty-four hours. Too much, maybe. I couldn't deal with more feelings now—mine or anyone else's.

He stepped backward a few paces before waving to us. "Well, good night, guys. Let me know what happens, Willa."

"Okay," I said, uncertain. I didn't want to let him go. I wanted to kiss him good night but he'd already moved away and Tre was standing between us. "Thanks for your help."

We split ways at the end of the aisle and Aidan walked toward his car. Tre was parked on the other side of the complex, and as we neared his Audi, I could hear Aidan's door shut in the distance. Then, the sound of him reversing loudly, skidding a bit, to get back out to the road.

"Sorry if I overstepped myself there," Tre said.

"Not at all," I said.

"Everything okay?"

"Yeah," I said, settling into the passenger seat.

I wasn't sure how much to tell Tre, or how much he already knew. This Aidan stuff wasn't the kind of thing Tre and I usually talked about. It was new territory for me, period. "Thanks for sending him to meet me at the animal shelter this morning."

"Thought you'd appreciate that." He smiled at me sidelong. So I had my answer. He definitely knew something was up.

I felt my face get hot. "I did. But I guess none of us really knew what we were getting into today."

"Somehow, I think that's kind of a Willa Fox thing. You're a walking adventure." Tre braked at a stop sign.

"Or maybe a walking disaster," I said, shrugging. "That's what it's starting to feel like, anyway. Can we stop at my house to pick up my school stuff?"

School. I'd already missed a day for the trial, a day for suspension, and a day for community service. I was thoroughly dreading my return to Valley Prep. There was a disciplinary-board hearing for my criminal transgressions to look forward to, not to mention the general hostility of the Glitterati et al, who were expert in making life hell for their enemies.

"So you're really going back, huh?" He gave me a look that said, *Good luck, kid.*

"Yeah," I said. "For tomorrow, at least. But I don't know how long I'll stick around."

"Why, you think they'll kick you out?"

"They could," I said. They probably would. "But even

if they don't, I might leave, anyway. I need to find my mom."

Tre frowned. "Willa, that would just be stupid. You'd be breaking your probation if you left town, you know."

There he was again, acting like my conscience. Tre had been through his own legal troubles—he was arrested for stealing cars and joyriding in Detroit, then shipped off to boot camp. After that, his mom sent him here to live with his dad in Paradise Valley, where he vowed to turn over a new leaf. Other than living vicariously through me and my exploits, he'd toed the line and stayed out of trouble.

He was setting a good example. I just wasn't following it.

"I know," I said. "But what am I supposed to do? If she's in trouble, I can't just stay here and read transcendentalists and do geometry proofs like nothing's happening."

He pulled up in front of my house. "I don't know her, but I'm pretty sure your mom would want you to do what you're supposed to do."

I cringed. I knew he didn't mean it, but the way he was talking about my mom, it was like she was dead, and it was wigging me out.

"Well, she doesn't want me to call the cops, either, so I'm out of options."

He nodded, looking thoughtful. "You have to do what you have to do. Just think about it, is all I'm saying.

Think about the big picture."

I hopped out of the car and ran toward the front step, trying to ignore the wave of anxiety when I opened up the door for the third time that day. What would I find now? Nothing. It was still a wreck but it was undisturbed from the way Aidan and I had left it.

In my room, I gathered together a few outfits, some makeup, a couple pairs of shoes, and my toiletries, and stuffed them into a bag. I also grabbed my backpack with my schoolbooks. It was a joke—I knew I probably wasn't going to be able to do much work, but I felt like I should at least go through the motions.

On the way back to the car, I stopped in the laundry room. Impulsively, I grabbed my mother's blue windbreaker to take with me. Maybe it was childish, but I didn't know how long I'd be away and I just wanted one more piece of her that I could hold on to.

FOUR

MY NEW ROOMMATE, decked out in a Madlib T-shirt and
striped pajama bottoms, knocked on the door. "Willz,
I'm going to sleep. You cool here?"

I'd changed into my own sleep gear and was sitting
cross-legged on the crisp-sheeted bed. Still, I knew
there was no way I'd be able to doze off—not for a
while, anyway. Not unless someone sedated me with
some hospital-grade medication.

"Nice pj's." I looked up at him and smiled, apprecia-
tive of his rock-starness. Tre had managed to put me up
in his fancy house like it was no big thing—he always
had a way of coming through like that, and modestly.
"Do you think I could use your laptop?"

"Hang on," he said, and went down the hall to his
room. In his absence, I stared up at the vaulted ceiling. The guest suite, which had its own bathroom with
whirlpool tub and spa shower, had been freshly done up

by the Walkers' maid Angela, down to the pillow plump-ings. From my window I could see the negative-edge pool surrounded by exotic plants and a swim-up bar, lit impeccably by dramatic pink and blue lights. Beyond that was a detached workout facility with indoor basket-ball courts and a gym. Tre's dad had obviously done well for himself, first as a pro baller and now as a coach. This place was nicer than some luxury hotels.

Not that Tre had it that easy. He grew up in Detroit with his mother for fifteen years before he even knew who his father was. After he was sent to boot camp, his dad and stepmom took him in but they still had years of making up to do. At least Tre had a relationship with his dad now. That made him lucky—in my mind, at least.

I mean, my own dad was a blank to me. Not only had I never met him but I had no idea who or where he was. My mom was a champ, raising me all by herself from the early days when she was only a teenager—just a year older than I was now. I didn't question that but sometimes I couldn't help but wonder about the life I might have had, with normal, married parents. Brothers and sisters. Grandparents. Aunts and uncles. Big family parties.

A mother who didn't just disappear one day, for no good reason.

But there had to be a good reason. Didn't there?

I touched the necklace at my throat. It was my only link to a past I didn't really understand.

When Tre came back, he handed me his computer in its neoprene sleeve. "There's a printer downstairs in the library if you need one." He pronounced the word *library* with a British accent to show me that this whole scene was still new and strange to him. "I'll be up at six thirty. I'm hauling your ass out of bed, too. So don't stay up too late zoning out on the net." He smiled, showing his dimple, and I couldn't help but find his parental concern cute.

"Six thirty? Jeez." I yawned just thinking about it. "You don't mess around."

"Just trying to stay out of trouble. And I suggest you do the same, Sly Fox." He saluted me. "See you in the A.M."

I opened the computer and brought up the email from my mom again. I figured that if I read it enough times, I might be able to figure out where she was. Maybe there was a hint in there somewhere.

hardest thing I've ever done

I wish I could explain why

no choice

Someone or something else had forced her to leave. That had to be it. I closed my eyes to hold back the tears that were finally coming, spilling out from underneath my eyelashes no matter how hard I tried to hold them back. My chest was heavy, too, but I would not let myself sob, not in Tre's house, not with his little brother, Kai, in the room next door. All I could do was ball myself up and hug the pillow close as fatigue and fear swelled through me.

When the tears finally subsided, I sat up again. I was depleted. Might as well try to go to sleep. I reached over to turn off the computer.

Before I could, I saw that a newer email had come in, this time from Aidan. Just seeing the arrangement of the letters of his name gave me a little buzz. He was thinking of me. I clicked it open.

> *Willa,*
> *I know you're probably mad. I'm sorry for earlier. I didn't want to start trouble. I really just wanted to make sure we were safe. Here's the photo of the painting we took. Write when you have a chance, okay? I want to help you figure this out.*
> *A*

I palmed at my damp eyes and gathered a clean breath. This email from Aidan made the world feel a little less bleak. Whatever anger I'd felt seemed small and distant now. How could I possibly be mad at him, after all he'd done for me today? Not to mention this was Aidan Murphy we were talking about. He could charm the mustache off a military dictator.

I opened up the attachment to look at the painting again. My mom could be anywhere by now, but I felt sure that the painting could at least tell me what was going on in her head before she left, and maybe that would lead me to her.

I zoomed in, magnifying the pixels on the screen. To someone else the picture might have looked like a bunch of blotches. But my mom was always talking about "visual vocabulary," and I knew that she used broad shapes and strokes of color to build up the energy or feeling of a place.

The paint was thickly applied—it appeared as though she'd spread it on with a palette knife, swirling it like frosting on a cupcake so that the white melded with the blue, and I could see now, looking closer, that the brown wasn't really brown at all but tiny bleeding patches of amber and yellow and green.

I zoomed out again, way out, and the image started to come together, all the pixels falling into an order. It looked like a beach scene: On the left-hand side were jagged-looking brown-, red-, and cream-streaked cliffs that seemed to meet a wildly crashing ocean.

It was a landscape, there was no question. And the place itself, or at least the general look of it, was starting to seem vaguely familiar. But I had never seen this painting before and I couldn't conjure up the name of the beach, or how I knew it. Without a title or some other words or landmarks to place it, I wasn't sure I'd ever be able to figure out where it was. What was the significance? Maybe there was no significance.

My in-box jumped with a (1). Another email from Aidan.

> *Willa,*
> *One more thing: I traced the IP address of your mom's email. It looks like it came from a hotel in Santa Barbara called the Hadley. Just thought you'd want to know.*
> *A*

My heart leaped. He'd found her!

I already knew Aidan was supposedly a computer whiz, but I was amazed and touched by his genius none-theless. I Googled the Hadley and it came up right away, a small boutique hotel. The photo showed a Mission-style building with white stucco walls and a Spanish tiled roof dripping with hanging vines.

> *A—*
> *Thanks for sending this info. And I'm not mad at you. I promise. I know you were just trying to help. You did the right thing, asking Tre.*

My fingers hovered over the keyboard. How could I convey my sincere thanks, the seriousness of the situation, and also the *other* feelings I was having—the dizzying, tickly feelings that had nothing to do with my mom's disappearance and everything to do with Aidan? No, I had to stay focused on what really mattered. This stuff with my mom was more important than my love life right now.

I'll be at Prep tomorrow, and I'm not sure where I'll be after that. I will let you know. Thanks for everything today. Might not be until after all of this is resolved, but I will make it up to you. Just let me know how. Sleep well, Aidan.

XO,
Willa

I crept down the hallway to the library and, trying to be as quiet as possible, plugged the laptop into the printer, so I could print out the address of the hotel and the picture Aidan had sent me. Then I took both pieces of paper and stuffed them into my overnight bag, along with the envelope of money from my mom. I had to be prepared. Just in case I had to leave.

I turned off the light and got into bed, resting my head against the now-damp pillow. Everyone else in Tre's house was asleep—I could hear Kai turning over in his bed, the mattress faintly squeaking, and I envied him for being a little kid with nothing to worry about.

I wished I were that young again, with my mom here to comfort me with one of her made-up fairy tales.

I tried to close my eyes and count backward from eight hundred by sevens, a trick that usually worked when I couldn't sleep. All I could see, though, was that painting, as if it were right on the backs of my eyelids. And that kept leading me back to my mom, the shock of her leaving, the pain of missing her. It was all too strange.

Should I follow her? The note said not to. I pictured her stern face, the pinched-up expression she made when she was angry with me, and wondered if I should listen, if I should do the right thing. But what was the right thing? Right, wrong. Stay, go. They were just words now. And words meant nothing when you were alone in the darkness.

FIVE

MY BACK-TO-SCHOOL STRATEGY was simple: Stay invisible. In the morning, I put on the most unimaginative outfit I could summon out of my overnight bag: jeans and a black T-shirt. Maybe there was no way to blend in after being outed as the mastermind of multiple robberies, but I didn't want to stand out any more than I had to.

I quickly dried my hair, tied it back in a ponytail, and put on a little bit of lip gloss. The final result was human but blank and nondescript, like a mannequin or a secret shopper. I stared back at myself in the mirror and saw my mother's blond hair and hazel eyes, all the features we had in common. Then I remembered she was really gone and I still didn't know what to do about it.

Tre made us bagels and coffee, which we ate, standing up, at the granite-topped kitchen island. His stepmother had already left for her tennis lesson, and Kai was waiting for us, dressed in his Prep uniform of khaki pants and a little blue blazer with the school crest. With his curly mop of hair and round glasses he looked like a serious second-grade scholar.

He watched over our breakfast impatiently. "Can we go now? You guys are taking for-*ever*."

He was still at an age where he actually looked forward to school. He was learning how to tell time and count to a thousand. He probably had friends there waiting for him and, I would've guessed, the only drama in his life took place on a baseball diamond.

"All right, little man," Tre said, moving our dishes to the sink. "We're out."

I loaded both my bags into Tre's car. I couldn't stay at Tre's house another night. It was nice here, but I didn't want to take advantage of his generosity. I wasn't sure where I'd go next—part of me really wanted to hit the road and find my mom, but I kept hearing her voice in my head, telling me off.

Don't be a hero, Willa. Just go to school like you're supposed to. Face whatever you have to face. Deal with your problems.

You're one to talk, my own voice answered her. *Didn't you just run away from yours?*

We drove to Valley Prep, with Kai in the backseat. The entire car ride, I could feel him studying us, his little forehead creased into a frown.

"Are you guys boyfriend-girlfriend?" he asked finally.

Tre looked at me and smiled sheepishly, apologetically. "No, Kai. Willa's my friend."

"Then how come she slept over? You never have girls sleep over."

Wow. I guess seven-year-olds like to cut to the chase.

"She's having some issues, man. She just needed a place to crash."

"Oh." He seemed to think this over for a moment. "Well, she's pretty."

"Thanks, Kai," I said, flattered by his assessment. I'd never been anyone's girlfriend—not yet—though my insides shimmied as I thought of those few hours of almost-girlfriendness with Aidan. If I went to California, would he wait for me until I got back?

Tre gave Kai the side-eye. "Don't you have anything else to think about back there? No homework to do?"

I laughed. I considered Tre just a friend, and I was pretty sure he had a lady love in Detroit. If so, she was a lucky girl.

Tre lived close to school—a little *too* close for my taste. At the sight of the white Valley Prep sign at the end of the school's driveway, I felt my stomach drop. I was *so* not looking forward to this.

I remembered the first time I'd ever seen the place—the day school started back in September. I'd ridden to Prep on my old Schwinn, feeling a little bit like a freak in the pack of Maybachs and Bentleys, not to mention the lack of bike lanes. And then, in the parking lot, Cherise almost ran me down in her VW. That's how we'd met. A classic story, really: I was knocked to the pavement and she helped me up. She felt sorry for almost killing the new girl and so she took me under her wing and introduced me to all of her friends. Which, looking back on it, was something she now probably regretted.

Ugh. Just thinking about my last IM exchange with Cherise, where she basically made it clear that she no longer wanted to speak to me, filled me with the sads. And now I'd have to face her in person.

I checked the clock on Tre's dash. There was still time to turn around, right?

Tre pulled up behind a line of luxury cars in front of the Lower School entrance. "Okay, buddy, why don't you get out of the car now and go embarrass someone else, huh?"

Kai shrugged, slipping the straps of his turquoise backpack over his little shoulders. "All right. See you later."

We watched him walk up the steps and go inside.

"Sorry about that," Tre said. "Kai's a little bit of a punk sometimes."

"He's cute," I said. "No worries. And anyway it helped take my mind off the situation."

"The back-to-school situation?"

"The my-mom-is-missing situation. The my-house-was-wrecked situation. The about-to-get-my-butt-kicked situation."

"Yeah, that's a lot of situations," Tre agreed as he smoothly steered the car around to the Upper School lot. He found a spot in the section reserved for the junior class.

Nearby, Drew Miller was getting out of his Beamer. He was friends with Nikki and Kellie. He was a Grade A douchenozzle. He was also one of the people I'd stolen from.

Oh God. It was starting before we even stepped foot on school property. I wanted to duck behind a car. I wanted to tunnel through the asphalt into my own personal cave. Was this how my mom had felt before she had to leave? This kind of impossible fear?

"You ready, Willa?" Tre asked.

"Not really," I said, forcing a smile, trying to be brave. "But I guess we have to go in, right?"

"Don't think they'll teach us much out here."

I wanted him to say, *It's going to be fine, Willa* or *There's no need to worry, Willa.* But of course he didn't. For one thing, you couldn't just write a script in your head and expect someone to follow it. For another, how could he promise me anything? We both knew there were plenty of good reasons to worry. I was screwed. Simple as that.

I grabbed my two bags and we headed toward the front courtyard. I'd only been away five days, but so much had changed in my own life in that time that I half-expected Prep to look totally different.

No way. Prep was exactly as I remembered it: the

modern concrete-and-glass buildings stretching out low and infinite against the red desert earth. Behind them, glimpses of craggy rock formations that looked like an altar to the sun.

The strategic, year-round plantings were all there— spiky cacti gardens, pale mesquite and yucca trees, and bright hanging bunches of bougainvillea. There was that very specific Prep smell of recent construction and fresh mulch, touched with a light hint of leather and a soup-çon of designer perfume.

And the courtyard was the same, too, spilling over with its usual morning bustle of students gossiping and tussling before class. The only thing that was missing was Aidan. When would I see him again?

I glimpsed Kellie and Nikki at their customary spot on the wall. Only now, instead of joining them, I was going to walk on by. Like a new girl. Like an outcast. I already felt the stares. I prayed they didn't see me.

I swallowed hard and looked up at Tre. He smiled at me in silent support. Nothing to do but keep moving. There was only one way inside the school. Besides, I was going to have to face them sooner or later.

As we passed, there were whispers and even some giggles, too. Try as I might, I couldn't not hear.

Did you see the news?

The thief is back.

Kellie said they found her fingerprints on everything. . . .

We were almost there. I fixed my eyes on the burbling

courtyard fountain. It reminded me of the background sounds they played at spas to relax you—which I only knew about from hanging around Nikki and Kellie and Cherise. I wished I could drown everything out, including my thundering heart, and focus on that sound. Only now the water was just adding to the cacophony. Another voice accusing me.

The door was in sight. But the chorus continued, the words closing in on us.

Is she suspended?

What did she steal?

Kellie's dad's going to sue.

I think it's awesome. The girl's got balls.

Tre put a protective hand on my back. I stopped and gave him a small, tight smile. I didn't need to be guided. "I'm okay," I said.

On the other side of the door, the cool, air-conditioned hallways of Prep offered little consolation. The scene was the same inside. The too-hushed sound of people stopping what they were doing, the crowds clearing as we advanced.

When I was part of the Glitterati, the same thing used to happen, but then people were moving away out of fear and reverence. People were staring at Kellie, thinking how hot she looked, how envious they were of her latest handbag or boots. Now they were stepping aside out of disgust and judgment.

Focus, Willa.

There were lockers, books, classes to think about—normal high-school things that would take up the hours between now and the rest of the day. I kept my gaze straight ahead. The only way out was through.

The harp rang over the loudspeakers, signaling the start of classes. Tre walked me past the library.

"Want me to see you to homeroom?"

I wished it were that easy. "No, I've got an exclusive engagement with Mr. Page. A VIP meeting." I wanted it to sound like a joke but my voice was too thin, too strained.

Tre grimaced. He had no sugar to coat this pill. "Ouch. All right. I'll catch you at lunch, then."

In some ways, at least, I was protected in the administration wing, where there were no sniping students hanging out. Just a blue-carpeted hallway leading to Mr. Page's office, lined with portraits of all the headmasters past of Valley Prep, silver-haired, suited, and solemn. Mr. Page himself was waiting for me behind his desk, wearing his usual bow tie and a dour expression.

"Have a seat, Willa."

I set my bags down, sat in one of the heavy antique chairs, and folded my hands over the wooden armrests. I thought of my mom and how she had worked her magic to get me into this school, how much she'd wanted me to get a top-notch education.

"You know why you're here, don't you?"

I nodded. No point in playing dumb. "Because of last weekend."

He linked his hands together in front of him. "Right. We have our disciplinary hearing scheduled for tomorrow and I just wanted to let you know a little bit more about what to expect. It'll be some board members, the head of student council, and myself. The hearing will require us to ask you some questions about what happened. Similar to a real trial."

But this wouldn't be like my court trial. When I went up in front of Judge Prendergast, my mom had stood by me. Now she was nowhere to be found. I needed her.

"And then . . . ?" I rubbed my fingers over the wood grain of the chair, trying to find a pattern.

"And then we'll decide if you can continue on here at Valley Prep. Do you have any questions for me at this time?"

I shifted forward in my seat. "So what are my chances? I mean, I've already been in the news and everything. How will people make a fair decision?"

He frowned. "I don't know. Nothing like this has ever happened in my twenty years here and I'm not sure the VP community is going to be very understanding. Look, Willa, I know you're a good student and you're new here and I want to give you the benefit of the doubt. But I'll be honest with you—I don't think the odds are in your favor. We'll just have to see."

"Got it," I said. *Don't you dare cry. Look straight ahead.*

The heavy bookshelves in his office were packed full of old volumes in color-coordinated rows. I felt an ache seeing them, knowing that they were probably neglected. And I'd probably never read them, either. Not now.

Then a wave of guilt. I'd totally blown this once-in-a-lifetime opportunity. My mom would be very disappointed in me. That is, if she ever came back.

Would she ever come back?

"Willa? You still with me?"

Mr. Page paused, pressing his lips together. A lot of kids complained about him and his stiff ways, his rules, his formal dress. I had nothing against the guy. He was just trying to do his job. But he'd given up on me. It was obvious.

I just wanted a chance to prove that I could change. That the Sly Fox stuff, that wasn't really me—or at least that was just something I did.

"Yes," I said.

"So I'll give your mom a call today and fill her in. Any other questions?"

Good luck getting ahold of her. I shook my head.

He reached across the table to grip my hand. "See you tomorrow, then. Good luck to you, Willa."

How come, I wondered, when people said, "Good luck to you," it always sounded so much worse, so much more final, than plain old "good luck"? As though you were really, really going to need that luck.

When I stepped out in the hallway they were waiting for me. Kellie and Nikki. Arms folded across their chests. Mouths curled up in scowls. Like mob heavies with evenly applied mascara.

Not so long ago, I'd excitedly searched for those familiar faces across the crowded dining hall, or in the middle of Neiman Marcus, because I thought wherever they were was where I belonged. Now dread seized me again, adding to an already-churning swirl of emotions.

My jaws clamped together. Could this day get any worse?

"Hey, Willa," Kellie practically sang, her well-pampered voice reverberating through the corridor. "Welcome back. How was prison? Make any new friends?"

It was her faux-sweet tone, the one she used to threaten me and Cherise when we dared to call her out on the horrible rumors she started about Mary, Alicia, and Sierra. The one that barely disguised the acid evil underneath.

"I hope so. Because you don't have any here," Nikki spat—as always, there to back up Kellie's every last word.

I kept walking. Kellie's eyes narrowed as she kept pace with me, whipping her shiny brown hair over her shoulder. "Real friends don't break into each other's houses. You know that, right?"

And then I felt the tiniest bit bad, because I heard the insecurity in her voice. I couldn't read it, though. Did she really think we were friends? Or was she just surprised that anyone thought she deserved to be robbed? Was it possible that she was that oblivious? If so, that was sad. But it didn't change how I felt about her.

"That's kind of basic, isn't it?" Nikki said.

I will not look at them.

It was like a scene in a storybook, because as soon as I made eye contact with the two-headed monster with matching Chanel handbags, I was as good as dead. They would see my weakness—any hint of the slightest bit of fear—and exploit it. But I was tempted, so tempted.

"Guess her mom never told her that," Kellie said.

"Clearly," Nikki said.

"Just leave my mom out of this," I blurted, unable to help myself. So much for ignoring them.

But they kept on with their despicable banter. "Yeah, well, maybe it's different when you're from the ghetto," Kellie said.

"Ghetto is as ghetto does."

Anger boiled up inside me now. I'd stolen from both of them, I reminded myself. They could make me feel a lot of things but they would never make me feel sorry about that. I spun around, fuming. "And once a bitch, always a bitch."

"Better to be a bitch than a busted loser," Kellie said. She glared at me, her diamonds glinting.

Busted. That's what she called those other girls. I felt like punching her pretty little face.

"Forget it." Cherise cut in and stood between us. She seemed to come out of nowhere but she must have seen us in the hallway. She must have been standing nearby.

"Don't be stupid, you guys. Do you know how small you look right now? She's been punished. It's not your job."

Cherise wouldn't meet my eyes but I could tell by her posture—her arms folded across her chest, her back straight and erect—that she was acknowledging me, as a human, with feelings. Maybe she wasn't ready to forgive me, but she wasn't interested in hurting me or attacking my dignity.

Unlike Kellie and Nikki, who were surely filling up the ValleyBuzz blog with mean-spirited posts, unflattering photos, and rude comments. If not at this very minute, then later, certainly.

In a rare moment of concession, Kellie stepped back and tossed her hair to the other shoulder, leaving a trail of her sickeningly sweet perfume in the air. "Yeah, well, I need to go to history. This piece of trash isn't worth our time, anyway."

Just then I noticed that others had stopped to stare at our interaction, with gaping mouths and narrowed eyes. Great. We were a sideshow now.

Freed, I hurried away down the hallway to class. So I'd made some bad decisions and I was paying for them. I knew that. But the worst part wasn't Nikki's and Kellie's taunting. The worst part was knowing that I'd lost my best friend and there was nothing I could do about it. Seeing how Cherise had resisted falling into their game only made me miss her more. The girl was golden. And I . . . well, I no longer really knew who I was. Sly Fox.

Skank. Loser. Criminal. There was a whole new set of names to choose from, and none of them covered the missing-mother part.

At lunch, I found a far-flung corner of the dining hall, an empty booth in the back. I promised myself I wouldn't let the Glitterati force me to skip a meal. I wasn't going to let them have that power. Lunch was too important. But I didn't exactly want to be a spectacle, either. The compromise was to sit where I could see everyone who would be watching me. Preemptive ogling.

I picked at my salad Niçoise with seared tuna, the day's special. Of all of Prep's luxuries, the gourmet cooking was one that would never cease to amaze me. Actually, there were many things I still loved about the school itself—if only I could've started the year over fresh.

So far I'd survived French and geometry. Comp was a little tougher, because Cherise was there. I'd sat four seats away and tried not to look over in her direction the whole time, wondering if she was as nervous as I was.

Then I'd spent my free period in the computer lab. I was supposed to be researching a civics paper, but I couldn't stop myself from checking the Greyhound site. There was a five o'clock bus that was leaving that afternoon. It was a twelve-hour ride with a transfer in L.A., so that would get me to Santa Barbara by the morning. I just needed to get to the station. If, that is, I decided to go. I was still wavering.

"Hey, Willa." I looked up. It was Mary, her black hair pulled back in a ponytail. Behind her was Sierra.

"Hey, guys," I said.

"How are you doing?" Sierra asked, looking down at me with a serious expression, her brown eyes lit with sympathy.

"I've been better," I admitted. I felt the hard shell I'd been cultivating all day starting to crack with their small act of kindness. Tears surged in my eyes.

Don't go there.

I took a sip of water and tried to pull myself together. If I started talking, I might tell them about my mom, my house, the money, how I'd lost everything. I might totally fall apart right there in the middle of the dining hall. No, I had to keep it together.

"Don't let them tear you down," Sierra said. "Those spoiled girls aren't worth it."

"It's not just them," I said. "It's everyone."

"Not everyone. We're rooting for you. You know that, right?" Mary said. "We'll never forget what you did."

"Those gifts made us feel like someone actually cared about us, and that meant a lot when—well, you know, when coming to school was pretty much a nightmare," Sierra said. "And you put those *perras* in their place. We don't have to take their crap anymore."

"Yeah?" I looked up at her, hope creeping in.

"You did something. That was more than someone

else would've done," she said.

"Well, we're here if you need anything." Mary shifted her tray. She was still hovering over the table.

I smiled appreciatively. "Thanks, guys."

I could have asked them to sit with me, but I didn't want to hurt their reputation. They'd already been linked to me and the crimes, as the recipients of my scheme. People had already questioned whether they were the ones doing the stealing—at least that was Kellie's and Nikki's theory at first, before I got caught. If anyone still thought they were involved, it would be terrible.

Besides, we weren't friends. Not really. They were people I talked to in gym class or the girls' room, but Sierra didn't exactly like me. It would be weird now, after everything that happened, for us to start hanging out. Like I bought their affection or something. Which had never been my intention.

They turned to go, and I felt some of the day's pressure lift off me. No matter what happened, it hadn't been a waste. And now I knew what I had to do. It was clear.

I watched them walk across the dining hall, noticing that neither girl was wearing the couture clothes I'd sent them. Sierra was in boot-cut jeans and a flowy fuchsia top, and Mary was wearing a flouncy green dress. Nothing fabulous, nothing expensive, but they looked like themselves—cute and normal.

Waiting at their usual table were Shane Welcome and

Bradley Poole, who were part of VP's A-list. So maybe I hadn't really been able to change their lives or make a permanent impact on their wardrobes, but I'd at least gotten them some dudely attention.

As I sat alone, their words rang through me. I did something. I didn't just stand by. I could be proud of that, at least.

And now that my mom was in trouble, how could I even think of not doing the same for her?

No, I had to get on that bus.

When I turned back again, Tre was approaching the booth with long strides, carrying a Gatorade and a panini. "How's your first day back going?"

I heaved my shoulders. "Eh. Girlfights in the hallway, threats from the headmaster, general alienation. You know, the usual."

He pointed his drink at me. "You're still here, right? No one's chased you away yet."

"I'm still here," I said. And as I opened my mouth again, I knew I had made a decision. There was no turning back. "But I'm leaving today, Tre."

He raised his eyebrows over the orange liquid as he took a swig.

"And going where?"

"I have to find my mom," I said. "I know you don't agree with me. But they're going to kick me out, anyway. Page said as much. And I have a plan, I think. Aidan traced the email to Santa Barbara. So all I need to do is get a bus this afternoon. I've got my stuff with me. And then I'll be out of your hair."

"What makes you think I want you out of my hair?" He put his Gatorade down. "How will you get to the station?"

"Call a cab or something."

He spread his long fingers out on the tabletop. "Well, I've been thinking, too."

"And?"

"And I think you're right. You need to go after your mom."

I stared at him, shocked. "What about all that 'you'll break your probation' stuff from yesterday?"

"The thing is, I know you, and once you get an idea in that head of yours, there's no way to talk you out of it. You knew all along you were leaving, didn't you? I did."

"I didn't really make up my mind until just now."

"And if it were my mom . . . well, I can't imagine what you're going through, knowing she might be in trouble." He paused and scratched at a spot behind his ear. "Of course, from a legal perspective you're playing with fire. Naw, if I had my choice, you'd stay here."

"Because you enjoy carting me around and making me breakfast?" I teased.

"Right." He shook his head, a smile hinting across his face. "I'm just saying that once you get involved in the criminal system it's real easy to keep getting sucked back in."

"But you did it," I said. "I mean, you managed to get out of it."

"Just barely. People are still trying to act like I'm screwing up, even when I'm not. Maybe it's easier not to fight that. Maybe you should just be who you are, you know?"

"A criminal?"

"C'mon, Willa. That's not what I mean. I mean the part of you that wants to fight, to change things." He looked away to drain the last of his drink. "That being said, I think you might need a little help with this half-baked plan of yours. Meet me outside when the final harp rings?"

I grinned. That I could do. Everything would be easier with Tre's help—it would be just like old times. Yes, I'd be breaking the law again, but this was different. This was about my mom. "Do I need to bring anything special?"

"Just your true self."

SIX

"MIND TELLING ME where we're going?" I asked Tre from the passenger seat.

He'd been silent for the past five minutes as he drove us along. Surprises were cute and all, but I was pretty sure I'd had enough of them in the past few days to last me for the next fifteen years.

I scanned the scene outside the window for more information. We were heading south out of the Valley on Route 51, I could tell that much. His Audi picked up speed as we merged onto a huge multilane highway lined with sound barrier walls, and passed under a big green sign indicating that the airport was five miles ahead.

"Are we flying somewhere?"

Tre just shook his head. "Damn, you're impatient. We're finding you an alternative means of transport. If you're going to skip town, you can't go taking public transportation or using your credit cards."

"So what do you propose?"

"What do you think?" He looked at me knowingly, keeping a palm on the wheel.

I thought he meant stealing something. But then I thought better. Tre wasn't doing that stuff anymore. He probably had something else up his sleeve.

I clutched my schoolbag in my lap. The overnight bag was at my feet. If his idea, whatever it was, didn't pan out, I still probably had time to make that bus.

The highway filled up with more traffic as we approached downtown Phoenix. It was getting close to rush hour. Being on the road felt good—at least I was now doing something instead of moping around school. There was a purpose to fulfill. And going after a goal always raised my spirits.

We were still headed toward the airport. I frowned. Planes didn't count as "alternative" unless it was a private jet. Or he was sneaking me into freight. Which could be a little extreme, but kind of cool. I pictured crouching in a darkened compartment with pets and baggage. Maybe we were going to use some other kind of airport vehicle, like a rental-car shuttle or a skycap buggy.

Tre signaled to exit the highway at Sky Harbor Circle. "We've got one more stop to make. Just stay with me, okay? I've got this on lock."

I was. I was right there with him, going along with his obviously thought-through scheme.

That is, until he pulled into a Chevron station.

Because sitting on the curb in front, legs splayed out and sipping a frozen coffee like he had no care in the world, was Aidan.

What the . . . ?

"You called Aidan," I said.

Tre honked the horn and waved to Aidan before turning to me. "Yes, I did. And dude actually took public transportation to meet us here. Imagine that."

As happy as I was to see him—and there's no describing the exact joy of watching Aidan stand up and shake out his mop of hair, sliding on the strap of his backpack, the crooked smile of recognition slowly spreading across his face—I was a little weirded out. These two were like peas in a pod. What was up with the conspiracies between them? Why were they always making secret plans to meet each other without telling me? Why did all the men in my life suck?

"Now look." Tre patted my shoulder. "Don't get mad. I knew you were going to try to do this on your own. And I knew if I asked, you'd say no. But there's strength in numbers, Willa."

I thought back to the previous night. Maybe that was true, but I still wanted to be in charge of my own plan.

Of course, as Aidan came over to the car and nodded at me through the window and got in the backseat, my twisted-up face relaxed into a smile. Involuntary response. I blame hormones.

"Hey, Willa."

"Hey," I said softly.

"I guess you're wondering why I'm here."

"Kind of."

"I wanted to help out, make sure you were okay. And I wanted to give you this."

He handed me a salted caramel, wrapped in cellophane. This was an inside joke between us, about his sweetness and my saltiness.

Touched, I took it from him. "I'll save it for later."

"Don't wait too long. They have a tendency to melt."

Like my brain. *Snap to it, Willa. We have a job to do here. You need to get to California, remember?*

"I won't forget it." I slipped it into the pocket of my jacket. "So can we move along with this, Tre? I need to hit the road soon."

"All right, we're going. Girl's got an attitude."

"Doesn't she?"

I ignored their jibes. As Tre drove, the scenery outside was growing more industrial with warehouses and docking areas full of trucks, plus the occasional motel or strip club.

Tre pulled off onto another street with a row of long-term parking lots. "Time to check out our options," Tre said.

"So we *are* stealing a car." My pulse quickened at the thought—anticipation, tingling and hot, burned in my hands. Then my brain flashed back to Judge Prendergast. The look on his face in the courtroom. My promises to be good.

Stealing was wrong. So wrong.

But it was so *exciting*.

"We can't. I mean, I can't do that." The feelings I was having, just thinking about it, were making me squirm in my seat. Bottom line: I didn't trust myself. I loved thieving way too much.

"What did you think we were doing?" Aidan asked. "Going to pick out curtains?"

"Look, Willa, I wouldn't suggest it if I thought there was a better way," Tre said, putting the car into park. "Don't worry. I've got a strategy."

"And what's that?"

Tre slipped back into crime-professor mode. "Simple. We pick a car." He pulled out a pair of binoculars from the glove compartment. "Then we wait for it to get dark."

I unclicked my seat belt, realizing that we'd be sitting here for a while on our stakeout. "We're just going to hot-wire it, right here in plain sight?"

He circled the area outside the windshield with his finger. "Hardly plain sight. No one's hanging around here at night. People park for weeks at a time, and security is a joke. These companies can't even be held responsible for break-ins. If we look like we know what we're doing, no one will notice us."

He was right—there were no pedestrians around, seemingly for blocks. Just litter, cracked, weedy sidewalks, and billboards with scantily clad women.

"But . . . you said you weren't going to do this anymore," I said.

"I'm not," Tre said pointedly. He looked around and shook his head. "I thought this was supposed to be a shady area. Please. Phoenix is wack."

Aidan laughed. "Sorry, dude. This is as shady as we get here. You'll just have to work with it."

I wasn't done with the previous line of conversation. "If not you, then who? Me?"

"No," Tre said. "Not you."

"I've got it covered, Willa." Aidan pointed to a gold Cadillac Escalade. "What about that one?"

"You?" I asked, incredulous.

Since when did Aidan know how to steal a car? And again, when was all of this decided and why was I the last to know?

"Too flashy," Tre said, lifting the binoculars to his eyes. "We need to think practical. We also need to look for the farthest end of the lot, on the edge where the cameras won't pick it up. Assuming there are cameras, which we have to do. Even if some of these lots just have them for show."

"Well, it's a long drive to California," Aidan said. "It should be a comfortable car."

"Just hang on. I'll pick the car," I said, not wanting to lose control. This was my mission, and I couldn't lose sight of that, not until I'd found my mom. "And I'm driving."

"No way. You don't even have a license," Aidan pointed out.

He was going to be a stickler for a little rule like that? "We're already breaking the law here. And how hard can it be to learn? All kinds of idiots know how to drive."

"It's harder than you think," Aidan said, raising an eyebrow. "Driving is a subtle art."

Forget Aidan. I had to appeal to the mastermind. "C'mon, Tre."

"'C'mon, Tre' what?" Tre's eyes rolled upward like he was pleading with an unseen god on the ceiling of his Audi.

"Let me try," I said, gesturing to an empty parking lot at an abandoned restaurant-supply store. "Let's go in there. I'll show you."

Tre looked at his watch. "Well, we do have some time. If you're serious, we'll give you a shot."

He did as I requested, driving into the lot and parking square in the middle. We traded seats.

I got behind the wheel and examined all the dials and buttons like I knew what I was doing. Then I adjusted the mirrors and the seat and waited. For what, I don't know.

"It's in park," Aidan offered. "All you have to do is put it in drive. The *D*."

"I know," I said, but my tone was too brittle to be convincing. Already I could feel my bravado slipping away.

You can handle this.

I'd done way scarier things than this recently, hadn't I? And my mom's life could be depending on me. I shifted the gear and put my foot on the gas. The car jerked forward as though sprung by an industrial-sized rubber band. Even I, who'd made this happen, was shocked by the force.

"Whoa whoa whoa," Tre said, laying an arm across me to hold me back—from the windshield and the road on the other side of it. "Gently. Hit the pedal gradually."

I tried again, a little less jerky this time.

Driving. I was driving. It was kinda like flying. I couldn't believe how powerful I felt.

I eased up on the pedal and let the car roll to the outer edges of the lot before braking. I hit the brake pedal with my left foot—more like a clomp. The left foot, apparently, was even less controlled than the right because we stopped all at once, eliciting a screech from the tires and an *ack* from the backseat.

Okay. Maybe it wasn't graceful but I had achieved stopliness.

I turned to my skeptical passengers. "See? I can do this."

"I think that's still up for debate," Tre said, rubbing at his temples.

"What's next?" I asked, ready to show them what else I could do. Wanting to get on the road already.

"All right, hotshot, why don't you reverse now?" Aidan asked, grinning. Unlike Tre, he seemed to be enjoying this.

Tre turned back to give him a look of death. "Maybe

you're forgetting this isn't your car, Murphy."

"What? If she's going to drive, she has to be able to go backward, too. Not to mention parallel parking."

"Psh. Forget it," Tre said, waving for him to shut up.

"Reverse." Reasoning that going back would be as easy as going forward, I moved the gear into *R* and hit the gas. Smoothly. Gradually.

As the car moved steadily backward, the empty lot and the warehouses in front of me grew smaller. It was almost too easy. I was going to do this. I was going to drive and find my mom and neither of them could stop me.

"Willa," Aidan said. "I think you're forgetting something."

I looked to my left and right. I readjusted my hands on the wheel. I glanced at the speedometer and the other dials in front of me, though I didn't know what most of them were for.

"What? What am I forgetting?" I turned around to face him. That's when I saw the wall coming for us. Well, technically, we were coming for it.

Looking back. I was forgetting to look back.

The bricks were a blur of red.

Aidan and Tre screamed.

I slammed on the brake pedal with both feet. The car halted, bouncing on its tires with a loud screech. Tre flew forward, almost hitting his head on the glove compartment.

"Okay, okay, that's it!" Tre yelled. "Put it in park. We've seen enough of your skills. Get out."

My hands clenched into fists of frustration. I'd screwed up. "I could learn—"

"There's no time," Tre said as we switched back to our original seats. "Nice try, but you obviously can't drive to California."

Aidan grabbed my headrest and leaned forward so I could feel his breath on my ear. "Look, I'm fully prepared to be your chauffeur. I've got some free time on my hands these days, with no school and all."

"But you can't," I blurted. I looked to Tre pleadingly, but he was too busy driving us back to our previous spot across the street from the long-term parking lot.

"Why not?"

I wanted him to—of course I did—but Aidan coming with me would complicate everything. How could I explain that? I couldn't. Not in so many words. I tried a softer line of reasoning instead. "I mean, do you really want to do this? It could take a few days for us to get there, find her, and come back."

"It's sounds like fun, actually. I've got nothing to lose. Except, you know, getting in trouble for breaking my probation, too."

I looked into his green, green eyes and got lost there for a moment. This was exactly the trouble . . . with Aidan around, I would totally lose focus. I would be reduced to jelly of the most inefficient kind.

"C'mon," he cajoled. "I'm the one who figured out where the email was coming from."

"But this isn't going to be a vacation."

"I know," he said.

I paused. I could use some company. It was a long trip. I didn't necessarily *want* to be alone. He was waiting, smiling hopefully, for my response.

"Fine," I relented. "You can come with me. Just don't . . ."

". . . don't what?"

Don't distract me.

"Don't get us lost."

"I won't. Because you'll be the navigator. You do know how to read maps, right? Or do we need to do a lesson on that, too?"

"Yeah, I know how to read maps." Didn't he know how important this was to me? "If you're really coming with me, then you need to be serious."

"I am serious." His face told me he was.

"Okay," Tre said, handing me his binoculars. "I think I see our car. Aisle 5G, on the end there."

By now the sun was setting, but I could still just barely discern the makes and models of the vehicles through the round lenses. The car Tre was referring to was a silver Volvo, probably from the midnineties.

"It looks kind of old," I said.

"That's why it's perfect," Tre said. "No built-in alarm. It's safe and sturdy. Drives well, too."

Aidan clapped his hands. "So how should I do this?"

"Just shimmy open the door and get under the steering wheel. Use this." Tre handed Aidan a screwdriver, a pair of wire strippers, and a roll of electrician's tape. "Take off the cap and get into the ignition wiring. Strip the wires and connect the brown wire with the red wires. Tape it together and you should be good to go. You have to move quick."

"I thought you knew how," I said to Aidan.

"Nope, never done it. But how hard could it be?" He looked at me, winking.

"Harder than you think," I said, echoing his own words back to him. So he was a newbie, after all. I didn't know whether to be glad or terrified.

Aidan stuffed the supplies into his pockets. "I think I've got it. Fingers crossed."

"Fingers crossed and legs broken, man. We'll wait here," Tre said.

We watched him slink toward the parking lot entrance. I wished Tre were doing the car stealing—I would have been much more comfortable knowing we had an expert on the case—but I understood why he wanted Aidan to do it. Besides, Aidan claimed to be good with technical things. He should be able to figure it out.

"Look, I'm sorry I had to do this to you, with Aidan and everything," Tre said, breaking the silence in the car. "But I really think this plan will be better in the end. You really don't know what's waiting for you on the other side there—you need someone with you. I'd go myself, but you know . . ."

He couldn't go. Not with his record. And he was right. I did need help, even if I was reluctant to admit it.

"Plus the driving . . . don't even try to front," he laughed. "When you get back I'm signing you up for driver's ed."

"Whatever," I grumbled. I looked out the window into the inky darkness. Planes were taking off overhead from the nearby airport, huge and roaring as they rose above us and lifted up into the night.

He leaned back and his leather seat creaked a little. "You don't have to answer this if you don't want to, but is something up with you guys?"

"I mean, we kissed or whatever," I admitted. "I don't know what's going on, though."

My face flushed. Maybe I was having a panic attack, or maybe Aidan was making me into a crazy person. And talking about it with Tre was uncomfortable. I felt certain he could see right through me to how I really felt—and I wasn't sure I wanted him to know all of this. I barely understood it myself.

"He's a cool guy," Tre said softly. "But I think he has a reputation. You know, for getting around."

"Like I said, I don't really think . . ."

"Just be careful, okay? I think he can help you out. Don't let the emotional stuff get in the way."

"I will," I said. "I mean, I won't."

I stared into his brown eyes and saw the genuine concern there. Also, something else, something fierce and protective just swimming underneath the surface.

"I want you to be safe, Willa." He gripped at the steering wheel, alternately tensing and releasing his fingers, and then turned away so I could no longer read his expression.

Just then we saw the headlights flaring out of the lot. They came toward the Audi, suddenly and straight on.

Everything behind that was dark, but when the car stopped short in front of us, I could make out the silhouette of a man chasing after it on foot, yelling, "Stop! Come back here!"

Aidan rolled down the driver's-side window. He was terrified. It was all over him. "Let's go!"

"Did he see you?" Tre demanded.

"I don't think he saw my face," Aidan rasped.

Tre looked at me with a furrowed brow. "Get in the car, Willa," he said slowly and evenly.

I looked from Tre to Aidan, hot with confusion and the chaos of the moment. I felt paralyzed by indecision. To go meant getting into a stolen car that was about to be reported. To stay meant risking getting Tre into trouble. Meanwhile, the guy was coming closer, yelling and panting. "But—"

"Just do it!" Tre bellowed. "Get the hell out of here!"

I did as he commanded, grabbing my bags and hopping into the passenger seat of the Volvo.

"We'll call you from the road," Aidan said.

"Don't call me unless it's untraceable," Tre said, sounding almost disgusted. He hit the gas pedal and tore out of there, the Audi fishtailing down the little street as he swerved away from the running man.

Aidan and I sped off in the opposite direction, heading back toward the highway. I watched in the side mirror as the silhouette of the man got tinier and tinier.

We were doing this. We were really driving away in our stolen car—now a getaway car. It had all happened so fast. Two laws broken.

No turning back now.

And that, ladies and gentlemen, was how I ended up in a stolen 1992 Volvo with my pseudocrush, sort-of makeout buddy behind the wheel, on a road trip to find my mysteriously missing mother.

SEVEN

BY THE TIME we crossed the state line it was fully night. We'd made good time—speeding through Tolleson and Goodyear and whole nubby stretches of desert. The traffic on the road had opened up. Through the veiled haze I could make out some mountains looming in the distance.

Aidan let out a cheer when he saw the sign. "Woo-hoo. California, baby. That makes how many hours to go?"

"Two, I think?" I studied the map.

We were both getting giddy now. Several hours on the road in a stolen vehicle will do that to you. It was all a little unreal.

The fact that this Volvo, which vibrated and made weird rattling sounds any time we went over fifty miles per hour, had gotten us as far as it had, seemed some-what miraculous. The other issue with the car in motion was that the window on my side was busted, the glass sliding down every so often. How had no one stolen this hunk of metal before us?

Still, none of that mattered. What was important was that we were on our way. Free. The breeze blowing into the car felt like a wind of good fortune, carrying us along. The classic rock pouring out of the radio was loud and heady. And we were going to find my mom. If only we could get there sooner. Like by teleport.

Ever since she'd gone missing I ached inside with longing. I just wished I could see her through some kind of crystal ball, like Dorothy looking in on her family in Kansas, just to know that she was okay, wherever she was. Though my mom was from Missouri. Originally, anyway. I reached up to touch the bird at my throat.

As though he were reading my mind, Aidan turned to me and asked, "What's the deal with your mom, anyway? What's she like?"

"She's awesome," I said. I pictured her in her tank top and shorts, pulling weeds out of the garden, building things. Hatching the next great plan for us. She was young and beautiful, and way cooler than any other moms I knew. She had a lifetime of travel stories, a wicked sense of humor, and a skeleton key tattooed on her ankle. If it weren't Aidan driving right now it could have easily been her, taking us on one of our summer trips or moving us to our next home. She was the queen of the road trip.

"I mean, are you guys close?"

"Yeah," I said. I couldn't really remember a time when we hadn't been together. We had our weekend movie nights on the couch, our pj's-till-five days, our summer camping outings, our long talks at the kitchen table. No matter where we were living we'd taken those things with us. At the same time, she'd always encouraged me to be independent, to learn how to do things on my own.

I wondered, suddenly, if that was because she'd known that something like this might happen. That she might one day have to leave. But that was paranoid, right?

I flashed back to her note. She'd known enough to leave the money. But then she was always prepared. She was the kind of person who wrote everything down, had a to-do list for every hour of the day.

"It's gotta be something serious, don't you think? I'm not even tight with my mom—she's either at the tanning salon or shopping twenty-four/seven. My dad's secretary, Wilma, has been more of a parent to me, practically, but I'm pretty sure a mother wouldn't leave her kid like that unless she had a good reason."

He was right, of course. But I just wanted to change the subject, because I could feel some tension gathering in my throat and the last thing I wanted was for Aidan to see me cry.

This was too raw, too close. And whatever was happening between Aidan and me was too new.

"Can we change this?" I reached toward the radio,

but Aidan held out his hand to block me.

"Driver's choice."

"Who made up that rule?" I asked.

"Dude, that's a *universal* rule. Everyone knows that the driver has to be relaxed on a road trip. If you were driving you'd get to pick."

"But I can't drive."

"And thus, it will be my choice so long as we're on this trip. I have excellent taste," he said, turning the dial so that the classic rock blared even more loudly through the speakers. "You, of all people, should know that."

My cheeks warmed at the compliment.

"Can you grab me a turkey jerky from my bag, please, copilot?"

"Righto." I dug out the snack for him, noticing that his bag was filled with at least one change of clothes, and handed it over. "So you knew all along you'd be driving, didn't you?"

His eyes dipped over in my direction and my insides fluttered. "I had a strong inclination, yes. Or I hoped, anyway."

I tried to ignore the trembling in my chest. This was real. There was something going on and both of us could feel it. I pointed to a sign for the exit coming up. "Maybe we can stop for dinner?"

"Yeah, good idea. I could use a coffee, too."

We found a Subway a few miles from the highway and pulled into the parking lot. I stashed the map and the printout of the painting in the glove compartment and left my schoolbooks, but I took my overnight bag, afraid to leave it and all my cash in the car with the busted window. It was much cooler here, in the middle of the night, and I quickly grabbed my mom's windbreaker and slipped it on.

All of a sudden I felt aware of the two of us being together as we crossed the parking lot, that people passing by might think we were a couple. Were we? He was here, even when it meant risking his own probation.

He was walking fast and aggressively, as he always did, his jaw set. I glimpsed his biceps poking out of his T-shirt.

Hello, biceps.

What was he thinking about? Was he worried about his parents? Was he afraid? There were so many things I didn't know about him. Things I wanted to know.

After he ordered, he turned to me. "What are you having? Only the finest here for the lady."

I scanned the menu. "Turkey and cheese."

"Excellent choice. One of my favorites."

The cashier asked, "Is this separate or together?"

"Together," he said, and a little shiver danced across my shoulder blades.

We sat down at a Formica booth to eat our subs.

"Thanks for dinner," I said. "You didn't have to—"

"Pay? Willa, my parents have more money than God, okay? I can cover a freaking sandwich."

I shrugged, embarrassed. That he was so direct about stuff like that, when so many Paradise Valley people acted like there was nothing special about having millions, set Aidan apart. But his having money was also something that would always be different between him and me.

"What's the plan?" he asked, popping a pickle slice in his mouth.

"I don't know," I said. "That's what I've been wondering." I'd been so focused on getting to Santa Barbara, I hadn't thought through the rest of the details.

Like the fact that we were really breaking the law now, as in brand-new crimes. And the fact that my mom said not to come after her.

I was so getting grounded. Probably before *and* after getting arrested. But what choice did I have?

"I've got it. Check this: We go in, bum-rush security. You steal a maid's uniform. We'll restrain the guards and tie them up, but it'll just be temporary. . . . Then we go up the service elevator. I'll hide in your laundry cart."

I laughed. "I don't think all of that will be necessary."

"No?"

"We can probably just go into the lobby and ask for her at the front desk."

"That doesn't sound fun at all. I thought you were supposed to be some kind of bandit. Sheesh." He balled up his paper bag and stuffed it into his soda cup.

"She's probably sitting in there watching pay-per-view," I said. Though I was saying this more to myself than to Aidan. And in my heart of hearts, I sort of doubted it.

She'd said she was in serious trouble. A fresh shot of panic thrust me upright. Where was my mom and who was she with? Time was ticking by as we sat here.

"We should really get going," I said, collecting all of our trash together and grabbing my bag.

"As you wish." He bowed and tipped an invisible chauffeur's cap.

We got back in the car and continued on. After a while we passed a sign for Coachella.

"Have you ever been to the music fest?" he asked.

"No, but I've always wanted to," I said. "Have you?"

He nodded. "It's fun. Maybe we can go this year." He didn't look over.

"Yeah," I said, a tingling sensation spreading over me like static on a wire. *He's asking me out. Like, on a real date.* "That would be cool."

Just then, the car flooded with blue and red lights, flashing and bouncing off the windshield. In the rearview mirror it was plain as day: a cop car speeding toward us.

"Oh my God," I said. "They found us. How fast are you going?"

"I'm only doing sixty," he said, glancing down at the speedometer.

"It's a fifty-five zone," I said. "Slow down!"

Aidan braked gently.

Panic welled in my chest as I remembered the night I was taken to juvie. The cop advanced, shifting into the left lane, so that he was almost beside us. "Is he pulling us over? What should we do?"

"I don't know," Aidan said, biting his lip. He glanced to his left and back again. "I don't know if I could outrun him, not with this piece of junk."

The black-and-white car held steady with us, going window-to-window for a bit. I squeezed my eyes shut, preparing for Aidan to hit the gas or for the cop to push us to the shoulder. Something.

But nothing happened. When I opened them again, the cop accelerated and zoomed forward, the lights pulsing out into the horizon.

We both exhaled at the same time.

"Holy crap," Aidan said, wiping sweat from his hairline. "I thought we were toast."

I looked down and noticed that I'd been gripping the door handle so tightly the blood had drained from my hand.

Aidan hit the gas and the car sped up again as we covered more ground that stood between us and whatever lay ahead.

I pumped my fingers, trying to regain sensation in them. This whole situation was putting me on edge. My mom, the cops, the stolen car. Of course, being stuffed into a small metal box with Aidan Murphy was nerve-racking in its own way.

"This is it, I think," Aidan said, ducking his head to see through the windshield. "That says Hadley, right?"

We'd been driving along the coast for some time, though in the dark we could barely see the ocean. Then Aidan turned off the highway onto a street with suburban homes. It was almost midnight as we reached the center of downtown Santa Barbara, and the Hadley Hotel was indeed straight ahead.

With its bell towers and observatory, it looked like it had once been an old convent. Now it was the type of place that cost four hundred dollars a night to lounge around in a fluffy robe and order up shrimp cocktail, or whatever it was that people did in hotels. I personally never had the pleasure of staying in one. My mom, ever the free spirit, had always acted like she preferred cabins and campsites. Maybe that's why she chose the Hadley, because it would be the last place anyone would expect to find her. Actually, the more I thought about it, the more I realized I might be the only person looking for her. We had no other family, and we'd moved so much she never really had any friends that I knew of.

I watched as Aidan parked the car. My legs were thrumming against the faux-leather seats, and it was all I could do to not jump out of the still-moving vehicle. We were finally here, and I couldn't wait a minute longer.

I pictured my mom sweeping down a grand staircase to greet us in the lobby. A long, tearful embrace. Maybe even a chamber orchestra. Who knew? I just needed to get in there.

I stripped off my seat belt and grabbed my overnight bag.

"Let's do this," Aidan said.

I felt like we were robbing a bank—that was how deeply my pulse was thumping. But it was a different kind of excitement now. A different kind of anticipation.

We marched through the sliding glass doors, past a gigantic floor-to-ceiling floral arrangement with green tentacles, and toward the check-in desk. The young Asian woman sitting behind it looked up as we approached. "Hello. May I help you?" she asked with a hospitality-trained smile.

"Yes," I said, breathlessly pushing out the words. "I'm looking for a guest named Joanne Fox. I believe she's registered here."

"Hold on," she said. Her fingers clicked on the keyboard as she consulted her computer. Her eyes dropped down along the lines of the screen. "Hmm, Joanne Fox, you said?"

"Yes," I said, my heart rising expectantly.

She cocked her head politely. "I don't see anyone here. Is it possible she checked in under a different name?"

Of course it was. Argh. Why hadn't I thought of that? If she was in trouble and hiding from someone, she almost certainly wasn't going to use her real name. I'd heard that celebrities always used pseudonyms, sometimes funny ones, to elude the paparazzi when they checked in to hotels.

Think, Willa.

"Maybe try Julie Christie?" That was my mom's favorite actress. She loved old movies, and she'd even imitated her haircut once. It was worth a shot.

The woman smiled. "I think I'd know if someone here was checked in under that name."

"Can you just look, please?" I asked, feeling increasingly desperate.

"Okay," she said, and scrolled down her screen again. "Nope. Nobody here under Julie Christie."

"She's a blond woman, about five foot six. Looks kind of like me?"

"I'm sorry, but we can't give out room information without a name. For security reasons—I'm sure you understand. Besides, I just started my shift, so I wouldn't have seen her."

I looked at Aidan, at a loss. He shrugged back at me and then pointed a thumb toward a plush-looking sofa across the lobby.

"Do you mind if we sit here for a bit?" I asked the woman.

"Be my guest," she said, then let out a tinkling laugh. "No pun intended."

Hotel humor. Awesome.

Aidan and I made our way to the seating area. I sank down onto its soft cushions, dropping my bag on the floor, and felt the weight of my own misgivings.

What had I been thinking? That I could just waltz in here and summon my mom to the front desk and drive away? In my fantasies, yes. That had been exactly what I was thinking.

"No other names she would use, huh?" he asked.

"None that I can think of," I said. "Besides, I didn't want her to start getting suspicious."

He leaned back and folded his arms behind his head. "No offense, but I think she might be a tad suspicious already, given that two teenagers have shown up to her hotel at an ungodly hour on a school night. What now?"

I ran my hand over the elegant embroidery on the throw pillows. The lobby was cool and comfortable, and pleasant flute music played overhead. It did nothing to soothe me. I was all raw edges.

The way I saw it, we only had two choices, and they involved staying or leaving. I still felt reasonably certain that my mom was here, and after driving all this way, I wasn't just going to turn around and head back to Paradise Valley.

"Let's stay. I mean, the email came from this hotel. So she must've been here, right?"

"Well, not necessarily," Aidan said slowly. "I was kind of thinking this over on the way up and it's possible she's not."

"What do you mean?" I demanded.

"Well, the email address I found could be a proxy— you know, a fake address people use to hide their real IP. If you wanted to disappear, you could set it up that way."

"No." I shook my head. "She's not that technical." What I didn't say was that I really didn't believe she wanted to disappear. I couldn't let myself believe that.

"Either way. She could be here but she might not be," he said, sounding as conclusive as a Magic 8 Ball.

"Why didn't you mention that possibility before?" I asked, feeling frustrated. "I mean, that might have been helpful to know before we drove all the way here."

"You seemed so excited about finding her. I didn't want to disappoint you. Besides, like I said, it's pretty much a fifty-fifty."

Fifty-fifty. The worst ratio ever invented.

"Well, I'm not leaving," I said. "If she *is* staying here, she's got to come through the lobby at some point."

"Okay," he said. "We'll wait." Then he proceeded to close his eyes and drop his head back against one of the throw pillows.

"That's cool," I said, realizing that we'd been up all night. I yawned involuntarily. "I'll keep watch. We can take turns napping."

But it's not like he needed my blessing. He was already snoring lightly.

While Aidan slept, I waited. Or tried to. After twenty minutes passed and hardly anyone had come in or out of the hotel, I was impatient.

I decided to do a little more footwork. The front doors slid open and I stepped out into the cool night air.

A valet in a red uniform stood by the entrance. "Hello, can I help you?"

Up close, I could see he was probably middle-aged— short and clean-shaven, with graying hair.

"Maybe," I said. "I'm looking for my mom. She kind of looks like me. I'm wondering if you've seen anyone like that over the last couple of days."

"Hmm." He frowned. "I see a lot of people coming and going all day."

"She has shorter hair and she's a little taller?" I prompted him.

He paused to consider this. "Actually, there was one woman like that, now that I think of it. Traveling alone. I remember parking her car—I think it was a Subaru."

I inhaled sharply. "A hatchback? Green?"

"Yes, I think that's it."

"When did you see her last?"

"I couldn't say. Maybe a day or two ago? It's kind of a blur, to be honest."

"Is she still here, do you think?"

"She could be." He shrugged. "Look, hon, I don't have a photographic memory or anything. That's all I got."

It was enough for me. So she *was* here. Or had been. At some point.

I thanked him and headed back inside. I could go back to waiting now, or at least waiting until Aidan woke up. He was still curled up in a sprawled version of fetal on the couch. Behind him, in the back of the lobby, I noticed a bar set up with tea and cookies and pastries. I was starving. Complimentary snacks? Yes, please.

I eyed the woman at the front desk. She appeared to be busy checking someone out of the hotel, so I proceeded to the bar and started to help myself.

A TV overhead played CNN news. In the background, it droned reports about tornadoes in the Midwest and a political scandal involving a sexting senator. Then I heard the words *teenager* and *suspect*. My head snapped up.

On the screen a brunette woman was standing in front of the long-term parking lot in Phoenix.

The lot where we'd stolen the car.

I dropped my croissant, and it tumbled to the carpeted floor, flakes of pastry crumbling to bread dust.

"A 1992 Volvo was reported missing yesterday, and now authorities are tying the crime to Aidan Murphy, son of Hanson Murphy, CEO of MTech, the technology firm headquartered here in the Phoenix area."

The camera flashed to a balding man in a striped polo. "I seen him myself. I'd just gotten back from vacation and I came to get my car and I seen him sitting in the driver's seat. He looked straight at me and kept driving. The little bugger almost hit me."

So the guy did see Aidan after all. They knew who he was.

Oh no oh no oh no oh no.

The reporter again. "Local police confirmed that Murphy's parents filed a missing-persons report today. Murphy has been on probation for an unrelated crime and was recently expelled from the Valley Preparatory School. Authorities have reason to believe he's on the run with the stolen car."

I didn't need to hear any more. I ran back to the couch

and shoved Aidan awake.

"Aidan, get up," I said through my teeth. "Get up right now."

He rolled over and draped an elbow over his eyes. "What? What time is it?"

"They know it's you," I said. "I just saw it on the news. That guy you saw . . . he went to the police."

Aidan sat up immediately. "Oh crap. This is not good. Really not good."

"I know," I said, alarm rising through my voice in faltering waves. "What should we do?"

"We can't stay here. That woman at the desk saw both of us. And who knows who else."

"The valet driver. I just talked to him. But he saw my mom. She was here."

"We'll have to come back," he said, standing and whispering fiercely. He took hold of my arm. "We'll have to figure it out. Let's *go*."

"Now? But what if she shows up?" We were so close. How could we leave?

"C'mon, Willa," he hissed.

I reluctantly followed him out through the lobby, looking back over my shoulder for any sign of my mom. But there was no one coming or going. The woman at the front desk didn't even look up.

EIGHT

"WE'RE SO DEAD," Aidan said, covering his face with his hands.

We were back in the Volvo, still parked behind the Hadley, hardly daring to look at each other. The road trip, maybe just a garden-variety bad idea to begin with, was quickly becoming a full-on, shaky-handheld-camera horror-movie nightmare.

"I can't believe you did this to me," I said. "You put the whole plan in jeopardy."

"Me? *I* did this to *you?*" His eyes widened and his voice flared to an incredulous pitch.

"Yeah, you. Screwing up with the car. Getting spotted. Now they know. They know we're gone. And they're after us."

My point was that we were supposed to be finding my mom and rescuing her and now we were devoting precious time and energy to saving ourselves. Now we were on the run like criminals. Which maybe we were, but the running wasn't part of the plan.

"It takes two to tango," he said.

"Actually, it only takes one person to botch a car theft."

He blew out a slow sigh and I watched it bloom on the windshield. "(A) This is my first time. There's a learning curve with this sort of thing."

I rolled my eyes. "Yeah, well, that's not what you were saying back in Phoenix. You were all, 'How hard can it be?'"

"I'm not finished." He held up a hand as if to hold back my torrent of anger and fear, and maybe his own. "(B) They only know about me, so you're still in the clear. And (C), I was only trying to help you out. So theoretically I could be just as mad at you right now, for putting me in this situation to begin with, but I'm not."

Was he even serious? After he and Tre conspired to make him my designated driver? Like they gave me any choice?

"For the record, I didn't ask you to come with me. I could've just taken the bus."

"And you would've been on the express route back to juvie. Look, Willa, we can blame each other all we want. It doesn't matter now. What's happened has happened. We need to move on. Preferably by getting as far away from the Hadley as possible."

I stared out at the velvety nighttime California sky,

the wrinkled folds of mountains in the distance, and the ocean, to our left. Hostage to the beauty, I felt time slipping away. The car was beginning to close in around us like a prison. In my grand scheme we were supposed to be on the road back home, my mom in tow. Now everything was up in the air again.

Even so, I felt bad. I didn't want to be fighting Aidan or blaming him. "Look, I'm sorry if I snapped at you. This whole thing is making me jumpy. But we still have a mission."

"I'm not giving up on that. We just need to think." He rubbed at his temples, staring ahead.

It was twelve forty-five A.M. I was overwhelmed with fatigue suddenly, realizing that I hadn't slept since the night at Tre's, which was now almost thirty hours ago. Aidan had at least gotten his nap in the lobby.

"I can't think," I said. "I'm exhausted."

"Well, you sleep. I'm going to drive a little, and then we're going to find another place where we can wait and stay the rest of the night. Like a motel or something."

"Just don't go too far," I said, trying to keep my eyes open. It felt wrong to sleep at a moment like this. And yet . . .

The forward movement was seductive and I could not resist the pull.

Just five minutes, I told myself. I felt my head lolling as Aidan drove, and I was out.

• • •

When I woke up, the car was stopped.

"Hey, sleepyhead," Aidan said, almost affectionately.

"Hey," I said, smiling at the sound of his voice, forgetting where I was.

It took me a moment to come back to reality. To remember what was going on. The stolen car, the Hadley, the news report. Then I saw where we were parked, in the lot of the Palms Motel. A neon vacancy sign glared at us, missing a few letters. There were only a handful of other cars around, most of them as beat up as the Volvo.

"You ready? We can check in for the night," Aidan said. "Then I was thinking we could ditch the car and maybe try to sneak back into the Hadley tomorrow."

"Okay." I liked the sound of that plan. We didn't need the car, anyway. Once we found my mom we could all drive back to Paradise Valley. Then we could explain everything to the police. I might have to go back to juvie but it was worth it.

With a little sleep under my belt I felt ready for the next phase of Operation Rescue My Mom. We got out and walked toward the entrance. Wherever we were, it felt remote and quiet.

"How long did I sleep?"

"About an hour. You looked pretty cute, with your mouth hanging open."

Oh man. That was mortifying. I was starting to think that there was an appropriate juncture in a relationship for road trips, and Aidan and I just hadn't gotten there yet. And now we were about to check into a motel like some creepy old people having an affair. Can you say cringe?

The lobby at the Palms was a one-eighty from the Hadley. There were no floral arrangements, no piped-in music, no freebie snacks. No one wanted to be seen in this place, let alone hang out in the lobby. There was, however, a desk with a woman behind it. She had bleached blond hair, a name tag that said Sherry, and a pink piece of gum that flashed between her teeth.

"We'd like a room, please."

Her eyes traveled over me. I prayed the woman didn't think I was a prostitute.

But she didn't say anything. "That's sixty-five dollars," she said.

"Let's see," Aidan said, thumbing through his wallet. "I only have forty bucks. Do you take AmEx?"

I yelped and grabbed for his hand, remembering Tre's warning. "No! We can't use that!" Seeing the startled look on his face, I took it down a notch. "I mean, we should just pay in cash."

As much as I wanted to save the money my mom left me, I knew this was what it was for. My survival. Which was now, for better or worse, bound up with Aidan's.

I put down my hand and felt for my bag at my waist, but I was pawing at air.

My bag. Oh my God.

"Hold on," I said, and bolted for the door, heading for the now-familiar boxy shape of the Volvo in the lot.

I'd probably just left it in the car, right? I mean, that would have been stupid, given the busted window, but we'd only been inside for five minutes, tops. It wasn't enough time for anyone but the most talented burglar . . . and no one was even around. . . .

I'd already gone through all the scenarios by the time I got to the car. Once you became a thief, you couldn't help but think like one.

I threw open the passenger-side door and searched the seat. Nothing. Just my bag with the schoolbooks.

Then I knelt down on the pavement and groped underneath, pushing my hand between the grubby floor mat and the sticky springs. But by the time I was reaching frantically into the crack between the seat bottom and backrest, I knew the bag was gone.

I walked back into the lobby, where Aidan was waiting for me.

"I lost it," I murmured as I looked at him in horror. "I lost the money."

"You what?" Aidan glared at me. Then to the floor: "Oh crap." And then to the lady: "I'm sorry. We'll have to come back."

The woman shrugged, as if she'd seen a thousand indecisive teens walk away from her desk before. We meant nothing to her.

But that motel room, it meant everything to me. It

was our shelter. Our means of sleeping, washing, and hiding until we could find my mom. We were rootless, homeless, moneyless. It was all I could do now to keep from falling apart.

With every step back to the Volvo, I was bracing myself for the onslaught of Aidan's anger. Not that I needed it right now—I was thoroughly furious with myself, enough for the two of us.

So. Freaking. Stupid. How could I have done it?

"Dude, I can't believe you," Aidan said, smiling at me sidelong.

"I messed up, okay?"

"I know," he said, his smile cracking into a deep chuckle.

He was *laughing*?

"It's so not funny," I said. "We have to go back to the Hadley. Like, instantly."

I pictured where I'd most likely left my overnight bag, on the floor by those couches in the lobby. If we hurried, maybe we could still get it before anybody noticed. Going back there now was risky but it was a lot of money in question, too much money to leave behind. We needed it. Besides, my wallet was in there, too, with my VP school ID. And all my clothes. With every passing second our total screwedness was reaching new heights.

Of course, I still had my Comp notebook and my copy of *Walden*. Because those things were really going to come in handy on the road. Maybe only if we could cook them or use them for a fire.

"Okay, okay," he said, trying to contain himself. "Let's go."

I stared at him as he calmly drove out of the Palms parking lot, signaled, and turned onto the road. "You're actually enjoying this, aren't you?"

He pressed his bottom lip out. "A little. I mean, at least I'm not the only one who makes mistakes."

"Clearly you're not," I said, leaning my head against the broken window. I wanted to yell and smash things. I wanted to cry.

He shook his head, still not even looking mad. "So maybe we're even?"

"Maybe," I said. It was no consolation, though. Because our being even did nothing to make our situation any less terrifying. It just meant we'd both been idiots.

"Look, Willa, it's okay. It was just a few thousand bucks."

"To you, maybe. To you, that's chump change, right?"

I thought of Nikki and Kellie. Not having any concept of what a few thousand dollars meant to us in this situation, or in any situation, for that matter, was pure Glitterati-tude. Having grown up without servants, a pool house, or a trust fund, I valued every single in my wallet. Which, of course, might be gone forever.

"I'm just saying, money is money. It's just a bunch of paper with green ink. It doesn't *mean* anything."

"How about our safety and freedom?"

"We'll get it back," he said gently. "Probably no one even noticed it."

And this was worse, this nice-guy stuff—I couldn't even be mad and take it out on him when he was being all supportive. How irritating was that?

I huffed out my misery, and it was sucked into the air through the busted glass. Freezing now. Couldn't Mr. Volvo Owner have invested in a little duct tape?

I was still wearing my mom's windbreaker, and I wrapped it tighter around me and shoved my hands in the pockets. As I did, my fingers brushed against a piece of paper on the right side.

I pulled it out and unfolded it. There was a doodle in the top corner, the kind she made while she talked on the phone. Beneath was a single column of words, written in her sloppy cursive.

Needles
Posts
Crest
Azalea
Drain
3RS

One of her shopping lists. Maybe she had used it on the way to Home Depot when we were settling into the house. I folded it up and put it back into the pocket. It was probably sentimental of me, but there was no way I was getting rid of anything of hers now. Not until I got to see her again.

"That's a nice jacket," Aidan said, probably noticing it for the first time.

"It's my mom's," I replied. Even referring to her in this way made me sad and angry and anxious. I was here to find her and the only thing I'd done so far was successfully steal her clothing. Stealing was the only thing I was good at, apparently.

We drove most of the way back into town in silence. The ocean came in and out of view through my window. Then I remembered that in all the time I'd lived in Arizona, I had been craving an ocean view. I should enjoy it now. I tried to watch the waves and let them wash away all my negative thoughts.

Okay, do-over. What's done is done.

What was it my mom always said about not letting your worries eat you up inside? Time to start thinking constructively.

"So we'll get the money," I said, trying to convince myself and lay out our goals. Saying them aloud would help us make them a reality.

Aidan nodded. "Then we'll find another motel. And in the morning we'll try to find your mom."

"That sounds like a plan," I said. Never mind that we had no details on how we would do that.

"I'm just going to double-park in front," Aidan said,

as he pulled into the driveway of the Hadley. "You can run in and grab it. Try not to make too much of a scene."

He was joking, and ordinarily I might try to zing him with a comeback, but it would be a long time before I would be able to find any humor in this situation. Like, a decade.

He pulled up to the hotel's entrance, with its flags of many countries and spotlit palm trees. The valet I'd talked to earlier was still standing by the doors, waiting to assist the next patron. As I neared, the glass panes swished open. Then they swished closed again. I was still standing in place.

Because I'd glanced inside and saw all that I needed to see.

"Aidan," I whispered as I climbed back into the car. "I can't go in there."

He bent down to look through the passenger-side window and took in what I was talking about: two uniformed policemen talking to the woman at the front desk.

"No," he said. "You can't."

NINE

WITH NO MONEY and the police on our tail, and the two of us desperate for sleep, we discussed our next step. We couldn't spend the night in the car—it was too exposed, too visible. We couldn't keep driving—not unless we wanted to prop Aidan's eyelids open with toothpicks.

There was only one option, really, and that was to find a place to squat. Which meant I would have to resort to my old tactics of breaking and entering. And pretend like I had probation amnesia. But what did it matter now? We'd already broken three laws and counting.

Aidan seemed to like this suggestion because it would give us a chance to shower and get off the road. Also, he just liked the idea of being a badass. It kind of came naturally to him.

"Finally, I get to see the Sly Fox at work," he said. "I can steep in the wisdom like a delicate tea."

"Eh, it's more like espresso. Coming at you hard and fast."

"Either way. It's gonna jolt me. Now where to, boss?"

"We need to find a second home," I said, chewing on my thumb. There wasn't much time to think. "A place that we know will be empty for the night."

You couldn't throw a bottle of Bain de Soleil without hitting a beach house around these parts—it was pretty much vacation central. But nothing near downtown Santa Barbara would do. It was too near to civilization, the houses too close to one another, with too many possible prying eyes.

Aidan drove on into the neighboring town of Montecito and then up into the hills where lights twinkled from distant ridges. Now that we had a purpose, the mood in the car was oddly calm, and I felt that with the decision to break into a house, however crazy it was, I had some control over the situation again.

Then there was that old giddy excitement pumping through my veins, the familiar sensation before I was about to go rogue. Bubblier than bubbly—it went straight to my head. I'd be lying if I said I wasn't psyched.

The road was winding and Aidan slowed to allow for the sharp turns as we ascended farther upward. Outside my window, the edge of the pavement dropped dramatically into dark woods.

"Keep going," I instructed. My instinct was that higher ground meant better views of the ocean and thus, more vacation homes on bigger, more isolated lots of land. If we were going to do this, at least we wouldn't be breaking into poor people's houses. We passed what looked like a vineyard and then turned around another curve. The road broke off in a Y, and I instructed Aidan to bear right, where we could see some glowing lights nestled in the carpet of darkness.

What I'd learned from my earlier forays into thievery was that there was a certain level of intuition involved— you had to go with your gut.

"Now turn here," I said, pointing to a stucco gate. "Let's try this one."

Aidan did as I asked. He was a trusty second-in-command, it turned out. Frankly, I was surprised he took direction so well. The road narrowed into a drive-way, which climbed still farther.

Finally, a home came into view. Well, technically, it was the pool we saw first: a turquoise diamond, lit up from the inside. The house, which seemed to be built around the pool and not the other way around, was modern, all glass and peachy-colored stone, flanked by huge columns and topped with square hip roofs. On the side of the building was a helipad, a round expanse of neatly trimmed grass.

"Why do you even need that?" I asked Aidan, who was going to have to be my go-to for all questions about rich people.

"I guess for when Madonna or visiting heads of state

drop by," he said as he pulled the Volvo around the circular driveway, palming the wheel like we owned the place—or, for that matter, the car. "Anyway, it might come in handy for us, if we need to make a getaway."

"But we'd need a helicopter, wouldn't we?" I said.

He pointed a thumb at his chest. "I got connections, babe."

I shook my head at this Aidanism. Of course he did. His parents probably had a whole fleet of helicopters. Clearly, I was going to have to be the practical one here. "We should probably try to hide the car."

"I'm going to park it behind the guesthouse," he said.

"Good idea."

We drove toward what looked like a miniature version of the mansion, sitting next to a six-car garage. Then we got out of the car and moved toward the main building. I went first, dancing into the darkest parts of the lawn, and Aidan followed.

Finding a shadowy wall, I pushed my face up against the glass and peered in. Sure enough, most of the furniture was draped in white sheeting, a good sign. The lights were clearly on a timer; the landscaping was probably maintained on a weekly basis.

It was always possible that tonight would be the night the owners showed up for their vacation, but since we were a week away from Thanksgiving I was willing to hedge my bets that they were at one of their other homes.

"How do you propose getting in?" Aidan asked.

I'd already been working this through in my head, thinking back to my lessons with Tre. "We have a couple of options. We can break a window on the first floor, then wait for the alarm. Sometimes the alarm system isn't more than a siren. If no one shows up, we go in. That's the longer, safer option."

He folded his arms across his chest. "And what's the shorter, riskier option?"

"Going in through a second-floor window, and, if we need to, disarming the alarm system from the inside. Second floor may or may not be wired."

Aidan seemed to be taking this in and making his own calculations. "I'm a shorter, riskier kind of guy, I guess. Option B seems more efficient. And look, I still have this." He lifted up the screwdriver and wire cutters he'd used to steal the Volvo.

"Perfect," I said. "Short and risky it is, then."

I led the way, enjoying, for the moment, the fact that I was in charge, which was a good distraction from the fact that I was totally nervous about the whole endeavor. With Kellie's house, at least, I'd had the security code. And every house was different. These big places almost always had custom systems, so you couldn't assume anything.

We circled the house on foot, stopping on the east side in front of a stone wall that enclosed what looked like the living room. Suspended above it was a wrap-around balcony that must have led to the master suite.

115

"Climb up there," I instructed Aidan. "Then we'll go in through the bedroom window."

Aidan scrambled up the wall, easily finding traction with his sneakers digging between the stones, and I followed. Then, like some kind of suburban ninja, he jumped up to grasp the balcony railing and hoisted himself over it, landing in a squat.

"C'mon," he said, whispering down to me as he straightened himself up. "Jump."

Easier said than done. The first time, I didn't jump high enough and I couldn't reach the railing.

I got it on the second try, feeling the cool metal press into my fingers. I knew I didn't have the upper-body strength to pull myself all of the way—stupid X chromosomes. As I dangled there, I realized I didn't have much grip strength, either—I could feel myself slipping.

Luckily, Aidan grabbed hold of my wrists and pulled me until I could reach his upper arms. (The biceps, incidentally, were as solid as they looked.) Then he had me by the waist and he swung me around.

"You can drop me now," I said.

"You sure?" he teased.

"Drop me, Murphy," I growled.

He let go and my feet touched down on the concrete.

We stepped around the balcony to the mountain-facing side. "Use the screwdriver to wedge open the window at the lower hinge."

"Okay," Aidan said. He bent over and edged the flat

blade into the crack of the window. I stood guard, watching over the empty darkness. The night was placid—but in a couple of hours the sun would be coming up.

People were way too trusting. *If I had a place like this*, I thought, *I would have a seriously mean pit bull. Or maybe a wolf dog for the pants-wetting factor alone.*

"I got it," Aidan said. He turned back to me and grinned, impish.

Then he lifted the window from its frame and crawled through it, disappearing inside. I went in after him, my feet touching down on thick white carpet.

No sheets up here. The room was minimally decorated but lush, with an enormous, floor-hugging bed, wall-sized flat-screen TV, and marble fireplace. Everything was white and gray and very clean, an oasis of wealth and good taste.

"Now wait," I whispered. "The alarm could go off any minute. If it does, we need to find the control panel ASAP."

We paused, crouching. Then we looked at each other quizzically. No sound. Maybe it wasn't wired.

"It must be a one-zone thing. Let's go downstairs." I looked back over my shoulder to make sure he was with me.

Like clockwork, the siren sounded.

Burr-rrip. Burr-rrip.

Loud and dissonant, like a school jazz-band reject.

Aidan covered his ears. "Painful."

"C'mon," I said, waving him along.

I wandered through the rooms looking for the wall-mounted box. The alarm kept going.

I knew from Tre that the wired systems were usually mounted in the basement next to the circuit breaker.

But we were in California. Houses here didn't have basements. Which meant the system was most likely wireless. Which meant that we couldn't just disable the phone line. Which meant I was just going to have to wing it.

"Maybe near the back door?" Aidan suggested.

We went through the kitchen and beyond that into a laundry room/mudroom.

I spotted the box next to the door. "Yep. Good call."

I snapped the box cover open and saw the code pad. "Screwdriver, please."

Aidan handed it to me and, my heart throbbing in my throat, I worked on the tiny screws, loosening them until I could remove the metal plate.

"Do you have those clippers?" I said to Aidan, stepping aside. "Cut it."

"Which one? The red, or the green? There's like twenty wires here."

"All of it. And quickly."

He did as I asked, leaning in and pinching away at the little threads.

"Now pull out the control pad."

He frowned. "Like, out of the wall?"

"Yes."

He reached and ripped out the metal frame, holding it up like the beating heart of an animal sacrifice.

Within a fraction of a second, the siren quit.

"Is that it?" he asked nervously.

"That should be it," I said. "That should disable everything."

I couldn't be 100 percent sure. We were still frozen, afraid to move.

We looked at each other. The alarm had gone on for less than a minute, but it felt like much longer.

Aidan waved his hand experimentally. Silence. I took a few steps. Slowly, then faster, making exaggerated movements.

"Clear," I said, dizzy with the thrill of getting it right, getting in. Finding the solution. Like those times when I'd pickpocketed someone or broken into their locker or car and it all fell into place like it was meant to be. Maybe this was our payoff for bearing all the stress of the past couple of days—our sign that we were doing the right thing on this trip. Maybe our luck was turning around.

"This place is amazing." We fist-bumped. "Sly Fox, you've done it again."

Tell me more, big boy. Some girls like to hear how pretty they are or how nice they are. As much as I hated to admit it, the Sly Fox talk stroked my ego in all the right places. Back at home it was still a painful memory, but now that we were far from Paradise Valley I was remembering what I'd liked so much about stealing.

We wandered back through the kitchen into the great room with its exposed beams sloping down on all four sides. The floor was tiled with veined stones like crystals and there were stunning views on both sides—the ocean in one direction and the mountains in another.

By now I'd been in some extremely fancy Paradise Valley homes, but I was still blown away by the wealth and beauty in which some people were lucky enough to live. Did they even know how lucky they were?

"Did you see their DVD collection? It's like an entire library." Aidan ran from one room to the next and back again, puppyish.

I followed him into the media room, which was more like a theater, lined floor-to-ceiling with shelves of movies, a screen built into the wood-paneled walls, and a row of white couches set up in front of it.

I would have expected Aidan to be less impressed, having grown up with this sort of stuff, but he seemed to be enjoying the walk-through tour as much as I was. "Look at that kayak," he said, pointing to a thirty-foot wooden boat that was suspended from the ceiling in the dining room, hanging over the enormous table that had to seat twenty-five people. "I think that's Native American."

It was hard not to get caught up in the excitement— in his excitement, specifically.

"What should we do now? I'm too pumped to sleep."

"Shower," I announced. Argh. I was inadvertently macking on him now. At least if I was going to make a move I should do it purposefully. "I mean, I need one. And I need to change." With my bag gone I had nothing to wear but my dirty old clothes.

"I have some stuff in my bag, but I guess that doesn't help you, huh?"

"No," I said. "But maybe they have something."

Upstairs, I found some shampoo and soap in the master bathroom—spa-quality, of course, with all-natural ingredients. I helped myself to a towel and stepped into the giant glass-walled stall. Like everything else here, it had a view. I could see the pool below, glittering under the lights.

When I'd toweled off, I found a robe that was thick as a rug and soft as down, wrapped it around me, and stepped out into the bedroom. Along the wall opposite the bed there was a large dresser. Surely there would be something in there I could borrow. I rummaged around in the drawers and I pulled out some men's pajamas and a pair of woolen socks.

"Hey, Willa, I've found the mother lode," Aidan called, his voice echoing from behind a nearby door.

I followed the sound into an enormous walk-in closet. There were racks upon racks of clothes for both men and women, built-in shelves of all shapes from floor to ceiling. The shoes alone took up a six-foot wall, coordinated by color in neat pairs.

It was so big that I couldn't see Aidan—I could only hear his disembodied voice muffled behind the shirts and pants and suits.

"I've been working on our disguises," he said. He emerged from behind the racks wearing a fedora and a three-piece suit. "What do you think?"

He looked good. Seriously good. Like red-carpet good. "Wow. I've never seen you this . . . spiffy."

"I'm thinking if you're trying to hide you should just go over the top with it. Maybe I can shave my head. Ooh, or grow a mustache. How long do you think it will take?"

He was smiling, clearly enjoying the process of dress-up. Now that he'd come closer to me, I was distinctly aware of the fact that the fabric of my robe, thick though it was, was all that was shielding me from him. He must have noticed it, too, because he briefly met my eyes and we paused there, looking at each other in awkward silence. Then he turned away and busied himself with the tie rack.

"These are all Gucci. I guess I should have been paying attention when my dad was explaining the Windsor knot."

I looked on the lady side. There were fur coats and handbags, evening gowns with sequins. I found a pair of jeans and a red bateau-neck tee that was a little basic for my tastes, but comfortable. Even better, it looked like the things were close to my size. From the shelf, I pulled out a fuzzy gray cardigan to wear on top, and I piled the clothes over my arm.

Aidan picked up the sweater. "That's it? That's your disguise?"

"Well, I can't go wearing one of these fancy dresses."

"You should do something about your hair. Maybe we can cut it."

"No cutting!" I said, grabbing it defensively in a side ponytail.

Back in the bathroom, I swiped at the mirror, which was still fogged up from my shower. My face was pink—whether from the heat or the proximity to Aidan in my near-nakedness, I didn't know. I rummaged around in the drawers of the vanity. Lo and behold, there was a bottle of women's hair dye. Mink brown.

"I've got a disguise. I'm going brunette," I called out to Aidan.

"Sweet," he said from the other side of the door. "Who do you think lives here, anyway?"

"I was wondering the same thing."

"I know one way to find out," he said. "Can I come in?"

I let him in. He opened up the medicine cabinet and handed me a pill bottle.

I took one look at the label and blinked to make sure I was seeing it correctly. "Aidan, you're not going to believe this."

"What?"

"It's Sam Beasley."

"As in, the Academy Award–winning actor and director Sam Beasley?"

"Yes."

"Give me that." He grabbed the bottle out of my hand. "Holy crap. You're right. And he takes statins for high cholesterol. I totally would've thought he'd have some more interesting drugs here. Some painkillers, at least."

I looked through the rest of the medicine-cabinet shelf. "Nothing much besides Band-Aids and mouthwash." I looked down at the robe. "Oh my God. I'm wearing Sam Beasley's robe."

Aidan grabbed me by my waist. "And it looks good on you."

"You think so?" I choked out the question, feeling his nearness.

He ran his finger along the bow I'd tied, tracing its infinity-sign shape. "I mean, you'd probably look better in my robe."

"You don't have it here, do you?"

"No. That bastard beat me to it."

His eyes. I was transfixed. I drew in a breath. "Thank you for today."

"We make a good team, you and me."

Now his face was close and there was no denying it. We kissed, his mouth pressing hard against mine. His lips parted and I got lost there, spinning, spinning, spinning.

He lifted me up so that I was sitting on Sam Beasley's bathroom counter, his hands planted on my hips. The steam in the bathroom swirled around us as I wrapped my arms around Aidan's neck, my legs around the backs of his knees, locking him closer. His hands drifted up my rib cage. Aidan dressed in Sam Beasley's suit. This was crazy. This was not my life.

My life was . . .

My mom. As we kissed, a pain stabbed me in the chest. I'd almost forgotten the reason we were here.

I pulled away. I couldn't do this. I couldn't just fool around with Aidan, no matter how tempting it was— not when my mom's life was at stake.

Aidan's eyes widened with surprise. "What?"

"Just. I don't know. I think . . ." I tried to summon my voice but it was hoarse, like it had been kissed into oblivion.

This was the problem with luxury, wasn't it? You could just wrap yourself up in cashmere and delicious-smelling lotions and shut out all your real-world problems.

". . . I should put this stuff in my hair. And then I think we should try to get back to work. On finding my mom. Do they have a computer in here?"

"Yeah, okay." He stepped back, nodding. But he was looking at the floor, so I couldn't really read his face. "There's an office-type room downstairs. I guess I should change, too."

When he was gone, I used a comb I found to work the dye in, remembering how my mom sometimes did her hair at home. It didn't smell that great. In fact, it was kind of eye-wateringly skunkish.

Then I showered again and dried my hair. It looked pretty awful—only one notch above a wig. You were given a natural hair color for a reason, and my reason was that I looked like the undead with anything darker than yellow. I imagined what Cherise might say if she saw this pathetic dye job. Oh well.

I changed into a pair of Beasley's pajamas, which looked a lot more comfy than the skimpy women's nightgowns in the drawers. I went downstairs, finding Aidan in a room off the kitchen. It had the same beautiful exposed-beam ceiling, yet another fireplace, and a bay window overlooking the mountain side of the property. My mom would love that, too, I thought.

Aidan was sitting down at the desk in front of the latest-edition Mac. The place was tricked out—if this was Beasley's beach house, I couldn't imagine what his regular everyday house looked like.

He turned around when I came in. "Your hair looks . . . different."

"Is it okay?" I said, touching the ends self-consciously and wishing I didn't care quite so much what he thought.

"Yeah. I mean, it's a good disguise."

Not the reaction I was hoping for, but then again, I

had just pushed him away. Maybe he had feelings about that. What kind of feelings? I wondered. Our timing was all wrong. But if we could both just wait until all this stuff with my mom was cleared up, maybe we could really be together.

I paced around the room, thinking. "The valet said he saw her there. He definitely saw her car. Can we look it up somehow? I don't know the license plate number."

"I might be able to figure it out. Where was her driver's license from? Arizona?"

"No. We just moved there." I tried to picture it. I couldn't remember ever having seen it. We'd lived in so many different places. "It could be Washington, Oregon, or Nevada. Maybe California."

Aidan shook his head. "You can't make it easy for me, can you, Colorado?"

That was the nickname he'd given me when we first met. It had been a little while since I'd heard him use it.

"Which reminds me . . . It could also be Colorado."

While he worked, I went into the kitchen to look for some food. The refrigerator was mostly empty, except for some diet soda and expensive-looking champagne. In the pantry cabinets there was canned tuna, ten thousand bottles of oils and vinegars, and a block of baking chocolate. I could get into the whole rich thing—I loved their toiletries and their fine fabrics—but would it kill these people to keep a little Kraft mac-and-cheese in the cabinet? I guess Sam Beasley had a boyish figure to watch.

I was definitely going to write him a thank-you note in the morning, I decided. An IOU of sorts. Because while I had willingly stolen lots of stuff from people I disliked in the past, this was something we were doing for survival, and I didn't want to take advantage.

Starved anyway, I cracked open a soda and a can of tuna. I offered some to Aidan, but he made a face.

"No, thanks. I've still got some jerky left."

I was way too hungry to feel self-conscious about repulsing him with my makeshift dinner. I sat down and looked over his shoulder as he typed in numbers and clicked on the mouse.

Then it occurred to me that someone like Beasley was as high profile as they came. There was no way that a break-in to his house would go under the radar.

"Do you think we should be worried?" I scraped up the last bit of my meal.

"About what?"

"About breaking into a Hollywood star's house. About *Extra* or *TMZ* getting the story."

"There's no extra penalty for crimes against celebrities."

"I just mean, will they be able to find us?"

"We'll cover our tracks. And we're going to have to keep moving, anyway. Like, first thing in the morning."

That worried me. What if she was still here and we had to leave town?

He rolled his chair away from the desk. "I've gotten through Nevada and Oregon. There's no sign of her."

"That was fast," I said. I wrung my hands, disappointed. "But there's still Colorado and California, right?"

"Don't worry. I've got skills with a *z*. You've got the break-ins and I'm good for computers and getaways. Give me a sip of that," Aidan said. I handed him my soda and he gulped it down, handing it back to me with just a tiny bit left.

"No fair," I said.

"I'm sure there's more in there. Besides, I need a little boost. This could take a while. California is a tough one to break into."

I settled in on the couch, watching Aidan work.

"You can sleep if you want," he said.

"No way," I said. "I'm staying up with you."

Fair was fair. We were in this together now. Besides, how could I sleep with Aidan so close to me? When we'd just made out . . .

Oh God. We'd just made out again, hadn't we? My stomach did a loop-de-loop.

"You'll never make it," he said, laughing at me.

"I will, too."

I watched his back, thinking how strange everything had become. How far away Paradise Valley seemed now.

Aidan was the only thing that was keeping me tethered to home, to who I was.

Within a few minutes, my eyes grew heavy. I fought as long as I could, but the rhythmic clacking of his typing and the firm couch overpowered the effort. Like a storybook girl—Sleeping Beauty? Gretel? Goldilocks was probably more like it—I was lulled into the quiet darkness of nothing.

TEN

AT SOME POINT I felt a hand on my shoulder—it was so soft it could have been my imagination—and what was that? Lips on my forehead?

"Willa."

A voice close to my ear called my name as my brain swam up to the surface of consciousness.

"Willa, are you awake?"

I'd been dreaming of Aidan and me on a canoe in the middle of a lake, which was weird because I'd never been on a canoe before. But the dream had a sweet, romantic sheen to it and I wanted to linger there. We were boyfriend and girlfriend and the rest of the world was far away. Like we had no problems, no worries, except paddling on to wherever it was we were going.

Now I opened an eye to see him leaning over me. *Aidan.* I smiled. We were still together. That part wasn't a dream.

He wasn't smiling at me, though. He was holding his cell phone, his face contorted in worry. Reality came pouring back in, clean and piercing as the sunlight through the giant bay windows.

"What's up," I mumbled, pressing the heels of my palms into my eyeballs to help them adjust to daytime vision.

"I turned on my phone. I thought I should at least check to see if anyone called us. We have a message. Should we listen to it?"

Up until now, we'd kept the phone off, not wanting to be tracked by the roaming signal.

"Do you recognize the number?" I rolled onto my side. I was still in Sam Beasley's pajamas and the buttons had been pressing into my cheek, leaving what was sure to be one of those embarrassing sleep wrinkles.

"It's a California number."

My nerves twanged like guitar strings and I sat up, knowing exactly who it was. *Corbin.*

"We have to listen to it," I said. "Can you put it on speaker?"

Aidan sat down on the couch next to me and set the phone between us, then pressed play. The voice that streamed out was low and gruff.

"This is a message for Willa Fox. Detective Corbin here, with the Federal Bureau of Investigation. I'm fairly certain you know who I am—I left a card at your house several days ago. Anyway, I've been following your case and I've found this number through police channels. As I'm sure you're aware, there are people looking for Mr. Murphy and they know you're involved now, too. A hotel clerk at the Hadley identified you both. My message to you: Come back and turn yourselves in before you get hurt. Don't screw around. It'll just make you look stupid. And I know you're not stupid."

There was a pause then, a clearing of his throat.

"Look, Willa, there's a lot you don't know about this situation, a lot you don't know about your mother. She's in big trouble right now. Those people who messed up your house? They were after her—they're still after her. We know that she left Santa Barbara yesterday morning. I'm only telling you this so you understand that you're in over your head. Leave now. It's my job to bring your mom back—not yours. I'm trying to look out for you guys. Please call me when you get this message so I know you got it."

He left his number and then hung up.

"They know I'm involved," I repeated. It wasn't much of a surprise. But still. This was the FBI. I folded my arms around my gathered-in legs. This was no joke.

"If you believe him. The guy sounds like a jerk."

I pictured Corbin the night in the restaurant, skulking around us, like he was the criminal. But I still didn't get how he knew so much about my mom or what the connection was. "He said they're after her. Whoever *they* are." I squinted as I processed the information. Who

133

would be trying to hurt her? "Did you find her car?"

He shook his head. "Not yet. But I think I'm close. Maybe another hour or two. So what do you think?" he asked.

My mind was going into acrobatic contortions. I picked up Aidan's phone and stared at the screen like it would reveal additional information. All it told me was that he'd left the message an hour ago. We'd made some mistakes and we were taking major risks. I was worried.

I just wished we had something to go on. Corbin seemed to know much more than we did. And that was really unfair. It was *my* mom, after all. He was just an interloper with government credentials.

"Look, I made some coffee. Do you want some? Maybe that will help us think better."

I nodded gratefully at Aidan and watched him head for the kitchen. He'd been up all night and he looked exhausted. I wanted to reach out and hug him. I was lucky that he was helping me sort this out. I was lucky he was so understanding. I was lucky he was here.

The phone rang again and I jumped. A 310 number. Corbin again?

Should I answer it?

The only thing in the way of finding out where my mother was, was the fear of getting caught. Maybe there was a way, somehow. . . .

The thing was, Corbin already knew we'd been in

Santa Barbara. Maybe he even knew where we were right now. And this was a life-or-death situation—I was desperate. I had to take my chances.

I pressed my finger to the screen. As I held the phone up to my ear, anticipating a voice, there was a beep: the sound of another call coming through. I drew the phone away and looked at it.

It was a text message, from someone named Sheila.

Haven't heard from you. Miss u baby.

My stomach roiled. *Baby?* Who the hell was Sheila, and why was she texting Aidan to tell him she missed him?

Distantly, I could hear Corbin calling out from the plastic device in my hand. "Hello? Hello? Willa?"

Aidan was standing in the doorway with mugs of coffee, smiling. Panicked, I hung up and threw the phone down on the couch.

It was too late.

His smile faded into a suspicious expression. "Willa, did that guy just call again? Did you pick up the phone?"

"I—"

"You know they can trace us, right?" He dropped my mug so quickly on the desk that the contents spilled over the side. "You know it's only a matter of time now."

"Sorry, but I just—" My thoughts were all tangled up. It was all happening too fast. I couldn't explain why I'd done what I'd done, or tell him what I'd just seen on his phone.

"Were you going to turn us in? Don't you think you could've asked me first? I mean, aren't we in this together?"

"We are. I wasn't going to turn us in. I wanted to find out more about my mom."

"The guy's FBI, for chrissakes. Do you even get how screwed we are? Get your stuff together. We have to leave."

He stormed upstairs.

I fumbled around in the office to find a pen and paper. Quickly, I scrawled a note.

Dear Mr. Beasley,
Thank you for the use of your home. We will repay
you for your services. Consider this an IOU.

I briefly thought about using another name, or not signing it at all, but what the hell did it matter now? Corbin said they knew I was involved. I put the pen back to the paper and wrote, *Best, Sly Fox*.

Aidan thundered down the stairs. He was wearing a sweater-vest and a driver's cap I didn't recognize and carrying his backpack. He threw me the (stolen) clothes I'd picked out the night before. "Get dressed. Let's go!"

As soon as we got back into the Volvo, we could hear the sirens, a distant whine.

"Is that for us? They couldn't have traced us that quickly, could they?" I asked, panicking.

He shook his head. "It's probably the local police. Maybe the guys from the hotel. Unless you want us to turn ourselves in, I'm just going to gun it."

I nodded, giving him my assent. "We're not giving up now."

He hit the gas and we tore up the driveway and out into the street. It was still early morning and the fog was thick, curdling close to the ground. Overhead the sky was gray. Darker than overcast. The asphalt was barely visible beyond a few feet.

The sirens were getting louder, but I couldn't see much behind us. "Where are you going?"

"I don't know, but I'm heading away from town. There's gotta be more cops down there."

"We need to get rid of this car," I said.

"Later. No time now."

We had no GPS, but if I had to guess, it seemed like we were driving north into the mountains. I turned around again and I could just make out the red and blue lights bouncing off the fog.

"They're catching up."

I had a flashback to the night I was caught breaking into Kellie's house, how the police chased me down, first on my bike and then on foot as I ran through the desert—how terrified I was in the dark, pure adrenaline fueling me onward. Then the horrible moment when they caught up with me, literally dragging me down into the dirt before they dumped me in juvie. No way was I going through that again.

"Faster," I urged Aidan, my voice scratchy and ragged.

"I can barely see."

"C'mon!" I shouted.

The yellow lines of the road seemed to drop off as we hit a fork. Aidan braked suddenly and scrambled to steer the car, choosing the right turn. "God, I wish I had my Mercedes right now," he said. "This thing's got no suspension."

We snaked around to the left, then around another long hairpin curve that had me grasping the roof handle so as not to slam my head against Aidan's. The turns were making me queasy. I'd never been good on long car rides and this one was like a roller coaster. The sirens droned behind us like a swarm of angry wasps.

"What if they shoot?" I asked, realizing suddenly that there was a fate worse than getting caught.

"They won't," Aidan said. "We don't have a gun, and we're just kids."

I wasn't so sure they saw us as "just" anything. And I didn't know how much longer we could keep going like this. Driving fast wasn't enough. At some point we would have to do something to shake them.

At the same time I felt sick. And sicker. Nausea gripped me as the car weaved and bobbed along the windy road. I covered my mouth with my hand and tried to gulp down some air.

"What's wrong?" Aidan asked.

"Carsick," I said.

"You picked a great time for that."

I waved him off. "Just keep going."

Aidan veered onto a small dirt road. The car bumped and rattled as he drove over rutted ground.

"How do you know where it's headed?"

"I don't," he said plainly.

The road was so rough that Aidan had to slow down. We could feel the engine vibrating as the old Volvo tried to weather the rustic conditions. My insides lurched with every bump.

The cops were undaunted by the off-roading. They were getting closer. I could see their car now from my side mirror, the headlights growing larger in the little square.

"You have to go faster," I said, wiping the sweat that collected on my brow.

"I can't go much faster. Not without blowing a tire here. This road is really rocky." He made another sharp turn, throwing the car to the left.

My stomach heaved. "I—"

"What?" he said, glaring at me. "You what?"

"I'm going to be sick now." I pulled down the window as quickly as I could and stuck my head out to barf.

"Oh my God," Aidan said, breaking into a grin. "That is so nasty."

"Shut up," I said, wiping my face. I was grossed out, and truly humiliated. "I couldn't help it." Did he think I actually wanted to do this? In front of him? And did he

139

have to act like a ten-year-old, now of all times, with the police chasing us?

"No, not you. Look behind you."

I turned. "I don't see them. Did they pull off?"

"You puke-bombed them." He broke into hysterical laughter.

"I what?"

"It's too good. I wish I'd thought of that." Aidan's eyes darted up to the rearview mirror. "They swerved. They're not behind us anymore. I thought my skilled steering might do the trick, but it was your projectile vomit. Classic."

I was still too stunned to laugh. My throat hurt and my mouth was sour. "Do you have any gum?"

He shook his head. "Sorry. Unless our buddy keeps some in his glove compartment."

I checked but there was nothing. Ugh. "Now what?"

"We keep driving."

We were headed into the deepest part of nowhere and yet the road continued to climb, with steeper drop-offs on either side. After a while, the ocean came back into view, and the openness felt like a temporary relief. At least we could gauge which direction we were headed in.

"Is this even a real road?" I asked.

"It's a real road. Whether it's meant for real cars or not, I don't know."

"It doesn't seem to be going anywhere."

"Of course it's going somewhere. All roads go some-where."

That wasn't necessarily true. I was thinking of dead ends. Cul-de-sacs. Circular drives. And a Talking Heads song my mom liked.

Aidan reached over to turn on the music. The car swerved a bit as he leaned away from the steering wheel.

"Do you mind if we don't?" I asked quickly. "I just feel like we should be concentrating."

"Since I'm the one driving and doing the concentrat-ing, I'd like to have some music. It helps me concentrate better." He flipped it on, and started to fiddle with the buttons.

"At least let me do that," I said. "Just keep your eyes on the road."

"Bossy bossy."

"Look, I just don't want us to die, okay?"

And then, like some kind of evil sign from the cos-mos, it started to rain. Hard. The water pounded in translucent columns into the earth. Within minutes, I could feel the dirt dissolving beneath us into slippery mud.

Aidan turned on the windshield wipers and they left a dusty smear across the glass. The Volvo went sloppily around yet another curve and I could feel that we were slipping. Sure, we'd lost the cops, but now we were driv-ing the most treacherous course I'd ever seen.

My entire body was clenched in fear.

"You could maybe slow down a little bit now," I suggested.

"Ah, now she wants me to slow. You can't have it both ways, Colorado."

That nickname again. I couldn't believe I'd ever thought I was special. Like I was the only one he'd ever kissed. Please.

Why should I be surprised? Everyone said he was a player.

My bottled-up fear exploded into anger. Why was I letting this person, this person who probably didn't even have any real feelings for me, be in charge of my destiny?

But being pissed at Aidan was a luxury I couldn't afford right now. We had to make it out of here first.

Aidan swerved to avoid a big pothole. The Volvo, losing traction on the back wheels, fishtailed, and we swung around violently. Aidan slammed on the brakes but the car careened sideways, skidding in the mud.

I screamed. He screamed.

We were face-to-face with the very edge of a cliff and, several hundred feet below, the ocean.

And the car was still moving.

I squeezed my eyes shut, bracing for the plummeting fall. I gripped the door handle and bit down on my lip.

Dead. We were dead.

ELEVEN

I COULDN'T BEAR to look. Not until the brakes squealed, Aidan yanked the wheel back, and we slammed into a tree.

The crash was so sudden, so forceful, that I was heaved out of my seat, the seat belt cutting into my chest the only thing bracing me from the windshield. That, and Aidan's arm, which was thrown across me.

Somehow, even in the insanity of the moment, I felt acutely aware of this gesture.

He's trying to protect me.

There was the ferocious sound of ripping metal and shattering glass.

Then, quiet. The sound of our breathing. The eerie stillness of the forest. The patter of fat raindrops drumming on the windshield.

I clutched at my stomach and chest and turned to him. He had a hand on his forehead.

"Are you okay?" My words sounded high and tight, my voice hoarse. It must have been the screaming.

"Seems like it." He shrugged his shoulders and rolled his head around on his neck. "You?"

"I think so." There was feeling in my fingers. And my toes. That was a good sign.

I reached down to unbuckle myself.

We slowly opened the doors and inched our way up and out of the car. Standing gingerly, I felt around to make sure I hadn't broken any bones. Aidan turned around and I examined him, too. Neither of us had any cuts. I could feel a bruise starting on my rib cage. I felt along my torso for other tender spots.

"Sorry if I hit you there," Aidan said. "I just didn't want you to go flying."

"No, it's okay," I said. We were strangely polite and formal, posed like two figures in a diorama. Maybe it was just that standing on the edge of a cliff in the middle of nowhere with our wrecked car seemed a bit surreal. Or maybe we were just in shock. Probably a little of both.

The rain clung to our eyelashes as we investigated the damage. The tree itself was nothing to write home about—a small squat thing with a spidery clutch of branches—but powerful enough to stop us. Powerful enough to drive a major dent in the front fender and crumple the hood, accordion-style, around its thick base. All of the front lights were bashed into uselessness. Steam rose from the engine, and the smell of burnt rubber hovered in the air.

"Good thing we were in a Volvo, huh?" Aidan said, reaching out to remove the dangling grille.

I laughed weakly, feeling my ribs ache. "Safest car in its class," I said, deliriously repeating the line from an ad I'd seen a million times on TV.

There was nothing to do now but try to reverse the car and detach it from the tree. We couldn't call anyone for help, and we couldn't just wait for someone to rescue us. Aidan said there were probably bobcats and bears up here in the mountains. Besides, there were bigger predators out there: men who wanted us in jail. We had no choice but to just get in the smashed-up hunk of metal and keep driving, which we did, wordlessly.

I felt the immensity of our situation then. How one little decision had spiraled into a whole mess of trouble. But I wiped my face and opened the passenger-side door. Robotically, almost.

Our fate was decided. For the moment, there was no other plan.

The engine, thankfully, turned on. The car creaked out of its accident position, rolled backward, and we were on our way with a new rattling sound.

A few hours later, the rain stopped and the fog lifted, and we found ourselves on a (thankfully) paved road again, driving through the Los Padres National Forest. It was a stunning landscape: the thick cover of pine trees on the curving mountains around us, the craggy rocks sheeted in snow. Giant birds swooped overhead. All signs of life. Signs of hope, even.

Aidan seemed to have recovered from the accident just fine. He was still listening to his classic rock—unfortunately, the antenna was unaffected—and singing along at the top of his lungs to Steve Miller Band. "Woo! Woo!"

How could he bounce back so quickly?

He looked over at me, shocked, apparently, that I wasn't joining in. "C'mon, Willa. Don't you know this song? It's, like, programmed in your head from birth, I think."

"My head rejects Steve Miller Band."

Now that we were safe, reality was coming back again. The numbness was wearing off.

I reached into the glove compartment for the printout of my mom's painting. I unfolded the paper in my lap, willing it to tell me something, wishing it were a map that could show us where to go next. She'd been in Santa Barbara; we knew that. And now she was gone again. How were we going to find her if we were on the run ourselves?

I stared into the rendering of what I'd thought was a beach, the brown shapes intersecting with the blue ones, looking for any sort of clue I might have missed. But the image told me nothing. I folded the now-wrinkled paper back up again and sighed heavily.

Why did she have to leave me?

I tried to get into my mom's head. What was she thinking about? Who was after her?

Ever since we'd moved to Paradise Valley, I'd been feeling the distance between us widening, the disturbing sense that there was much more to her than I knew . . . that maybe she wasn't who I thought she was.

I bit my lip. This line of thinking was getting me nowhere.

Sure, I didn't understand everything about my mom—and according to Corbin, there were lots of things in the unknown category. But I wasn't about to start questioning the fifteen years of my life that I'd spent with her. No matter what sort of lies they told you, or what kind of secrets they were hiding, the essential truth of a person, and how you felt about them, was still there beneath it all, wasn't it?

I had to believe yes.

"Aidan," I blurted, interrupting his singing. Suddenly, it seemed important to know. Because there were things going on in his head that I couldn't access. Because I already felt him drifting away from me, and right now he was all I had. Because we'd just almost died. And because I wanted whatever this thing was between us to grow. "Why did you get kicked out of Prep? What did you do?"

He groaned, dropping his head back. "This again."

I had asked him repeatedly what had happened, why he got kicked out, and why he was sentenced to community service. More and more, I realized how much this bothered me—that he didn't seem to trust me enough to tell me what was going on. If he kept this a secret, what else was he hiding?

Then he faced forward again, gripping the wheel tightly. "You know I can't say. As much as I'd like to, Willa, I can't."

"But why? I've told you everything," I said. "I mean, this stuff with my mom is as personal as it gets."

"I know. It's not that I'm trying to be all secretive. Really. It's just that some things are better left untouched."

"Poison ivy, maybe, or sulfuric acid," I said. "But we're talking about the truth here. Isn't the truth supposed to set you free? The Bible, and all that?"

"There's another saying: The truth is rarely pure and never simple. Even if I told you the truth, you probably wouldn't believe it."

I looked at him plaintively. Why didn't he see that I needed to know? "That would be for me to decide, wouldn't it?" Why didn't he get how important this was?

Now he shifted in his seat, impatient. He exhaled a forceful sigh. "C'mon, Willa. Stop, okay? I said I can't."

"Fine. Whatever." And then, before I could help myself, the words slipped out. "Tre warned me about you, you know."

His brow furrowed in surprise. "He did? I thought we were cool. What did he say?"

"That I shouldn't get emotional about you."

"Well, are you?" I felt his green eyes drilling right into me and I knew that my skin, my muscles, my bones were no cover at all.

"Not at all," I said, turning away to look out the window.

By the time we got to Carmel it was late afternoon and we were running low on fuel. We'd traveled through the forest and back out to the ocean, silently winding around the rocky coastline. Our journey without the detour through the mountains would have been nearly two hours shorter, but hey, then we might not have had the opportunity to scale death-defying heights on dirt roads in the rain and/or decorate the Volvo with the latest in wood accessories.

In any case, the town was a beautiful sight to behold, all stone cottages and thatched roofs, Tudor-style storefronts and little manicured bursts of color in all the window boxes. I wish we could say we'd been smart enough to plan it, but our arrival here was purely by chance—and now we just had to get out of the jumbled-up wreck of a car. Plus we needed to do some more research, which meant finding an available computer.

"This is strictly a survival stop," I warned Aidan. I didn't want him to get too many ideas, even though I was light-headed about the possibility of another Sly Fox maneuver. *Pickpocketing is a gateway drug*, Tre had said.

If only he knew how right he was.

"Go up there," I said, pointing to what looked like a residential street. We drove around for a little while, checking out houses. I was looking for something quiet, easy to get into, and obviously empty.

"What about that one?" Aidan pointed to a modern home that was all glass boxes.

"No way," I said. "It's like an aquarium. Think discreet."

We debated the merits of trying a house for sale or a guesthouse on a larger property. Finally, we settled on a neatly kept yellow stucco cottage with blue trim and a rustic-looking wood garage door. It was the garage door I was counting on.

"You know best." He winked. "I'm just the apprentice here."

It wasn't a vacation house like the place in Santa Barbara. But it looked like a risk worth taking. We parked at the end of the block.

In the passenger seat, I closed my eyes for a moment and tried to center myself to prepare for another break-in. This would take concentration and we couldn't afford to make any more mistakes. No, from now on we needed to be superslick.

"Let's take all of our stuff and ditch the car."

Aidan slung his knapsack over his shoulder. All I had left besides my schoolbag, which was proving fairly useless to me at this point, was the pepper spray and the papers with the painting and my mom's email. I grabbed the bag, throwing the other stuff inside, and put on my mom's jacket.

"Before we go I need something from the car," I said. "Can you open the hood?"

Aidan frowned and reached over to pull the release lever. "I don't know. This thing is pretty crunched up."

We got out and he put his fingers underneath the hood to wedge it open. It took a few tries, but the thing finally gave, releasing a few more puffs of smoke that we waved out of our eyes. "What do you need?"

"That stick thingy for the oil." I was not well versed in my car vocab.

"The dipstick?"

"Yeah."

He reached in and pulled out the wire, giving me a funny look. "I'm not even going to ask why you want this."

I grasped it between my fingers. "Then you'll just have to watch."

"Oh, I'm watching." He tried to slam the hood closed but it bounced back up. "Ah, screw it."

We walked quickly and purposefully down the street toward the house. There was a stone wall encircling the property, which we hopped over easily, and we stepped onto the paved stone circling in front. My body ached from the hours in the car, and the bruise radiated from my ribs down my torso, but it felt good to move again. I saw that there were two newspapers on the front step—an excellent sign. And some weeds tangled in the bushes. Even better.

Don't worry, lonely house. We've come to keep you company.

I peered in through the tiny porthole window on the side of the garage. No cars inside, either. And there was a little gray box mounted on the ceiling. Very good.

Now, it was onto the door. It was supposed to look like it was original to the house, with cutesy wrought-iron hinges and handles. But that was just for show. It was actually electric and probably only a few years old.

I bent the wire into a hook shape. "Can you lift me up?" I asked Aidan.

Aidan flexed his biceps, and I tried not to notice. "I can manage that."

He leaned down to grab me by the legs and heaved so that my feet were at his chest and I could reach the crack between the garage door and the frame. I slid my wire up beneath the rubber flap concealing the opening and pushed it through, feeling around. It was a technique similar to the one I'd used to break into lockers at school. All I had to do was find the latch. . . .

"You're getting heavy," Aidan grumbled.

And how was it that a minute ago he was doing his Mr. Universe routine? Paging the men of the world: No girl ever wants to hear that she's heavy, under any circumstances—home invasions included.

I scowled and rotated my wrist so that the wire brushed against smooth plastic. That was the gray box—I was sure of it—and then, as I lowered the wire, a little lip. I hooked around the edge with the wire and pulled down, feeling the lever release. "Got it."

Aidan lowered me and I pulled open the door. Triumph. Success. *Entrez.*

"Damn." He grinned. "You never cease to amaze me. What's that trick called?"

"The Disable the Garage Door with a Dipstick? Don't know. We'll have to think of something catchier."

We breezed by the pristine rows of shelving, the neat arrangement of tools hanging on the walls. "Whoever lives here does not use this stuff," Aidan said.

He grabbed a wrench and an extra screwdriver.

"What are you doing?" I hissed.

"Stocking up for later. You never know when we might need it. This is a survival stop, right? Besides, these people aren't using them."

I shook my head and put my hand on the doorknob leading into the house. I was willing to bet it was unlocked—nobody kept the door between their garage and house locked—but I was also preparing to deal with another alarm system inside.

I looked at Aidan. "Ready, klepto?"

He nodded. I turned the handle. The door was open. Awesome.

Unfortunately, there was a very large, very angry gray pit bull charging toward us, barking. Not so awesome.

We were already inside, standing in some kind of laundry room. Pride kept me from turning back. Also, the dog, which was jumping all around, circling both of us, and staring with his rheumy eyes.

"Down, boy!" I whispered loudly. I'd never had a pet myself. Other than my day at the animal shelter, my experience with the canine species was limited and I had no idea how to handle a mean and attacking guard animal. The dog seemed to know this, because he ignored my command and leapt on me, scratching at my legs and gnashing his teeth.

"Down! Down!"

"Uh, Willa? That's not gonna help. Not now."

"What do we do?" I yelped to Aidan.

"This way," Aidan said, rapping the dog on the nose with the back of his hand. The dog let up for a few seconds, and Aidan pulled me into a powder room and slammed the door shut.

"Oh my God," I said, reaching around to examine the tattered hemline of my shirt. "He bit me."

"He just bit your clothes," Aidan said. "Don't be a drama queen."

The dog was barking outside the door, clawing at it so his nails clicked on the wood. My heart was still racing wildly.

"We're trapped in here. And he's gonna keep barking

until the police come. Now what, dog whisperer?"

"At least there's no alarm," Aidan said, grinning.

"So our death will be silent and peaceful."

"Calm down, Colorado." He opened the vanity under the sink. "We need to confuse him. There's gotta be something in here we can use."

I folded my arms across my thundering chest. "I'm not going to poison a dog, if that's what you're thinking."

"Are you crazy? You think I would do that?"

He looked genuinely offended. Then I remembered seeing the way he was with the animals at the shelter. How his affection and playfulness with even the mangiest mutts just about melted me into syrup that day.

No, not really. But how well did I even know Aidan? Less and less all the time, it seemed.

"Never mind. I got something here." He produced a family-sized bottle of talcum powder and a hair dryer. "You get the door, and I'll get this."

I frowned. "How is this going to work?"

"Just trust me, Willa."

I just looked at him. The problem was I didn't exactly trust him, not anymore. Not after that text message.

"I got this, okay?"

The dog's barking had turned to vicious growls. I could practically feel his breath through the crack in the door. A few more minutes and a neighbor would hear us and call the police. Then we'd be dunzo.

Aidan plugged in the hair dryer. "On the count of

three. Ready? One . . . two . . . . three!"

I flung open the door and the dog burst into the bathroom, jumping on his hind legs. Aidan flipped on the hair dryer and simultaneously squeezed the plastic bottle so that the powder blew up and out into a white cloud, surrounding the dog's muzzle. The dog dropped down to all fours and paused, shaking to clear his head, trying to find his way through the haze.

In the meantime, we slipped by him and shut the door. "Now," Aidan said. "Step two. We need to stop the barking."

I followed him back into the laundry room, where he found a ten-pound bag of dry food. He opened the bathroom door a crack and slipped it inside. "That should keep him busy for a while."

He dusted off his hands and looked at me, waiting for my approval. Even I had to admit that he'd done a good job. "Nice one," I allowed.

We walked through the house into the kitchen. It was a small house, much smaller than Beasley's place, but it was neat and charming. Perfectly round windows like the one in the garage hung over the cabinetry, and frosted white beams arced over the ceiling. The floor was lined with wide planks and finely woven oriental rugs, and the walls were embellished with colorful paintings.

In the attached living room, the plush armchairs and polished end tables looked as if they were waiting for guests. A potted lemon tree sat in the corner, giving off a faint citrus fragrance.

"It's like a fairy-tale place," I said, wishing suddenly that I could stay here. Like *really* stay here. Move into this cottage and hide forever. Maybe if I could, things would all work out okay. Maybe that foreboding cloud, which had been hanging over my head ever since we found my house ransacked, would finally lift.

I opened up the stainless-steel double doors to peer inside the fridge. It was stocked with food.

"Lasagna!"

I brought the dish out and set it on the butcher-block counter. We ate quickly, with our hands. I tried not to think about it too much but the freshness of the food kind of messed with my theory about the owners being away for a while. I had no idea how much time we had here.

"This is disgusting, you know that?" Aidan said, licking tomato sauce off his fingers.

"Dude, beggars can't be choosers."

"What about thieves?"

I chewed on a mouthful of noodles. "How about 'Thieves can't be whiners'?"

Aidan found a laptop on the kitchen desk. We washed our hands so as not to leave marinara fingerprints, and went to work.

I opened up Google. The first thing I wanted to do was search for my mom and see if there were any news reports or other mentions of her that might help us in our quest. Obvious, maybe, but at this point I had to try everything.

I typed in "Joanne Fox," and about a hundred entries popped up right away. Most of these were on LinkedIn—networking profiles for a communications specialist, a real estate agent, a biologist, and a town mayor somewhere in Rhode Island. There was an Australian water-polo player by that name, too, and a woman on Facebook who looked like she was sixty-five. Six Google pages of results in, there was no trace of anyone remotely resembling my mom.

"This is weird," I said. "It's like she has no online presence at all."

"Well, that happens with some people," Aidan said. "You said she's not on Facebook or anything. Maybe she's just old-school like that. Analog."

I kept scrolling down. Nothing. Then I tried doing a news search. That brought up something, a news item about Joanne Fox on a site called Obituary.com.

I looked up at Aidan, blood rushing to my head, breath burning in my chest. My stomach plummeted. I felt like I was going to puke again.

Dead? Could she really be dead?

This is what I'd been fearing all along, wasn't it? I covered my face with my hands. I didn't want to look. I didn't want to know.

But I would know, wouldn't I, if that's what happened? I mean, was this how I was supposed to find out . . . if she were?

"Go on. Click on it," he said softly. "Remember what

you said about the truth setting you free? If something happened, you should know."

My hands shook as I moved my finger over the mouse pad. "I didn't mean . . . this."

"Want me to do it?"

I nodded.

He reached over, placing his hand over mine, and guided the mouse.

> *Joanne Elizabeth Fox*
> *October 12, 1997, St. Louis, MO*

I exhaled all the breath I was holding in when I saw the date: 1997—that was fifteen years ago. My mom was still alive.

I ran my hands through my hair. "This isn't her."

"Thank God," Aidan said. He moved his hand to click away, but I stopped him, remembering that my mom was from St. Louis.

> *A search crew from the St. Louis County Sheriff's Department discovered the body of a sixteen-year-old girl, identified as Joanne Elizabeth Fox, in Luther Ely Smith Park yesterday. Reported missing from her foster home since December 1, Fox was a runaway who had left multiple foster homes many times over the past three years. An autopsy revealed she was two months pregnant at the time of her death. Police*

suspect there was no foul play and have ruled the
death an accident. She has no surviving relatives.

I leaned in and squinted at the screen. The photograph looked nothing like my mom—this girl had dark hair and blue eyes and was much more petite. Yet there was no denying the name. Was that just a weird coincidence?

"No," I said to myself out loud. "It can't be a coincidence."

"I don't get it," Aidan said, looking over my shoulder. "This is a girl who died fifteen years ago. What's the connection?"

"Yes, but this girl died around the same time I was born," I explained, trying to articulate the thoughts that had flashed through my head and wound themselves together. "My mom would have been the same age and pregnant then, too. My mom has the same name and she grew up in the same town. That's too many same things, too many links for a coincidence."

"So you think it's her, that she's still alive? That she duped the police somehow?"

"Maybe, or maybe she's living under this person's identity for some reason." Even as I said it out loud it hardly made sense. "She must have changed her name along the way and assumed Joanne Fox's."

"But why?"

I pushed myself away from the island and took a few steps back from the computer. "I don't know. Because she knew she was in trouble with these guys who were after her?" I said. "Whoever they are."

For a moment I thought of my father, who I'd never known. Could this have something to do with him? He could've been anyone. Was she trying to escape him? That thought was disturbing, too.

When it came down to it, I really knew very little about my family history. I knew that my mom had left her parents' house when she was pregnant with me because she was only sixteen and they hadn't approved. I'd never even met my grandparents. All I had was the bird necklace around my neck—that was my only connection to them.

But if my mom's real name wasn't Joanne, then what was it? And what other things about her were lies? Everything, all that I'd assumed to be true, was unraveling in front of me. And with that came a crippling wave of vertigo, a feeling like my body had gone liquid.

Aidan's hand was on my shoulder. "Are you okay?"

"It's just . . . so strange. I mean, why do you change your name?"

"I don't know, Willa. But there's usually a good reason for everything, you know? We have to keep believing that."

Fine, but what was the reason for us being here, in the middle of this strange house, in an unfamiliar town? What was the reason for any of this?

"I guess," I said. I was drowning in uncertainty. In maybes. In what-ifs.

He hugged me and I felt his stubble brush against my cheek. "Don't worry. We'll figure it out. I'm going to work on finding her car, okay? Why don't you wash up or do whatever you need to do? Then we can get back on the road."

I moved aside so that Aidan could sit down. As he logged on, I looked away to give him privacy, though I couldn't help but wonder if he was going to get more messages from Sheila, whoever she was. For all I knew, he had an in-box of long-form sexts in his Gmail account. Ugh. Or maybe there was a good explanation for that text. I told myself that there had to be.

I found the master bedroom, a cozy enclave with a sloped beamed ceiling and a huge weathered armoire. In the bathroom, I scrubbed my face and brushed my teeth with my finger. I grabbed another pair of jeans and a mom-like ruffled button-down from the closet, quickly changing and stuffing my old clothes into the laundry hamper. I also found a baseball hat for Aidan and a pen and pad and wrote another note and left it on the nightstand.

"I found her car," Aidan said when I came back. "It was last seen in Tahoe."

Tahoe. Why Tahoe?

"And guess how I did it? I hacked into the E-ZPass database. Don't let my brilliance overwhelm you."

"That's our next stop, then," I said, handing him the hat. "And I won't. Let your brilliance overwhelm me, I mean."

"You see?" He stood up and stretched his long limbs.

"It's all coming together. We're getting close. And there's a reason for everything, right?"

I wanted to believe it. I really did. I wanted us to be a team, a winning team. If only I didn't have so many doubts . . .

He turned on the little television mounted underneath one of the cabinets. "Just want to see if anything has happened since this morning."

Things had happened, all right. Ho-ly.

There we were, the top story on CNN. Photos of us side by side appeared on the screen with the caption: FOX & FRIEND ON THE RUN.

"And now, to the news that's captivating the nation— the story of two affluent teens turned criminals. Willa Fox, also known as Sly Fox, and Aidan Murphy, son of Hanson Murphy, CEO of MTech Corporation, have skipped probation, stolen a car, and are now thought to be in California. After a high-speed chase this morning, the pair eluded police outside of Montecito."

"Dude, we're famous," Aidan said, grinning.

If that were true, then it was only a matter of time before we'd be recognized, even with our disguises. I felt a new kind of panic setting in. "We also have a lot of people looking for us. We have to find my mom before they find us."

The screen flashed to an image of Aidan's dad. He had a thick flap of silvery hair and glasses, and his head bobbed in a box next to the anchorman.

"Joining us live now via satellite is Hanson Murphy. Mr. Murphy, what is your family going through right now?"

"Shock, Bill. Just shock. Aidan was always a good kid. We never expected this from him. All we ask is that, Aidan, if you're out there watching this, that you come home. Your family needs you here. We just want you back, safe and sound."

Aidan's father's eyes filled with tears. I looked at Aidan and his expression had changed from awe and delight to something darker.

"What do you think?" I asked him.

"I think I need to find us another car." He wiped at his face. I could see the red tracing his eyes—he must have been completely burnt-out with so little sleep over the past few days—and I suddenly felt the urge to hold him again. Protect him.

Before I could, he grabbed his bag and turned abruptly, heading for the door. "You stay here and map our route to Tahoe. Let the dog out and shut the doors and I'll meet you outside in a few. And erase our browsing history from the computer."

The voices were still droning on about us. I shut off the TV. I tried to shake off the uneasiness. It hadn't told us anything we really didn't know already. We just had to keep moving. Like, ASAP. We had to get to Tahoe.

TWELVE

A FEW MOMENTS later, I watched through the kitchen window as a hunter-green Land Rover came speeding around the bend and pulled up in front of the house.

"Get in," Aidan called from the driver's-side window.

"A Land Rover?" I asked, my hand on the door. "Really?"

"What's wrong with it? I felt like we needed an upgrade. None of that broken-window crap. Just get in, okay?"

"Why not a Bentley?" I gave him a sardonic look as I relented, stepping up to the SUV seat. I shut the passenger-side door and buckled in.

Aidan hit the gas and we sped away. It was a smooth ride. I didn't think engines could actually purr— I thought that was just something car dorks liked to say—but this one actually did. The inside smelled like perfumed leather, and was trimmed with real wood and tortoiseshell accents.

I was pretty certain Tre would not approve of this flashy choice. I was pretty sure Tre wouldn't approve of anything we were doing anymore. This wasn't the simple trip I'd thought it would be; that was for sure. Things were way out of control. Every crime led to more crime. But I didn't know how we could stop it, at least not until we found my mother.

And there was a little part of me—okay, maybe a medium-sized part—that was loving every minute. Here we were, the two of us cruising down the highway in a Land Rover. Which we'd stolen. And that was pretty badass. Wrong, but badass.

Aidan was busy pointing out the advantages to our new ride. "It has satellite radio, so you don't have to listen to classic rock anymore. And here," he said, reaching over and handing me an eyeglass case.

I opened it up and found a gorgeous pair of Barton Perreira sunglasses, square frames with metal trim and smoky lenses. "These cost like five hundred bucks," I said. I remembered because Kellie had pointed them out to me at Neiman Marcus once.

"Only the best for your priceless face," he said. He turned off a side street to drive through the center of town so we could get back on the highway. "Try them on."

I shook my head, putting them on reluctantly, trying to ignore the surge of joy I got from him saying my face was pretty. That was what priceless meant, wasn't it?

"They're the perfect disguise," he said. And when I looked in the sun-visor mirror, I saw that indeed they were. He was making this hard for me. Here he was again, distracting me with shiny things. Of course, Aidan was the prettiest, shiniest distraction of them all. He belonged on top of someone's Christmas tree.

I snuck another look over at him. I could barely decide how I felt about Aidan Murphy from one minute to the next. Well, more accurately, what I couldn't decide was what I *wanted* to feel.

There were already a number of factors making me nervous. Namely:

(A) That he was clearly getting off on breaking the law.

(B) That he was getting sexts from some hoochie mama.

(C) That I still had no idea why he was kicked out of school.

(D) That I was still obsessing over that moment in Sam Beasley's house when we'd started making out in the bathroom.

(Not necessarily in that order.)

All the things that had seemed so appealing about Aidan back in Paradise Valley—the devil-may-care attitude, the flirtatious smiles, all the mystery surrounding him—now seemed like more of a liability than ever. Tre was right: My feelings were mucking everything up. I had to stay focused. I had to stay, well, professional.

"I can't believe you did this," I said. I took the glasses

off and put them away. No, I couldn't wear them. I shouldn't be enjoying this.

"What? Ripping off another spoiled rich person like my dad?"

So this was about his dad, then.

"He seemed so upset on the news. Didn't that bother you at all?" I thought of how I'd feel if I were in his position. Right now there were no parents looking for me, and that was exactly why I was here in the first place.

He shrugged, and I glimpsed the Aidan I'd first met at Prep, the one who set off a fire alarm just to see if the school would have the guts to bust him even though his dad was a board member. "He's on TV. What else is he going to say?"

"So you don't think he means it?"

"Who is he concerned about, really? Me or his reputation?"

"I think you're underestimating him. He seemed sincere."

"Maybe. But you don't know my old man. Anyway, I don't really want to sit here and analyze him. The guy doesn't deserve that much brain power."

I took in a deep stream of a breath, trying to make my voice level. I needed to lay down the law. I needed to create some limits.

"Aidan, thank you for the glasses. But we can't go around stealing for fun. It's really only something we

168

can do for survival at this point. We can't take any more chances."

"I thought you'd be proud of me. I'm just getting into the Sly Fox spirit."

He was certainly getting into it, all right. A little too much. And I was, too. We had to calm down.

"When I did it in Paradise Valley, it was to help other people—and get revenge on Kellie and Nikki."

"Well, now we have a purpose, too. Finding and helping your mom. That's even more important, isn't it?"

It was. "But I'm not trying to get back at anyone."

"So what am I supposed to do, steal from poor folks?"

He was getting me all mixed up again. "No, no. But we can't, like, celebrate it. And I'm writing all of this down," I said, looking through the glove compartment for a pen. "We're going to leave a note in this car, just like we did in the house. I want there to be a record so we can pay it all back."

I wrote down the glasses and the car in my Comp notebook, along with the other places we'd been and things we'd taken, and put it back in my bag. At least the notebook was serving some function, finally.

"You've gotta admit that this thing is pretty sweet, though," he said. "The cupholders have cupholders."

I smiled, and an easier mood settled between us.

"I'm not complaining," I said, jamming my finger on the satellite radio console. "Though you do realize you have ceded control over our musical fate."

"I can be open-minded. Sometimes."

I hit a button and smooth jazz pealed out of the speakers, pseudosexy saxophones and hissy cymbals. I looked over at him, testing his reaction.

"Agh. You're skating on thin ice," he said.

"I thought you were open-minded."

I scrolled on further and landed on a woman talking.

"What I don't understand, Jack, is why this is becoming such a craze. I mean, you have these two kids who have everything. Privileged beyond belief. And they go and throw it away to run around, acting like lunatics—stealing, squatting. And for what? I don't get it."

A man's voice responded. "Lisa, the point is that the media—people like you and me, I'd like to add—are only adding fuel to the fire. This story is on the cover of every tabloid this week, not to mention newspapers around the globe. Are we silently condoning this behavior by paying it so much attention? Perhaps. We have to admit our culpability here. And hey, who can blame kids out there for looking up to this Sly Fox and her accomplice, Mr. Murphy?"

Aidan and I looked at each other across the front seat, our eyes widened in amazement. I felt my face warm, almost as if I'd walked into a room and heard someone talk about me. Only this was *national radio*.

"They're good-looking kids. Smart. And let's face it: They're getting away with it."

Aidan gave himself a little pat on the back. But I

couldn't joke about this.

The woman interjected. "That's not the point, Jack. We need to stop glorifying crime in this country because it starts with this kind of folk heroism but it's a slippery slope. The next thing you know, the kids will be running around mugging one another. . . ."

"Oddly enough, that's *exactly* what I was thinking of doing next," Aidan said. "Mugging. In fact, I was just working on my fake gun."

He reached around and poked two fingers into my shoulder. Startled, I drew back a little.

How could he be so calm? I ignored him, difficult as it was to pretend he *wasn't touching me*, and reached up to change the station. I'd heard enough. It was plucking my already-frazzled nerves to worry about the media and what people thought about us. And they didn't get it. They'd never get it. They only had one side. They didn't know anything about my mom—though of course that was for the best, because they saw things only in black and white. A mother abandons her daughter. The daughter is a criminal. Yes, those things were true, but they were not the whole story.

The host answered a call. "Hello, this is Radio Issues. You're on the air."

"Yes, hi. My name's Kaycee and I'm calling from Columbus, Ohio. I just wanted to say that Sly Fox and Aidan aren't hurting anyone. They're doing what a lot of people wish they could do, which is to stick it to the man. I mean, it's like an adventure story, and they're the heroes—"

The woman's voice broke in. "This is exactly what I'm talking about, Jack. This kind of talk has got to stop. There's got to be accountability, responsibility for our young people. . . ."

That did it. I hit the button.

"Hey, why'd you change it? I wanted to hear what our fans have to say," Aidan said. "That's a good thing, right? That we have fans?"

"No, it's not." I wrapped my arms around me. "Not if everyone knows about us."

"But that's more people that can help us. Maybe we don't have to go it alone."

"We're not alone. We're both here, aren't we? And we've done well enough so far." I paused, letting the ridiculousness of my statement sink in. Well enough? We were on the road to hell. "I don't want to bring anyone else into this."

Before he could answer, Aidan's phone rang. We both jumped a little in our seats. "Who is it?" he asked.

I looked at the screen. "It's Corbin. Should I answer it?"

"No, let him leave us a message."

A minute went by and then the words *1 new voice mail* appeared on the screen. I grabbed the phone and pressed play, putting it on speaker.

"Willa, Aidan. Corbin here. How're things on the

road? Getting rough enough for you yet?"

Aidan and I looked at each other and I rolled my eyes. Corbin was like someone's annoying uncle. The kind of guy who would shake your hand and squeeze it hard and pretend you were hurting him.

"Listen, I'm wondering if you want to meet up. No pressure—just talk. No police. Only little old me. C'mon. We can sort some things out. I just want to help you and your mom, okay? Call me."

"*Call me*. Like he's our buddy. This guy just won't let up, will he?" Aidan said. He reached over to delete the message and I pushed his hand away.

"Don't." I bit down on my lip. A new idea was forming. "I'm thinking maybe we should do this. Maybe we can get some information out of him."

Aidan looked at me like I was nuts. "We already know she's in Tahoe. Why would we actually meet with him now and risk having him haul us in?"

"Well, we don't know where she is exactly," I reminded him. "I think he might, though. Besides, we wouldn't actually meet with him. We'd just get him to be in a prearranged spot. . . ."

"Ballsy." His eyes shone. "I like your thinking. But would it work?"

I shrugged. "Only one way to find out."

"All right, Colorado. Call him back."

I dialed Corbin's number and he answered right away.

"This is Agent Corbin."

"It's Willa. We'll meet you. In Tahoe. No police, right?"

"No police."

"Text us the location," I said, and I hung up.

"That was short and sweet," Aidan said.

"Next time I'll ask about his family."

"Hey, everyone's got one."

"For better or worse," I retorted.

An hour later, Aidan pulled off at an exit near Gilroy, and followed signs for a gas station. We needed to refuel the Land Rover and caffeinate for the next leg of the journey. I waited in the car while he went outside to pump. Another truck pulled in front of us. A man got out and cast a glance in my direction before unscrewing his gas cap.

Don't look at me, buddy.

I drummed my hand against the door's wood trim and watched Aidan walk into the office to pay.

I didn't like being left alone—not with people on the hunt for us, not in this elevated car. I peered into the rearview mirror to see if we were being watched. The truck in front of me pulled away and the station seemed empty, but I slumped down a little lower just in case.

Aidan's phone sat in the change compartment between the driver's and passenger's seats, where I'd left it. I looked up. Inside the store, Aidan had his back to me as he picked out sodas from the glass refrigerator case.

I reached over and quickly snatched the Droid. It was turned off, as we had both agreed it should be until further notice.

We could still be traced. Anyone from the police or the FBI could find us through satellite tracking.

I knew it was dangerous. I knew I should be doing everything I could to keep our cover. But—how can I explain this? Something much more powerful took over, an undeniable urge. The need to find out who Aidan was.

One way or another, I had to know. I didn't want to keep kidding myself.

I snuck another look inside the store as I hit the power button. Then, grasping the phone in both hands, I thumbed through the screen, looking for his text messages. In the received column there were at least ten from Sheila.

Not a total surprise. That's what I was looking for, wasn't it? But I felt my body clench up nonetheless.

I selected one, dated from a week earlier.

Where are u baby?

Then another:

Miss u. Can't wait to see u.

And another:

Hey sexy. When can we meet?

A sputtering swirl of rage and hurt boiled up inside me. Aidan was definitely fooling around with this girl, whoever she was. I counted the days backward on my hands. One of these messages was sent the day we kissed in my driveway.

Does she know about me? Do I even mean anything to him?

I couldn't believe I'd ever thought of him as anything like a boyfriend. For a moment there, I'd thought he actually liked me.

So stupid.

He was a player. Everyone said so.

And then another, more unsettling question. How could I possibly stay with him? Clearly, I hardly knew this guy. And here I was, relying on him to help me find my mother, relying on him to help us stay out of trouble.

I watched as he emerged from the front entrance to the store, holding the door open for a little old lady. That was just like him, I thought, sickened. Trying to charm everyone when he was the ultimate in shady. He flicked his hair out of his face and came closer to the car. I quickly shut his phone off and tossed it back into the change compartment.

He got into the front seat and set a paper bag on my lap.

"What's this?" I snapped, on edge.

"Um, snacks?" He switched on the car and, setting his arm around my headrest, turned back to reverse out of the lot. "Your blood sugar drop or something?"

I looked inside the bag. There were cupcakes, pretzels, Swedish fish, and more turkey jerky, plus two Cokes. It was a junk-food bonanza. "Did you steal this stuff?" I demanded.

He frowned. "Of course not. I had a little money left over. Why would I steal it?"

"You seemed pretty excited to be stealing stuff before." My tone was sarcastic and accusing.

"Well, I didn't. I wouldn't risk something like that unless we had to." He looked out onto the road, and then back to me. "Jesus, Willa, what's wrong with you? All of a sudden you seem really pissed."

"Nothing," I grumbled.

"Obviously there *is* something wrong. You've been really weird for days now. Hot and cold. At first I didn't say anything because I thought you were worried about your mom. But now I'm starting to think it's just because you hate me or something. It's like you can barely stand to look at me, even."

Aidan was acting like someone who cared, but I knew better. The text messages were proof. He was just good at pretending. This was all a game to him. A way to get back at his dad and entertain himself. He was using me to get his kicks, tagging along on my drama.

Then I thought of my mom. Joanne wasn't even her real name. Was there anyone in my life who didn't lie to me? Was there anyone I could actually trust? Tre, maybe. But he was so far away. I made a mental note to call him the next time I had a chance. In Tahoe, hopefully.

Aidan was waiting for a response.

I looked down to the floor of the car at my own feet. How could I look at Aidan? If I looked at him I would get sucked back into those killer green eyes.

For now, yes, I was depending on him to drive me, but only until we got to Tahoe and I could find my mom. And then I was no longer going to have room for Aidan—or his lies—in my life.

"Forget it," I said, not wanting to have this confrontation. What was the point? There were too many things I couldn't say out loud. "Okay? You win. Just drop it."

"You're no fun anymore, you know that?" he said.

"Yeah, well, you're no . . ." I trailed off as he merged onto the highway.

"No what?" he asked.

"Nothing."

What I had been about to say was that he was no *good* anymore. But even I had the sense to know that that would have been a little harsh.

THIRTEEN

I'M NOT PARTICULARLY proud to report that we spent the night in another squat. We'd gotten stuck, at around one A.M., in the middle of nowhere. Well, not exactly nowhere, but close to a town called You Bet, which we both bet was probably not worth stopping in. Aidan was too tired to drive and we were down to our last few dollars.

So we broke into a pool house. By "pool house," I mean a house for an indoor pool. The place was on a Mediterranean-style estate that had to be over a hundred acres, and it was so far from the main residence that it almost didn't matter whether the owners were home or not. (For the record, they didn't seem to be.) Inside, the air was humid and smelled like chlorine, but there were padded lounge chairs, which were cozy enough, and the suspended stillness and the sequins of light reflecting off the water were soothing.

Still, I hadn't gotten much sleep. I was too worked up about Aidan. I watched him doze soundly on the chair next to me as I cycled through waves of anger, disappointment, and loneliness—then just plain jealousy that he'd managed to set off for dreamland while I was still stranded on the shoreline of bitterness. I kept telling myself I would feel better in the light of day, but when the light of day came I was exhausted and dreading another long car ride.

By six A.M., I shook him awake. We snuck out and were back on the road again, closing in on Tahoe.

"So was that the last of your money yesterday?" I asked Aidan, unwrapping the final cupcake. Not exactly the breakfast of champions—or even semiphysically active outlaws—but what are you going to do?

"Pretty much," he said. "I have about twenty bucks left. And we'll need to get gas at some point."

"Well, we can't keep stealing," I said. "It's only going to attract attention."

"I know that," he said quietly. Ever since our discussion the day before he'd been treating me differently, less like a road buddy and more like I was an insect he'd picked up by the wings and trapped in a jar. I pretended not to notice, even though his distant tone chilled me.

Well, that was fine. We were simply carpooling now, until we could finish off our journey. Strictly business.

"I'm thinking we can call Tre when we get to Tahoe. Maybe he can wire us some cash. We need to get a different phone to use, too." Now that Corbin had sent us the location to meet him, which was in a Denny's parking lot, we no longer needed to use Aidan's Droid.

"You're the boss." He handed me the contents of his wallet.

"Thanks," I said.

I should have been looking tough just then, or at least basking in the glow of my leadership skills. I *was* the boss, wasn't I? This was my mission. So why did it feel sort of terrible?

I was bone-tired and heartsick, that's why. And being the boss of Aidan was no remedy for that.

Aidan found us a Kmart about twelve miles outside Tahoe. I put the fancy sunglasses on before I went inside, aware that I was probably going to be caught on camera. In the electronics aisle, I zeroed in on a prepaid cell phone for fourteen ninety-eight and bought it at the front counter with our last twenty-dollar bill.

"Tre better be home," I muttered to myself. Otherwise I was going to have to Sly Fox us some cash.

I felt the stare of the clerk behind the counter, a skinny dude with a baseball cap and the standard-issue red vest with the name Chris embroidered on the front. It was hard not to stare back. For a moment, I wondered if he recognized me. Probably he just thought it was weird that I was wearing sunglasses inside, I told myself.

But his eyes lingered just a little too long as he handed me back the change. "Have a good day," he said, smiling. "Be safe out there."

I said nothing, but my hands were shaking as I went to stand behind the store near some Dumpsters and dialed Tre's number. *Be safe out there?* I couldn't prove it, of course, but I was pretty sure the guy knew who I was.

Pick up. Pick up.

His voice was a familiar comfort, pouring through the receiver like maple syrup. "Willa! What's up?"

"We're still on the road," I said. I leaned into the wall and cupped a hand around my mouth as I talked. "In Tahoe. We haven't found my mom yet but we think we know where she is."

"You've got to get to her fast," he warned, his tone sharpening. "I've been following on TV and the cops are on the trail."

"I know," I said. "We're trying to lay low."

"Seriously, Willa. I've been worried about you—you guys. I should have never let you go on this trip. It's craziness."

There was a pause and I pictured Tre in his house, sitting on his living-room couch. For a moment, I ached to be back in Paradise Valley, too, where everything was safe and clean and comfortable. Where I didn't have to think five steps ahead. Where I could just hang out with him and watch cartoons like a normal person. "Well, I have a little favor to ask. We're short on cash. I was wondering if you could find some to wire us. Maybe a couple hundred? I'll pay you back—I swear."

"I can do that," he said. "No problem. But where should I wire it from and where should I wire it *to*?"

"Go to the Finer Things Pawnshop, in Scottsdale," I said, remembering the place I'd gone to when I started hocking stolen goods in order to buy Sierra and Alicia and Mary new clothes. "The woman there is blind and she won't give you much trouble. And you can send it to the Kmart on Emerald Bay Road."

"Emerald Bay Road. Got it," he said. "I'll send it to A. Murphy."

"Perfect." I exhaled relief. "You're the best."

He laughed a little. "Yeah, what else is new. So . . . how are you otherwise? You sound upset."

Where to begin? "We're just not getting along that well, I guess." As soon as the words were out, I felt my throat closing up with a sob.

"Is he messing with you?"

"Kind of," I said, trying to gulp down my tears. I was afraid if I started to cry I would completely fall apart, and I couldn't afford to do that right now. "It's complicated."

"If he's messing with you, I'll come straighten him out."

"No, no." I smiled at his protectiveness. "It's okay. I can handle it."

"You don't have to do this alone. I'm here for you," he said quietly. "Always. You know that, right, Willa?"

"Thanks, Tre." I looked down at my shoes. I could hear the soft rattle of his breath through the phone. I couldn't bring him into this. That would be asking too much. "We just have to find her."

"I know. And you will. But listen, if you get stuck for any reason—if something happens, and you need backup, you can call Rain Gladstone. I'm gonna text you her number. She's Cherise's cousin. She lives right there in Tahoe and she knows all about you guys."

At the mention of Cherise, I felt a twinge of regret. Before I could ask more about Rain, or how Tre knew about her, or how she knew about us, Aidan drove around to the back of the store. Through the windshield I could see him waving me into the car. "I've gotta go. Thanks a million, Tre."

"No problem," he said. "The money should be there within the hour. I'll text you when it goes through. And promise you'll watch yourself, Willa."

"I will," I said. But given all that had already happened, and how desperate I was to find my mom, I was no longer really able to make that promise with much conviction.

I wiped my face and tried to compose myself before I got back into the Land Rover.

"How can you just stand out there like that?" he asked me.

"No one was back there. And I wanted some privacy."

"So you could talk about me?" he challenged.

"No," I said, my face hot with the fib. "I had other things to talk about. Anyway, the wire should be here in an hour. And Tre is going to send us Cherise's cousin's number. He said we can call her if we need a place to go. I guess we should just hang out for a while. Then we can go meet Corbin."

He nodded, staring straight ahead. "You're the boss."

"Stop saying that," I said. His new attitude was really starting to bug me.

"Well, it's true, isn't it? It's your mom who's on the lam. I'm just a chauffeur."

"Don't play martyr now," I said, my tone sharp. "You're in this as much as I am. It doesn't matter to the cops whose mom it is. If you want to back out, be my guest. Or if you want to help, then be helpful."

"I didn't say I was backing out, did I?" He traced his finger on the window, making a line through the condensation.

We sat in tense silence for a while.

When he spoke again, his face had changed. "But I was thinking . . . maybe we should be trying to play it safe. We could just go to Cherise's cousin's house and hide out there for a while."

"And do what?"

"Wait, until we can gather more information. We could do some more research online. Forget about this Corbin thing. It's too risky."

I shook my head vehemently. I was tired of sitting

around and looking for the answer on a computer when we could find it with our eyes. "No way. We're so close. We're *here*. I know he can help us."

He sighed. "Did anyone ever tell you you were a tad stubborn?"

I smiled despite myself. "Yes. Many people have told me that. I just refused to listen."

"I should have seen that one coming." He rolled his eyes. "But just for funsies, tell me again how we're going to outsmart an FBI agent?"

"I'm working on it," I said. "Any input is welcome."

He shook his head slowly.

"What?" I said, indignant. "These things don't just come all at once. It's a process."

"Let's hope your process speeds up. We only have a few hours here, okay?"

After a while, the phone buzzed with the text from Tre, and Aidan went in to pick up the money. I sat in the car, waiting, while people came in and out of the store. I watched as the kid from behind the counter stepped out for a smoke break, skateboard under his arm. He lit up, and an idea flashed in front of my eyes, bright and perfect as a pearl.

"Got it," Aidan said when he came back to the car holding the envelope. He handed it to me and I tucked it into my bag.

"I've got it, too," I said. "A plan."

• • •

The Denny's was in a strip mall on a busy intersection of two four-lane roads.

"Why'd he choose this place?" Aidan asked, steering us into the parking lot. "It's so public."

"That's his thing," I said, remembering Corbin's meetings with my mom at the Target back in Arizona. "Listen, just wait behind the bank over there, and when you hear Chris yell, come get me. Chris, you know what you're looking for, right?"

I turned around to face him and he nodded from his place in the backseat. "Totally. Silver Nissan."

"Are you sure we can't give you some money for this?" I asked.

"No way," he said, grinning. "It's just so cool to meet you guys after seeing you all over the internet. I feel like I'm making history, you know?"

"History or infamy—take your pick," Aidan said. His tone was dry, but I knew him well enough by now to know that he was excited about our plan.

"We really appreciate it. Please just be careful," I said. I looked at the clock. "He should be here in five minutes."

Chris gathered up his skateboard. "If he's on time."

"Oh, he'll be on time," I said. "He's uptight like that."

"Fan out and take up your stations," Aidan said, dropping us off before he went to wait behind the bank in the middle of the parking lot.

I was dressed up in Chris's vest, my hair tucked inside

his baseball hat. The clothes were baggy enough that I could, from a distance, look like a boy. I went to wait by the shopping-cart trolley and tried to make myself busy.

Meanwhile, Chris hopped on his skateboard and started carving along the blacktop, swooping in and out by the entrance. I pulled a train of carts, one by one, clinking them together so that they fit in a neat succession, never taking my eyes off Chris and the cars coming into the lot.

A black SUV pulled in. Then a pickup. Shoppers moved toward me, sending new carts my way, and I received them, adding them to the stack.

An elderly woman bundled up in a wool coat came over to me just then.

Not now, lady. I tried to send her a signal with my body language that I was not available.

She was undeterred. She raised a gloved hand to touch my shoulder and her pocketbook, hooked around her wrist, dangled tantalizingly close. *I could just grab it,* I thought.

She's an old lady. Are you going to mug an old lady now? Seriously, Willa. Get your head in the game.

"Excuse me, sir, can you help me with my groceries?"

"I'm sorry," I said, trying to think fast and speak low. "I'm not authorized to do that. You have to ask a bag boy."

Just then, I spotted the Nissan coming around the corner. Chris saw it, too, because he gave me the signal we'd agreed on—a heelflip—and I gave him mine, pulling the brim of my cap down.

"But you're right here."

"I'm—busy."

The woman began shuffling away. "Some job you're doing."

As the Nissan pulled into the lot, Chris skated over, flinging himself onto the hood, hitting it with a thump. Corbin's brakes squealed the car to a halt, but it was too late. Chris had already rolled over the front and—a bit dramatically, I thought—he'd flailed himself onto the pavement, landing chest first and crying out in imaginary pain.

Watching him, I let out an *oof*. That's how bad it looked. But it was beautiful, really—an elegant ballet of wits and deceit, unfolding in slow motion. We'd taken a page out of the pickpocketer's handbook—one of the oldest tricks in the game. And Chris pulled it off perfectly.

Now it was my turn.

Corbin got out of the car and walked over to where Chris was lying and tried to talk to him. Chris played unconscious. A few other shoppers were working their way over, forming a huddle.

A young woman at the scene held up her cell phone. "I'll call 911."

There was a general buzz of chatter and medical advice, a man kneeling down beside Chris and taking his pulse. The crowd was reaching critical mass, about twelve people now.

This was my cue. I pushed the carts back into the trolley. With Corbin's back to me and everyone looking at Chris, I made a dash for the car and snuck up to the backseat. I opened the door and squeezed in, ducking down to the floor.

I could see his briefcase on the front seat.

Payday.

I grabbed its leather handles and dragged the bag through the space between the driver's and passenger's sides. I fumbled to open the latch and then unzip the main pocket. Inside was a laptop and several file folders. I made a quick calculation. There was no time to go through it all and there was no way to get the laptop. That was a disappointment—I knew we'd have everything if we could only take that computer. I had room under my clothes for just a few folders, so I grabbed the two thickest and stuffed them into my waistband, pulling my shirt and the red vest over it.

In front of me I could see Corbin still talking to Chris. Chris was showing signs of life and starting to wiggle his extremities. The supermarket manager had stepped out to help them. Corbin's arms were raised, hands upstretched to the sky, and I didn't have to actually hear him to know that whatever he was saying was something like, *I just didn't see him. I wasn't even going that fast. He came out of nowhere.*

Damn straight. That's exactly the way we planned it.

Behind me, Aidan pulled up in the Land Rover. I scrambled out of the Nissan and got into the passenger seat with my stolen goods.

"Got it?" Aidan asked.

"Let's get out of here."

Corbin was just turning around to notice us as Aidan put the car in drive. I pulled off Chris's baseball cap, letting my hair fall loose around my shoulders. I rolled down the window and threw the hat out, watching it sail across the pavement and land at Corbin's feet. He looked up and I could see recognition suddenly flare in his eyes. But by the time he probably put it together we were well on the road.

"That hat thing was a little much," Aidan said.

FOURTEEN

WE FELL INTO silence as we sped away from the strip mall. We were headed toward the casinos. A sign said STATELINE, NEVADA. We were crossing another state line.

Words felt impossible. My heart was beating in a primal rhythm of fear and elation, my head spinning and weightless. I felt like I could fly out into the layers of white—snow-covered ground, snow-dusted trees, snow-capped mountains—and over the turquoise swirl of lake water.

Forget Nikki's wallet. Drew's watch. This was the biggest job I'd ever pulled by far. And it had *worked*.

Slowly, the world returned to me. The leather smell of the car. The sound of the radio. Aidan's presence a few inches away.

"So what's in there?"

I got down to business, digging through the contents

of the files. The top folder was fat with pages covered in jargon and abbreviations. Might as well have been in another language—I needed a glossary to understand any of it.

"Crap," I said out loud as I impatiently thumbed through stapled packs of forms and letters. I didn't know what I was looking for exactly, but I figured I'd know when I saw it. Now I wondered.

"Anything?" Aidan asked.

"A whole lot of nothing." My bottom lip caught under my front teeth. "Generic stuff."

Please let there be something in here. All that work, all that risk, our brilliant plan—please let that not have been for nothing. It would be beyond ridiculous. It would be embarrassing.

Then my eye caught on a dark corner sticking out of the rest of the paper—a black-and-white picture. I pulled it out from the other pages.

It appeared to be taken from a distance, but there was no mistaking the frame of my mom's body, hunched over her purse like she was looking for her keys. It was something I'd probably seen her do hundreds of times in my life. Behind her I could make out the shape of the Subaru.

"Hang on." I paged back to the beginning of the file and looked at the top document more closely.

PROFILE: Leslie Siebert aka Joanne Fox

My hands instantly went cold, my fingertips numb.

"This must be her real name." My voice dragged into a hoarse whisper. "Leslie."

"Your mom? Her real name is Leslie?"

"Leslie Siebert." I frowned, trying it out again.

It just felt wrong. She didn't even look like a Leslie. And yet there it was. Typed out on an official FBI document with official letterhead. It had to be true then, didn't it? How did I not know this?

"What else does it say?" Aidan asked.

I squinted at the page. There were some cryptic letters and numbers underneath—FD-204, UFAP—more FBI code. But there were enough regular words that I could make out the gist of it. "It's an email from the head office, establishing permission for surveillance."

I flipped back to the photo. On the reverse side there was a date: September 26. That was last fall, right after we moved to Paradise Valley. Which meant I was probably there with her, maybe even sitting in the part of the car that was cut off by the left side of the frame.

Beneath it there were other photos, too, from October and November. It was like a slide show of our lives, albeit a creepy one. "They've been watching her for a while," I said.

"But why? Does it say anything about an offense?"

"If she was wanted for a crime and they'd tracked her for all these years, they would have taken her in by now, wouldn't they?"

"So why else would they watch her?"

"Maybe she's an informant," I said, my pulse speeding with the onrush of thoughts. "Like, part of the witness protection program."

Aidan nodded. "That would explain the name change."

"And the moves. And the secret meetings with Corbin." It did hang together. Enough that I could fill in the rest of the details in my head. She'd said all those moves were for artistic inspiration. Well, it made more sense now. Apparently she'd been trying to keep us hidden.

I swallowed hard. She'd left Paradise Valley abruptly. After I was on TV. Of course. They'd found her. And it was my fault. No wonder she'd been so angry with me. I understood now why she'd gotten rid of the phones, too.

But the file, as far as I could see, didn't say anything about where she was now. We needed a better lead. "Let's find another computer. You can check in on the E-ZPass."

"Right now? In broad daylight?"

"We have to act quickly before she gets too far."

Aidan rubbed at his hairline. "We're really pushing it, Willa."

I looked at him, pleading. I knew we were being wild and sloppy, but that's the thing about being a criminal. Once you start giving into that urge, you find it hard to stop. We just needed one more chance. One more clue. We'd put our skills together—my ability to break in, Aidan's ability to track her online—one last time. That's all we needed. But I couldn't do this part alone. Besides, we were on a roll. We were in a gambling town and I was feeling lucky.

I pointed to the view through our windshield. "Look, there's a big condo complex up there on the hill. They're probably time-shares. A quick check—fifteen minutes is all we need—and then we're out of there."

Aidan put the fleshy part of his hand on the wheel and looked ahead at the asphalt. I could see his doubt—it was in the slight arch of his eyebrow, the tiny twist of his mouth. But he did what I asked.

The skylight fit me nicely. For Aidan, who was a good thirty pounds heavier, it was a tighter squeeze and involved some self-squashing.

"I don't like this," he was muttering. "Not at all."

After a prolonged push, he landed with a muffled thump on the carpeted floor. We looked around to find ourselves in a kid's room, outfitted with a lime-green race-car bed.

"Is this your room?" I said. "Why didn't you tell me you had a place in Tahoe?"

"Why didn't you tell me I was going to lose three layers of skin?" He pushed past me, rubbing his chest. He wasn't smiling. "Let's just find the computer, okay?"

The condo was comfortable but basic. The rooms were cluttered with stuff, piles of clothes, and papers and books and knickknacks. The layer of dust over everything suggested that there was no maid in this home. The more I looked around, the more I knew this wasn't a house I would break into to steal anything. In fact, I felt really bad being in there.

There was a laptop in the master bedroom, on the floor by the dust ruffle on top of a heap of laundry.

Aidan turned it on and dove in. I sat down on the bed and opened up my schoolbag, where I'd stored the stolen papers. I spread them out in front of me like a deck of cards. There was another folder tucked inside the folder that I hadn't noticed before, labeled with the name Chet Tompkins.

CRIMINAL RECORD

FBI No. 356B290D
4/17/1994
Criminal trespass, private home
St. Louis, MO
Arrest Precinct: 2nd
Arrest Number: 9823
Prosecution Charge(s): CTTL, CTTP, SOL
Disposition/Sentence: Found guilty, issued a
  citation.

1/3/1997
Suspected robbery, First Federal Bank
St. Louis, MO
Arrest Precinct: 2nd
Arrest Number: 781
Prosecution Charge(s): None; not enough
  evidence.

On the page there was a pink Post-it, with a hand-written note.

10/22/1997
Suspected murder, Brianna Siebert
St. Louis, MO
Suspect was questioned in his home. No arrests made. Case still open.

Murder? Goose bumps broke out on my arms.

Then I saw the mug shots. A thickset man with a beard staring angrily into the camera. In another he was clean-shaven, a tattoo of a flying bird tracing the length of his neck. My eye traveled up to his face and then down again.

I'd only seen his back before. Still, I knew it in my bones. Flannel shirt guy.

Oh my God.

Before I could show Aidan, he turned around, his face taut with disappointment. "We lost her," he said.

"What do you mean, 'lost her'?"

He peered at me from under his brow. "I mean the car's gone. No record. Poof."

"We just saw her, though. She must be in there some-where."

He shook his head. "Willa, I've checked all available records in California and Nevada."

"So maybe she switched cars?"

"That, or she could have taken back roads. Or, I don't

know, maybe she's walking. There are a thousand possibilities."

I wasn't going to just let this drop. "Aren't there cameras on those tollbooths? Is there a way to hack into those?"

"I thought of that, but it means sorting through hundreds of thousands of records—maybe millions. We don't have the time or the resources for that."

"But we have to. We can't just—"

I was interrupted by a sound coming from downstairs. A sound like metal clinking.

Aidan's eyes widened in fear. I grabbed his wrist and clutched it tightly while we listened, frozen still.

A sound like a key in a lock.

Every muscle in my body clamped up. We had to get the hell out of there.

Tre always told me to leave the way I came in. Only this time it was impossible, at least without a ladder. Which we didn't have, obviously.

My mind raced. I gathered up the files as best I could and stuffed them into my bag, throwing it onto my back as we scurried around, looking for an exit. There was a wooden deck off the master bedroom, but it was three stories up. Maybe we could swing down to the deck on the next story? I quickly made the calculations. It was a weird angle. Dangerous. But no more dangerous than popping through the skylight, was it?

Meanwhile, the front door squeaked open, the bottom pulling on the carpet. Then we heard the footsteps, the creaking of floorboards. The rustling of bags.

We had seconds to make a decision. Or meet the owner of this house and go straight to jail, do not pass Go.

Aidan glared at me, demanding a solution.

You're the boss, I could hear him thinking.

Crap. I so did not want to be the boss right now.

I slid open the glass door as quietly as I could and we stepped out onto the deck. I silently gestured to him, showing him my plan.

He waved his hands across his chest like I was crazy.

I heaved my shoulders, letting him know without speaking that it was this or nothing. This or wait to get caught.

He pointed me to the snowdrifts on the ground, which sloped down a hill beyond the condos into a thicket of trees.

Fine. Whatever, I mouthed. My only comforting thought was that if I hurt myself I'd send him the hospital bill.

I climbed over the railing of the deck, edging my feet on the other side. I looked over my shoulder. He was watching me, flapping a hand to tell me to hurry up.

"Hey! What are you two doing?" We turned to see a man. The man. The owner of the condo, who was tall and balding and wore little round glasses, and now he was racing for the door. After us.

Oh no. OH NO.

Here goes everything, I thought, and let go.

FIFTEEN

LOOKING BACK, I guess we were pretty lucky. I mean, we could've died right there, landing funny from the three-story jump. Backs and necks had been broken on shorter heights. Or we could have gotten lost in the woods, frostbitten and buried in a snowfall only to be discovered a week later, two teenage Popsicles. We could've been shot down by the bald man, or by cops. The worst-case possibilities were endless, really.

But somehow, whether it was luck, or my closed-eye wishing, or fate or whatever you want to call it, we made it. Because now, after running for what felt like an hour, we'd finally reached an opening. We were coming back to civilization.

"Quick," Aidan said, pointing to a white bus with the words *Tahoe XPRESS* painted on the side. It was stopping in front of the entrance to the Blackjack Hotel across the street. "The shuttle."

Energy surged through my bones, pushing me down the home stretch. I followed Aidan as we dashed over the pavement, racing to the bus. The door was already open, and we climbed up the steps, gasping.

"No hurry," said the driver, a lackadaisical white-haired gentleman with a baseball cap. "I would've waited for you two, you know."

"How much?" Aidan demanded, reaching into the pocket of his pants.

"Shuttle's free," he said. "I make stops at all the major hotels, casinos, and the airport. Get on and off as you like."

Aidan nodded and made his way down the aisle to a seat, and I followed him into our getaway vehicle.

It was only as we sat down, sweat-dampened, wheezing, fried with adrenaline, that I noticed that everyone was staring.

"That was close," I whispered, because two young guys sitting in front of us had given us an especially lingering eye. My heart was still racing, even as the squat little bus pulled away from the curb and lumbered down the street.

We'd made it.

Aidan brushed snow off his sleeves. "Too close."

"Look, I didn't know he would come home," I said.

He turned away to stare out the window. "That's just it. It wasn't thought through."

I felt myself tense, all the adrenaline flaring and

burning out into frayed ends. "I made a mistake, okay? You could've stopped me."

I looked up as I said the last part, knowing it wasn't entirely true.

He pressed his palm on the glass. "I wanted to believe you. Just like I've been doing all along."

"What's that supposed to mean?"

He peered back in my direction and I felt the plainness of his gaze. The cocky, flirtatious Aidan was gone. So was the rich, tech-genius Aidan. There was just Aidan now.

"It means I don't know anymore. I don't know if we're going to find her, Willa." He sighed heavily. "It just seems like she doesn't want to be found."

The words cut into me—I actually winced as he said them. This was a line of thinking I could not—would not—tolerate.

"Well, she said she didn't," I said matter-of-factly. "But we can't let that stop us."

"We've been away for almost a week and we've got nothing."

"That's not true. We know she left for a good reason. We know her name. And . . ." I struggled to come up with a third thing.

"We know she's in trouble. So maybe we should back off and let her do what she needs to do. If that's going away for a while, then maybe . . ."

"Maybe what?" I challenged him.

"Maybe you have to learn to live with that. Maybe we have to stop meddling. No offense, but her life seems pretty messed up." He gave me an apologetic shrug.

She's not messed up, I wanted to say. *She's just got problems.* They happened to be big problems. Fine. But it wasn't like she was crazy or a bad person.

How would he know, anyway? He didn't know the first thing about her. He'd never even *met* her.

And then my own doubts started to seep in through the cracks between thoughts. My mom had lied to me, then she'd abandoned me. She had some secret past, dark enough that she had to change her own name.

Maybe she *was* messed up. Maybe we both were. Maybe she was even dead by now. Maybe everything I'd done was wrong. How did I know?

Tears brimmed in my eyes, and everything around me—the vinyl seats of the bus, the fir trees outside the window, Aidan's face hanging squarely in front of mine—was going hazy.

"No," I said. "I will never learn to live with that. And I will never stop *meddling.*"

Aidan slung an arm around the seat back and rearranged himself so that he was facing me. "Listen to yourself, Willa."

I folded my arms across my chest and tried to breathe, tried to suck the tears back in, but it was too late because a couple had already escaped and were sliding down my cheeks.

I listened. What I heard was Aidan trying to tell me I was stupid. That I was foolish and naïve for trying to find my mother.

I couldn't accept that. What else was I supposed to do? Give up and walk away?

No. Screw him for even suggesting it.

The bus was pulling into another casino. A family of older parents and what looked like their adult children got on, a big, happy, laughing family wearing matching baseball caps with the letter *Z*. They came down the aisle toward us and I felt shamed by their smiling faces.

"You'll never understand how I feel. You'll never be in this situation."

"I know what it's like to care about your parents." He cleared his throat. "And I've been thinking, maybe you were right. About my dad, I mean. Maybe I need to go home and give him another chance."

"And what do you expect me to do?" I asked finally.

"I—I don't know. Come with?" He looked down at his feet. "I just think we're grasping at straws here and we really don't have enough information. We're not detectives, Willa."

"Yeah, I realize that." My voice squeaked with sarcasm. I hated that he was seeing me so upset, so unbalanced. By now he'd seen a lot more of me than I wanted him to, including my awful quivering cry-face. Did it even matter, though? It was obvious there would never be anything between us.

"It's a needle-in-a-haystack situation. Maybe she was here. But maybe she's left. The point is that she could be *anywhere*."

I closed my eyes, which were sticky from the tears. "No, the point is that you're sick of looking. You're ready to give up."

"I didn't say that exactly. I just think we should consider calling the authorities before we get *killed*." Aidan's voice had lifted a few decibels with the last word.

The guys in front of us turned around again. They looked at each other, murmured something, and went back to their plastic cups full of tokens. I probably should have been worrying about whether they recognized us, but instead I was mentally counting the tokens. They were each carrying about four hundred dollars' worth. I was disgusted with myself for even thinking about it. It was like my kleptomania knew no bounds.

"We can't," I whispered. "Or, I can't. I can't go back to jail. Not before I find her."

"Moving forward like we are, with no backup, is a bad idea." He ran his hand through his hair. "Frankly, at this point, I think this whole trip has been a bad idea."

That stung.

"If it was such a bad idea, then why did you go along with me all this time?"

I turned away from him and looked across the aisle out the window on the opposite side. We were crossing back over into California. The mountains were coming into view again, and more thickets of trees. I was sick of seeing scenery from cars and buses. I wished I could get off this bus and get on my bike, ride around.

"You needed a driver. I didn't want you to do it alone. And, I don't know, at first it really was kind of fun, like an adventure. Running from the cops. Seeing our names on the news."

"So you were *humoring* me? You were being a good sport? This is just some kind of game to you?"

"No, no, no, Willa. You make it sound—"

"—like you don't really care."

Now the two guys were really staring.

"Can you turn around, please?" Aidan asked them. "This is a private conversation."

They smiled at each other and turned back. Whispered some more. I wanted to deck them. Both of them.

"Anyway, that's not it," he said to me in a low tone. "You know I care."

"Is it me you care about, or is it Sly Fox?"

"You, Willa," he said, staring at me, shaking his head gently. "You."

There was a pause. I wanted to believe him. I wanted things to be the way they were before, back in Paradise Valley. Before we kissed, even. When all of that was in the future.

But that was another time. We were practically different people now. Too much had happened for it to ever feel like that again. It was spoiled.

"No, you don't," I said.

His face opened up in surprise. "How can you say that?"

"Because I've seen your phone, Aidan." I was going for broke now. Cashing in my chips. Whatever gambling metaphor you wanted to use.

"What?"

"I know there's some other girl. Or is it plural?"

His face reddened and he grasped the back of the seat in front of us, nearly grabbing one of the guys' hoodies. "Did you read my text messages?"

"They came through when I was using the phone."

"And you just couldn't help yourself? Dammit, Willa!"

I shrank back a little. His face was red. I'd never seen him so angry.

"What? It wasn't like I was looking for them."

Well, maybe not the first time.

"But you didn't have to read them. I mean, you could've just put the phone down. Those were my personal, private messages. That's low."

"Obviously, if you didn't want me to read them then you had something to hide."

"Brilliant logic." He choked out a laugh. Then he put his hands on his face and shook his head side to side, like he was trying to wake himself up from a dream. "So this is what it comes down to, huh?"

A knot of suspicion and unease had lodged itself between us. I could feel it as certainly as I felt the vibrations of the bus engine beneath my feet. I remembered the first time we kissed, only a few days ago, in my driveway.

Maybe I'd gone too far. And yet there was no way to take it all back. "What do you expect me to do?" My voice dropped down to a lower register. "You haven't given me any reason to actually trust you."

The bus was slowing down now, stopping in the center of Celestial Village, a big town at the bottom of the mountain. Crowds of people were gathered outside on the walkway for some sort of musical performance. As we got closer, I could see it was a children's choir.

Holiday carols. They must have been singing holiday carols.

I didn't even know what day it was anymore. Had we missed Thanksgiving? How long had we even been on the road now? Real life, routines, normal breakfasts, calendar days had slipped out of my grasp.

"No reason, huh?" He looked angry. More than that. He looked disgusted. "Well, if you don't trust me, then there's really no point in me being here, is there? Maybe I should just go now."

People were coming and going, getting on and off the bus, but we just stared at each other.

Those green eyes. With eyes like that, Aidan Murphy had the potential to be the greatest thief of all time.

"Celestial Village. Last call." The bus driver's voice yanked me out of my spell.

Something inside me went hot and angry and anarchic. It was a feeling I'd had as a little kid, when a friend from third grade and I stole matches and set napkins on fire in his mother's bathroom sink. It was the rush you got only when you destroyed something.

"Maybe you should," I said slowly.

Aidan stood up then, slinging his backpack over his shoulder, and headed for the exit. I didn't watch him go. I didn't need to look to know that he was disappearing into the crowd.

SIXTEEN

ON THE BUS, sitting by myself, there was a moment of giddy elation. I'd done something stupid and terrible, and the freedom of it, of shutting Aidan out so I could be alone to enjoy my stupid terribleness, was amazing.

The thing is, you can't stay like that for too long— your body can be trembling and your heart can be racing and your mind can be bouncing all over the place, but at some point it all wants to go back to normal. And, unfortunately, normal means breathing complete breaths and feeling really, physically where you are, and that means seeing the true situation for what it is.

This was mine: I was on my own.

Aidan freaking left. He just . . . left.

The words sank in. That's when the regret sank in, too. Then the fear. And loneliness. And the missing-him.

The missing-him was the worst part. An ache in the

back of my throat like biting into something too cold too soon.

No, it didn't take long for my euphoria to wear off. Even before we got to the next stop, I knew I had made a terrible mistake.

I had to get off the damn bus. I reached up and yanked on the hanging cord repeatedly, signaling my stop.

Ding, ding, ding, ding.

"I think he hears you," one of the dudes in front of me said.

I didn't care. How could I care? My heart was breaking.

I kept pulling on the cord like it was an emergency tab, like it was my last gesture.

The driver pulled over at the SkyView Casino and Resort. I bolted for the door, flinging myself off the bus, and sprinted back the way we'd come, back toward the last stop.

I was going to find Aidan and apologize. I couldn't do this thing on my own, and I didn't want to. I wanted him with me.

He couldn't have gone too far, could he?

It took me about five minutes to run back to the center of the village, past rows of benches where tourists were sipping hot chocolate and past an ice-skating rink over which strings of lights in the shapes of snowflakes had been hung. There were dozens of people gliding across the ice and dozens more standing around it, watching.

I kept on going across the tiled pavement, which was inhabited by visitors bundled up in ski jackets, women carrying shopping bags, families with little kids trailing behind them.

As the crowd thickened and my visibility narrowed, I stopped to scan the crowd for Aidan's familiar shape, stretching up to my tiptoes to see over the tall people.

Nothing. Strangers, all of them. What was I going to do if I couldn't find him?

I panted, trying to catch my breath as I watched it drift in little clouds in the air. It was cold out now but my face was hot. More people were spilling out from the glowing interiors of shops and restaurants, smiling and having fun. The mountains hung high and wall-like behind them, and behind that there was a rising full moon. I peered up at it, silently asking it to help me find Aidan.

But its stoic face seemed to be mocking me.

You idiot. You let him go.

My eye caught on the pavilion and the bus stop where Aidan jumped off, about thirty yards away. A crowd of people were gathered around the still-singing carolers. They finished their song, "I Wonder as I Wander," and everyone clapped.

The concert was over. People were shifting, moving away, and as the throng opened up I thought I caught a glimpse of a gray sweater-vest.

Aidan!

I called out his name and ran toward him. But as I got closer, I could no longer see the gray vest. I stopped and spun around. And around again. Maybe I'd imagined it because there was just a sea of blue and red and green. No gray to be found.

It occurred to me that this was all we'd been doing the past few days—wandering blindly, trying to find the impossible. *A needle in a haystack.* Wasn't that what Aidan said?

I started circling the pavement, passing the ice rink again, and the pavilion and the giant statue of a horse. I walked up and down the rows of stores and cafés.

He must have really left, I thought.

And then, *Of course he really left. You told him to leave.*

I shivered. An hour or so had passed since I'd gotten off the bus. I wrapped my arms around myself as I passed Celestial Coffee for what felt like the twentieth time. Looking in through the windows, I scanned the room for Aidan. There was no sign of him. Just people sitting around in twos and threes, talking and drinking from steaming mugs.

Coffee. I still had Tre's money. I knew I had to be careful with it, especially if I needed to buy a ticket home. But I could get something warm to drink, couldn't I?

I was inside before I knew it, driven by pure caffeine lust. I slid into a vinyl booth behind a guy and a girl who were my age and looked like they were on a date. Even if they weren't, they were definitely about to hook up—I could tell by the way she was giggling and the teasing way he was grabbing her arm.

I felt bitterly, bitterly jealous.

A waitress came over to the table. She was my age, too, with brown hair tied into a long braid. "Can I get you something?"

"A coffee, please," I said, resisting the urge for a more expensive latte. I eyed the biscotti in jars on the countertop and the pies behind the glass. I was starving. But I couldn't eat now. I had to make the money last. I would have to wait until tomorrow. I didn't know how much longer I'd be on the road.

But what was I going to do now that Aidan was gone? Was I really going to keep on keeping on? I had no car. I didn't know how to drive. I could hitchhike, assuming I had a destination. Which I didn't.

They were playing a Robyn song that came out last summer. I remembered listening to it at Cherise's house over and over, dancing around her room. I smiled a little at the memory. We had so much fun together.

Then, as my eyes adjusted to what was in front of me, the espresso machines and the sugar bar and the two kids getting handsy, the reality of my situation came flooding back. The tears came back, too.

It was time to face the fact that I was alone. Really alone now. Maybe more alone than I'd ever been.

I remembered the nights I'd spent in juvie, staring at cinder-block walls and feeling the most profound despair I'd ever felt, like my life had ended.

But at least then I knew my mom would come to help me get out. This time I had to figure out how to get out of this mess by myself. And even if I did, would I really go back to Paradise Valley? There was nothing for me there. Certainly no friends. Sure, there was Tre, but he would probably be against me, too, when Aidan told him what happened. How I blew it again. How I'd been too greedy, enjoying the stealing too much. Wanting too much from Aidan.

When the waitress came back toward the table, she set down a coffee and a slice of flourless chocolate cake in front of me.

"I didn't order—"

"This is from that table over there."

I followed her painted fingernail to the couple in front of me. They waved shyly.

"Thank you," I said, confused.

"You're welcome," the girl said, giggling. "Foxy."

I smiled. They knew who I was. I wasn't supposed to be glad about that, but right now, it felt good to be recognized.

The cake was rich and fudgy and pretty much the most delicious thing I'd ever eaten in my life. The world, and all my worries, seemed to stop as I ate. You literally could not be in a bad mood while shoveling this thing into your mouth. And for a few moments, the kindness of the two kids in the booth next to me was enough.

Maybe this wasn't going to work out in the end, but at least there were still some people who were on my side.

I was finishing up the coffee and the last bite of cake when the server came back with a refill. "How was it?"

"Perfect. I needed some chocolate therapy," I said.

"Nothing like it. Can I get you anything else?"

"Actually," I ventured, "is there somewhere I can use the phone? Like in private?"

"The office is in the back," she said, pointing me to a closed door behind the counter. "Feel free."

In the room, I took out the temporary phone and then pulled the card out of my pocket. By now it was worn and soft, like cloth. My hands shaking, I dialed the number. I needed to figure out what my options were.

"Willa," he said. The voice was familiar instantly.

"Corbin," I said.

"I've been waiting for you."

"I know," I said, chewing on the edge of my lip. I studied the bulletin board hanging over the desk; on it were posted work schedules, a Heimlich maneuver poster, and a phone number for sanitation pickup. The room was like a closet, and I felt the smallness of it suddenly, like everything was closing in on me.

"That was some stunt you two jokers pulled in the parking lot. I could have you arrested for fraud, you know." His voice was taut with the threat. "Or worse. Stealing federal property."

I wasn't afraid of him, though. Because by now I felt

like I understood more. He needed me as much as I needed him. "But you wouldn't do that, would you? Not while my mom is still out there."

There was a pause, and in that pause I heard all I needed to know. Corbin cared about this case, and not just professionally. He cared about my mom, for some reason that I did not totally understand.

"Goddammit. No," he said finally. "I wouldn't."

"So where is she?"

"We don't know. We think she's gone off the grid."

"Off the grid?"

"She's not anywhere our satellites can detect," he explained. He actually sounded worried.

"Who are these people she's running from? Can you tell me that?"

"I can't." His voice sharpened to a warning pitch again. "Look, do you want to end up in a ditch on the side of the road? I've been telling you it's dangerous. When will you get it through your thick teenage skull that this isn't your mess to mess around with?"

If he was trying to convince me I needed to give in, he wasn't doing a very good job of it. Saying it was dangerous and not giving me any real answers only made me feel more panicky, more determined.

I pressed on with my questions, anyway. I had to know. "Just tell me this. Why'd she leave me behind this time? She took me with her before."

"They were getting too close." Corbin's voice was

ominous. "Once you were on the news, she couldn't take any more chances."

"So it was my fault she had to leave?"

He paused, as if he was thinking about it. "In a way, yes."

I felt a lead weight in my gut. Of all the reasons that I could feel sorry about what I'd done, this was the biggest. If I'd only known . . .

"Did she break the law?" My heart quickened. What if he was going to lock her up? I had to get to her before he did.

"I can't tell you any more than I already have. Not without putting both of you at risk, and that's the last thing I want to do." His voice went hoarse.

That wasn't much of an answer.

He cleared his throat. "You need to come home, Willa."

Big surprise. It's what he'd been saying all along. But I knew that when I dialed this number. And I wouldn't have called if I wasn't seriously considering it myself.

"I'll get you a ticket," he offered. "I'll make sure it's safe. We'll get any charges against you dropped. But you need to leave there. Alive."

"How do I know I can believe you?" I asked quietly. "How do I know I can trust you?"

"Well, you don't, I guess. You can never know one hundred percent about anything, and I'd be lying if I said different," he said, and I thought immediately of Aidan.

Of the look on his face when he told me he was going to walk.

I *couldn't* trust anyone. That was the problem, wasn't it? How could I start now? I wanted to give in. I was tired. But I couldn't abandon my mom.

"Can I think about it?" I asked.

"I'd prefer if you didn't," he said.

"Or I could just hang up now," I warned.

"Okay," he said. "Okay. Why don't you take the rest of the night? Call me in the morning and let me know what you decide. Just make sure you guys get yourselves somewhere safe."

"All right," I said.

I couldn't bring myself to tell him that there was no longer a "you guys." He would probably come find me and take me away in handcuffs. Then again, for all I knew, he'd been watching us the whole time and already knew that Aidan had taken off.

"And, Willa? One more thing. We've found her car. In Crest, California. Not too far from the Nevada border."

I gulped in air excitedly. "You found her car?" *I knew it!* She'd been in California the whole time. We hadn't even been that far off course. "So you should be able to find her soon, right? I mean, if her car's there, she can't be far behind."

Corbin's voice cracked slightly on the other end of the line. "Not exactly. The car was burned out. Left in the bottom of a quarry. We think it'd probably been there for at least thirty-six hours."

Silence came over the receiver. I felt my hopes sinking to the pit of my stomach, churning sickeningly. A burned-out car? It sounded horrible. And scary. Where the hell was my mother?

"So what does that mean?" I asked, my voice registering my alarm. I'd called him for answers, to figure out my options, but now I was as frightened and confused as ever.

"I just don't know, Willa," Corbin said. "We're working on it."

"Not fast enough," I said, and hung up.

SEVENTEEN

BY MY ESTIMATE I had about five more minutes left in the café's back office before the clock on the server's goodwill gesture ran out and/or she became suspicious.

But I still had one number left to call.

I held the phone pressed close to my ear and listened to the echoing ring. Four times. The silences in between seemed to go on forever. Biting a corner of my lip, I made a little bargain with myself—if no one answered, I would turn myself in. If someone answered, I wouldn't.

"Hello?" It was a girl's voice, high-pitched but a little raspy and breathless, like maybe she'd just woken up or run some distance to get the call in time.

Okay, maybe I wouldn't.

"Is this Rain?" I asked.

"This is she. Who is this?"

"This is . . ." *Should I use a code name?* I couldn't come up with anything original. "Uh, this is Sly Fox. Tre said you might be able to help."

"Willa? Is that really you? Oh my God," she said. "You're here? I can't believe it."

"I'm here," I said uncertainly. It was weird, how she was acting like she knew me. Like we were old friends.

"You're in my town. Holy crap." I could hear her smile. Then she cleared her throat, like she was trying to sound more official. "I've been waiting for your call. So where are you guys?"

"It's just me," I said, praying she wouldn't ask me about Aidan over the phone. I couldn't explain it now. Not without seriously losing it. "I'm at Celestial Coffee. In South Lake Tahoe?"

Gone was the professional voice again. "That's my favorite place! They have the best lattes. You, at CC. How crazy is that?"

It didn't seem all that crazy to me, certainly not any crazier than any of the other events of the day. I realized then that I knew nothing about Cherise's cousin, and she sounded very young. This was our contact?

I tried to steer the conversation back to the matter at hand. "Listen, Rain, I need help."

"Whatever you need! Do you need me to come get you?"

If you're old enough to drive, was what I thought.

"If that would be okay," was what I said instead. "I could use somewhere to stay overnight."

Forget the little bet I made with myself. I was pretty

sure I'd be turning myself in the following morning. But for now my main objective was to get somewhere safe and quiet, behind a closed door. A good night's rest in a real bed. And then I could at least start to think straight.

"That's no problem," she said. "Be there in a few minutes. Wanna meet out front?"

"How will I know it's you?" I asked, paranoid suddenly that I could be set up. What if this was some kind of trap?

"Don't worry," she said, giggling. "I'll make sure you know. I'm going to send you a sign so it'll be totally obvious."

"Not too obvious, though, right?" I looked around me. "If it's okay with you, I'll wait here inside the café. I think I feel a little safer that way."

"No problem. Totes magotes," she said.

As I hung up I wondered how I was entrusting my fate to what sounded like a ten-year-old. For all I knew she was coming to pick me up on her dad's snowmobile and I'd be staying in her backyard tree house. But what choice did I have?

I went back to my booth to wait. The couple in front of me had gone home. In fact, most of the people had left. It was now ten o'clock at night. I hoped Rain was really coming because it seemed like the café would be closing soon.

I stared into my empty coffee cup, stirring air, thinking about my mom. And Aidan. How the hell I got here.

And how the hell this was going to end.

Wallowing. I believe it's called wallowing.

Ten minutes later, the front door opened with a jingle. I looked up, startled to see a familiar face framed by the entrance.

Cherise! And behind her was Tre.

What the . . . ?

Cherise raised an eyebrow of recognition when she saw me, her mass of russet curls bobbing as she crossed the room. So this was Rain's sign.

I stood up and threw my arms around her, almost knocking her over. "What are you doing here?" I gasped in disbelief.

She did not, I noticed, return the hug. Not quite. It was more like she stood still and allowed me to do my embracing.

"Long story," she muttered. "The bigger question is, what are *you* doing here?" She stood next to my table and I smelled her familiar perfume, a vanilla scent she bought from Jo Malone.

Tre opened his arms wide and I fell against his chest. He, at least, seemed happy to see me.

"I can't—this is—you have no idea—I mean . . ." I could barely speak I was so flabbergasted.

Tre gestured toward the door. "C'mon, mumble mouth. We should get going. The car's just in the south lot."

I followed them back out into the shopping area. As

in the café, people were clearing out. The village center, which had been so crowded an hour before, was now nearly empty and our footsteps echoed as we crossed the paved walkway.

Tre, with his long legs, naturally loped ahead of us and left me and Cherise a couple of paces behind. If I sort of half-closed my eyes, it was almost like old times, me and Cherise at a shopping mall—albeit this place wasn't as ritzy as the ones we frequented in Paradise Valley. Also, Cherise was bundled up in a cute fuzzy blue scarf and mittens I'd never seen back in the desert climate of Arizona.

I snuck a glance at her and smiled.

Did the fact that she came to get me mean that she was ready to forgive me? It almost didn't matter. She was here, wasn't she? I felt like we would have a chance to start over, or at least move on from everything that had happened.

Until she looked at me sidelong. "Girl, you look like you've been hit with the tacky stick. And that *hair*," she said, leaning in to take a lock in her hand.

"It'll grow out," I said. "Or maybe I'll bleach it back when this is all over."

"Let's hope. You look like a low-rent Natalie Portman, after she goes cray-cray in *Black Swan*."

Tre coughed, fisting his chest to stifle a laugh. "Damn."

Okay then. She was still pissed at me. I was going to

have to take her abuse in stride.

"So how did you get here? I mean, what happened?" I asked Tre, sensing that he was more likely to give me a real answer than Cherise was.

"After that phone call, I knew you needed backup. So I called Cherise here and we decided to trek out to Tahoe. See if we could save your ass."

"And you came." I looked at Cherise hesitantly.

"He told me it was life-or-death. What was I going to do? Let you die out here?" She rolled her eyes.

"But what about your . . . law situation?" I asked Tre.

"I'm here strictly for support but I'm not getting more involved than that," he said.

"But isn't any kind of help 'aiding and abetting'?" I recalled my civics class lessons from freshman year.

"Technically, yeah, I guess so. But I'm just talking about my own personal boundaries here," Tre said. "So where's Murph?"

"We had a fight," I said, feeling my chest tighten.

He shook his head. "That's what I was worried about."

We stopped in front of a sage-green Prius parked at the end of the second row of cars.

"It's *so* nice to meet you, finally," Rain said, turning to shake my hand as I slid into the backseat. So she *was* old enough to drive. She looked only vaguely like Cherise. She was darker-skinned, with close-cropped hair, and she was wearing a hot pink puffer jacket that Cherise wouldn't have been caught dead in. And she didn't seem

227

to be drinking the same haterade as her cousin, either, because she was grinning widely. "You're all anyone talks about at my school for the past week."

"Thanks," I said. "I really appreciate your coming to get me. You're an angel."

"Rain's your biggest fan," Tre said. The two of us got in the back, and Tre's long legs were crunched up behind Cherise's seat.

Rain faced forward as she switched on the car, and her smiling eyes met mine in the rearview mirror. "Hey, I'm just happy to help out the cause. It's just so cool, what you're doing. Stealing from rich people—showing them who's boss."

I wasn't so sure anymore. I certainly wasn't doing the same kind of work I'd been doing in Paradise Valley, and I wasn't really showing anyone much of anything, except that I needed money and shelter to survive. What had I given back, really?

"Drive carefully, Rain," Cherise hissed. "Keep your eyes on the road."

I ducked down low, remembering there were police out there, there was FBI, and now there was the condo guy probably looking for me.

"So I still don't understand exactly," I said. "How did all of this happen?"

"You mean, how'd I get involved?" Rain asked. "You guys are huge. You know that, right?"

Tre turned to me. "We were worried you were going

to get caught. After we saw that you had a following going we thought it would be better to organize everyone and pool together to actually help. So we set up the official Sly Fox Facebook page."

"You did that?" I was sincerely touched.

"We both did—me and Cherise." He reached around the headrest and gave her shoulder a squeeze.

They did it together? Since when were these two friends? Before I'd left, they hadn't had much interaction—but that was partly because Kellie disapproved of Tre's criminal past and had attempted to make him a social pariah at Valley Prep. A pang of jealousy zinged through me. My friends were hanging out without me. Well, one of my friends and my ex-friend.

But if she was still my ex-friend, then why was she helping me? Was something more going on between these two? And why did that idea bother me?

"No one knows about your mom besides us, though. I hope you don't mind that I told Cherise," Tre added. "Anyway, we opened up a Kickstarter account. That money I wired you today? That actually came from your fans."

"Fans," I repeated, blinking and shaking my head, trying to wrap my brain around everything they were saying.

"Well, fans, likers, whatever you want to call them— you have five hundred and sixty-two thousand of those people. Did you know that?"

My mouth dropped open as I stared at Tre.

The number was incomprehensible. This whole thing had gone beyond the beyond.

"Everyone loves an underdog," he said.

Rain turned off on a dirt road leading into the woods. "We're actually not far now," she said. "My parents live, like, in the middle of nowhere. It's so boring out here."

"It's pretty, though," I said. Just then, I would have traded lives with Rain in half a millisecond.

I looked out my window at the shadowy mass of snowy trees, not unlike the woods Aidan and I had run through just a few hours earlier. For all I knew they could've been the same ones.

She turned on her wipers to swish away falling ice. "And I'm so sick of snow. Can it just be summer already?"

Two lights emerged from the darkness. The form of a pickup truck became clearer as it approached from the opposite direction. The vehicle slowed down and I locked eyes with the driver through the glass, a thick-necked man with a few days' growth of beard, and a flannel shirt. . . .

Oh my God.

My body trembled as I remembered the mug shot and list of offenses.

Is that Chet?

I covered my face and slunk lower in my seat. But it was already too late. The man, whoever he was, had seen me. I was sure of it. He would turn around and then come after us. He would kill me, too.

"Y'okay there?" Tre asked.

"I saw something," I murmured. "Someone bad."

Tre craned his neck to watch the receding truck through the back window. "'We Plumb 4 U,'" he recited. "That's what has you freaked out? Is your sink backed up or something?"

I turned around to look. I saw the vanity plate Tre was talking about. It was indeed a plumber's truck. And it was driving steadily onward, not turning around to tail us as I'd imagined.

Okay, fine, maybe I had been hallucinating.

"But—" I looked back again, just to be sure.

"Doesn't seem too threatening to me. Man, this trip has really done a number on you, hasn't it?"

"It hasn't been a Carnival Cruise, no," I said, facing forward again.

Cherise turned around. "So you need to tell us. What exactly happened to your right-hand man, Murphy?"

"We sort of parted ways," I said, in the understatement of the century.

She frowned. "But why? Did he go home? Where's he now?"

"I don't know where he went," I admitted. "All I know is we had a fight, and he got off the shuttle bus at Celestial Village. I tried to look for him. But he was just . . . gone."

"Well, we need to track him down," Cherise said.

"Before he gets caught. Does he even realize how close the cops are?"

"That's the thing. I think he's probably going to turn himself in. He was sick of running. And, I guess, he didn't really think we could find my mom. That's what we were fighting about. That, and other stuff," I mumbled.

"But you guys have come so far," Rain said, furrows appearing on her tiny brow. "How can he turn back now?"

I shrugged. "He wanted to go home."

"I don't buy it," Cherise added. "Aidan's your classic trust-fund rebel. Dude lives for trouble."

She had no idea what we'd been through, did she?

"Actually," I admitted sheepishly, "I'm thinking of doing the same thing. Going to the FBI tomorrow morning."

"FBI?" Cherise's curls sprang violently as she snapped her head around. "Uh-uh. We're not letting you do that. After Tre and I came all this way to help you? You have to keep going."

She *wanted* me to keep going? Back in Paradise Valley she'd told me in so many words what she thought of my lawbreaking. Now she was condoning it? I leaned against my seat and let my head drop against it. "They're going to get us sooner or later. And Aidan was right. We haven't been able to find my mom yet, so what makes us think we'll be able to get to her now?"

"And what makes you think this is a good time to give up?" Cherise shot back.

"I'm just really tired." The more I said it, the more convinced I was that it was the right thing to do. Even with the help of these guys, the whole thing was too risky. And being on the road was getting riskier by the minute, it seemed. There were scary people out there. People who wanted to hurt my mom. I shivered again involuntarily, thinking of Chet. So maybe that wasn't him just then, but the real guy was still out on the loose, somewhere.

"I'm a criminal," I said out loud, like it was a confession. Like they didn't know already. "I should do my time."

"You're not a criminal. Murderers are criminals," Rain said.

"She broke the law," Cherise said. "That makes her a criminal. But you shouldn't give up."

"I don't know. Maybe Willa's right," Tre said. "Maybe turning herself in would be the safest thing. She's had a good run."

Rain pulled the car up a gravel driveway, the little frozen stones rattling against her tires. In her headlights, a three-story house emerged, a rustic structure built with granite pillars and redwood logs.

As we got out of the car, Rain grabbed my hand and squeezed it tight. "I agree with Cherise. You can't give up now. Not with all these people on your side." Her round dark eyes peered at me with earnestness. "Your mom's still out there, Willa. And you're going to find her."

The lights outside, sensing our motion, flipped on as we neared, guiding us to the house, where we would be warm and safe. Rain's words hung in the air like the mists of our breath. But there were other things to think about besides those strangers on Facebook, weren't there? There was Aidan, and Corbin, and my mom.

"Maybe we shouldn't pressure her so much," Tre said, as if sensing my thoughts. "It's her life, after all. Whatever she does will be the right choice."

I smiled painfully, wishing like anything that I could believe him.

EIGHTEEN

"FIRST THINGS FIRST," Tre said as we entered the house through a tiled hallway. "Let's find out what's going on out there."

We walked into Rain's living room, a cozy wood-paneled nook with sofas and bookshelves. Before we could settle in, Tre reached to turn on the TV.

We landed on a commercial for a lemonade drink—a bunch of kids played around a backyard pool while a mom poured sunny juice into tall glasses. The cleanliness and shininess of it reminded me of Paradise Valley, and I realized how much I missed it. While I didn't want to go back to *my* life there, I remembered what it used to be like, with hot showers, and school, and friends, and a real family home. Like heaven.

Then the commercial ended and a news report came on. The line at the top of the screen said, *Stateline, Nevada.*

They were *here*. They knew I was here.

Cherise looked at me and shook her head. "Could you be any more of a headline hog?"

"I'm not trying to be," I pointed out. "Believe me. This isn't by choice."

The reporter, a blond woman bundled up in a silver parka, spoke gravely into her microphone. I immediately recognized the condominium complex behind her.

"Officials say a home break-in was reported here tonight. Police are already linking it to the Sly Fox, aka Willa Fox, a fifteen-year-old fugitive, and her associate, Aidan Murphy. Both are on the run and wanted for crimes in Arizona, California, and now Nevada."

Dramatic pause.

"With me now is Thomas Baden, who saw the two leaving his condominium just this afternoon."

The camera panned to the bald man I recognized from earlier. "I was coming home, and I heard a ruckus upstairs." He spoke loudly and clearly like a language teacher. "Next thing I know, the sliding glass door is open and these two kids have jumped off my deck into the snow."

Back to the reporter. "Baden got into his car and chased after the two suspects but says they disappeared into the woods behind his house before he could apprehend them."

Baden again. "It was like, poof. They were gone as quickly as they came in. They didn't steal anything,

236

either. Just seems like they used my computer."

The reporter stared solemnly into the camera. "While the suspects seem to be enjoying their notoriety, police are growing concerned about their next steps and are worried the two could be armed. They're now combing the area and looking for clues."

"Armed?" I said. "Give me a break." If you counted my pepper spray and my English books, maybe.

Cut to police headquarters and an officer in full uniform: a square-headed man with bushy eyebrows and a soft jowl. "They may be kids, but this is a crime spree, plain and simple," he said. "The longer it goes on, the more dangerous they become, to themselves and others. We're taking this very seriously. And we *will* find them."

"That's what I was afraid of. They're pretty close by," Tre said, clicking off the TV and folding his arms in front of him. "What do you want to do? And what about your boy?"

"He's not my boy," I said. That was exactly the problem, wasn't it? "Tre, you were right. I can't trust him."

Tre shrank back a little. "Did I say that?"

"The day we left. You told me not to get too close, remember?"

"I was probably just exaggerating. So you didn't get too distracted. Dude's flirtatious, but I didn't mean you couldn't trust him, period."

I frowned. Now he was taking it back? "I mean, I spent all this time with him and we're supposed to be together but he still won't tell me why he got kicked out. Not only that, but I think there are other girls. . . ."

Cherise whistled. "Murphy, Murphy."

"I don't know about the other girls," Tre said. "But as far as I know he's under a legal agreement not to talk about what happened at Prep. So that part is definitely not about you."

I thought about this for a moment. Aidan was willing to go on this crazy jaunt and break all sorts of laws, yet he was somehow still concerned about breaking a measly legal agreement with the school? It didn't exactly make sense, but then I was learning that everyone had their own boundaries, to use Tre's word.

I sighed. How much did it matter, anyway? "Well, regardless, he might already be in custody by now, or on his way home. I don't know where my mom is. So I guess I have to turn myself in."

No one said anything this time. Not one word of resistance. We all sat in silence, and the truth weighed on us like a leaded X-ray shield.

"Just sleep on it," Cherise said. "You're all wacked out right now. Just wait until morning at least."

"Before you go anywhere, I want to show you something," Rain said. She got out her laptop and logged on to the Sly Fox Facebook page.

She handed me the computer and I scrolled down, running my finger along the mouse pad to read the messages on the wall.

Sebastian Kerry You rock, Sly Fox. :D

Jenny Kaiser Sly Fox and Aidan Murphy are so cute together. I hope they get married.

I winced. That one got me in the gut.

Sam Jenkins Free Willa and her friend! They're just kids.

The Great John B They r so brilliant. I don't know what the big deal is. They never hurt anyone. They just stole stupid possessions that people didn't need, anyway.

Tina James If only the police would spend time trying to catch real criminals and murderers and the crooks on Wall Street instead of bothering these two. They're just trying to live their lives. Yes, they've made mistakes but who hasn't? They must have a good reason to do what they're doing. None of us are in their shoes so we can't judge.

The page went on and on. It was so easy to get sucked into the flattery, all the people rooting for us. I didn't want to start believing all of my own hype. But I did have to admit that we had a mission. We stood for something, even if it wasn't quite what our fans thought it was.

As those thoughts cycled through my head, I had to wonder again whether all of this was really happening to me. From the moment my mom disappeared life had gotten more surreal by the day. Reading Facebook posts about Aidan and me took the cake.

Aidan. I couldn't believe he was actually gone.

Rain wrapped her tiny arms around her chest. "Well, I'm going to go up to bed, you guys. Cherise, you want to show Willa her room?"

"Okay," Cherise said quietly. "G'night."

I reached over to hug her. "Good night, Rain. Thank you for everything."

"I'm going up, too," Tre said. "Unless you need me."

"No, that's okay," I said. "Get some sleep."

"I'll see you in the morning?" He eyed me as his question curled around itself.

I gave him a hug, too. "Yup. I'll say good-bye before I go."

Cherise and I started up the stairs behind them and she led me to the guest room at the end of the hallway.

It was a sweet little setup: a fluffy, down-comforter-covered bed with a wooden four-poster frame, a full-length mirror, and a brightly colored Turkish rug on the hardwood floor. On the walls were some postcards that I assumed came from places Rain and her parents had traveled.

I sat down on the soft mattress, feeling my weight sink into it. Cherise handed me two towels for my personal hygiene needs—which at that point were pretty major—and a pair of pajamas.

"You should be good, right?"

"Cherise," I ventured. "How come you decided to forgive me?"

She looked up at me from under hooded lids. "I don't know if I have yet exactly."

"Well, you know what I mean. How did you decide to come here?"

She leaned back against the wall, setting the sole of her foot on it and crossing her arms. "I still think the stealing was wrong. But I guess, the more I thought about it, the more I could understand what you were trying to do. And those guys, well, they're kind of hideous. I'm not really hanging out with Kellie and Nikki too much these days. You were right about them. I'll give you that."

So she'd disassociated herself from the Glitterati. This came as a shock. I thought back to that day at school when she'd stood up to them. It couldn't be easy for her to cut ties like that. "What happened?"

"Well, you know Kellie and I had a beef back in the day. It was just like Lower School all over again. I defended you and she started in with the blog, calling me names, starting rumors that I was a thief, too."

I drew in a breath. The last thing I wanted was for Cherise to be caught up in this. "And then what?"

"I found a wallet they planted in my locker and I confronted them, in front of Mr. Page. I told them I wasn't going to be their puppet. I was done."

"Are you okay?"

"It hasn't been the best time at VP. Let's put it that way. And to be honest, I was starting to get sick of hearing about you all the time from everyone." She arched an eyebrow.

"So then, why are you here?"

"Tre was the only one who'd talk to me at school. He was really there for me. And when Tre told me what was going on, I knew we could help, me and Rain. No matter what's happened, I want you to find your mom. I know how tight you guys are."

"Thank you," I said. "It means a lot to me. I hope we can—"

"—be friends again? We'll see, Fox." She gave me the side-eye as she stepped out. "Bathroom's in the hallway. Good night."

"Good night," I called after her, feeling almost foolish for my sudden lift of hope.

I showered and then came back to change. As I toweled off my hair, I looked at the wall with the postcards. One was a street scene in Mumbai, India; another was of London. Then my eye fell on the one on the end: wave-like hills with bands of bright colors.

I untacked the postcard from the wall and looked at the back.

Painted Hills, Oregon, it said.

My heart started racing. I was afraid to even be thinking what I was thinking. Still, I went into my backpack and pulled out the printout of my mom's painting.

All along I had been holding it vertically, thinking it was cliffs. Now I rotated the paper and held it so it was horizontal. This way, the ragged edges of stone now looked like the ground, and what I'd thought was the water now looked like the sky. Could this be the same place? I held the paper up against the postcard. There was no mistaking the bright colors, the unusual layers of green and brown and red.

No no no. So it looks a little bit like the postcard. So what? You can't keep doing this, Willa. You're losing your mind, on top of everything else. You need to give up.

I put down the paper and pinned the postcard back. Then I got into bed and slipped under the covers and pulled them to my chin and stared up at the ceiling.

I was probably just hallucinating, I told myself. That's what sleep deprivation could do to a person. Hadn't I thought I'd seen Chet just an hour before? Well, no more fooling myself. No more playing detective. In the morning I was going to turn myself in and let the authorities take care of finding her. I put my hand over my heart and felt it still beating hard.

What I'd done was wrong. Cherise had said it herself. And if it was wrong then, it was wrong now. I had to quit.

In the dark, I mentally rehearsed what I would do when I woke up. How I would call Corbin. How I would get Rain or Cherise or Tre to drive me to the bus station. How, if they wouldn't do it, I would call a cab. It was resolved.

The search, or at least my part in it, was over.

It was almost completely silent, except for the sound of snow sliding off trees in the woods. Another night in another bed. I tried not to think about where I would be sleeping next. I tried not to think about the fact that I might not even make it through the night. They could show up at any moment. I would surrender. I was ready to surrender.

My limbs were leaden with fatigue. I used my counting-backward trick to slow down my mind and lull myself into the sleep I so desperately needed.

Eventually, it came.

My mom and I are hiking up a steep hill. The woods are strangely dark for morning. There's no trail, so we just make our way through the brush. Thorns scrape at my ankles and mud sucks at my shoes but I don't care. She's with me. And she always knows the way.

"This is easy, isn't it?" she says, looking over her shoulder at me, her smile dazzling and wide. She turns to face forward again, and I notice her hair hanging in a long blond braid down her back. It's about a foot longer than I remember it. Has it been that long since I saw her last? In this place I don't have a sense of time.

There are no trees here. The land stretches out in front of us in bands of blue and purple and red. It's bald and spare, but the colors are like jewels. I want to grab handfuls of sand and stuff them in my pockets.

We're reaching the top of the hill and I can hear birds now, calling back and forth to one another, and the sounds of small animals scampering on the ground. I look down at my feet and see nothing except the footprints we've left.

"Can we stay here?" I ask.

"Now? No," she says, like it's obvious.

But it's beautiful, *I want to say.* We love this place.

Don't we?

For some reason I can't say these things out loud. I'm out of breath. I'm just trying to follow her, trying to keep up. Her braid bobs in front of me.

"Mom," *I call.*

"I have no choice," *she says.*

The bird chirping is getting louder, like we're walking straight into the nest. And then it becomes a rattling sound, like bricks or stones being thrown. I'm worried that this is an earthquake. That the color-splashed ground is about to split open and swallow us.

"Mom," *I try again.*

She stops, finally, and cups her hands in front of her face. "I've got to go," *she whispers, like she's afraid someone is listening to us.* "I have no choice."

That's when a gloved hand reaches out of the brush and grabs her around the neck. Another hand covers her mouth. I can't see whose hands they are but they've got her and they're dragging her away. She doesn't even fight them. Her body is limp as they take her.

"Mom! Mom!" *I yell out for her, even though the rattling sound is louder now. Even though I know that it's already too late.*

NINETEEN

I SHOT UPRIGHT, eyes open, electrocuted by fear. The sheets were half-torn off my body and I felt hot all over.

My mom. Oh God.

My vision adjusted, pulling the room into sharp focus. Even though I could see I was in Rain's house, I couldn't shake the lingering feeling of dread and terror, the burning images in my head. And I could still hear the rattling, like it was inside me.

She's okay, I told myself. *It was just a nightmare. Breathe.*

I tried to focus on inhaling and exhaling, allowing my breath to catch up with itself.

But the rattling continued, so I knew it wasn't just in my dreams. It was a noise from real life. And it sounded like it was coming from the front of the house.

Someone was trying to get in.

I threw myself over the side of the bed, feeling for the

door in the dark, and stepped out into the hallway.

"Willa?" It was Cherise—I could make out the shape of her in the inky half darkness. She grabbed my arm. "The police. We can hide you. C'mon."

Tre was in the hall now, too, his T-shirt half-tucked into his pajamas. "We can't hide her. Where are we going to hide her?"

"She can slip out the back door," Rain hissed. "It's not too late."

"We can bundle you up," Cherise said.

"Be real, you guys," Tre said, grasping his elbows and pacing back and forth. "We can't play around anymore."

"He's right." I stepped out a little farther, feeling the bass beat of my heart pulsing through the bottoms of my feet. I was barefoot, for crying out loud. Half-asleep. There was no good way to escape even if I wanted to. This was madness.

I started for the stairs.

"Willa! Where are you going?" Rain cried out, holding out her arms to block me.

"There's no point in hiding now," I said. I was going to turn myself in, anyway. Isn't that what I'd decided earlier?

The noise at the door continued. We all looked at one another for a moment, listening.

"Are you totally sure this is what you want?" Cherise asked.

I wasn't. How could I be? What sane person would

want to walk into police custody? And there was something else, some other doubt nibbling away at the back of my mind that had to do with the dream. But right then, I didn't know what else to do. I'd come as far as I could. Too tired to fight anymore. In a way, it felt like a relief.

Cherise gave me a worried look. I nodded to let her know that I was okay, that I appreciated all of her help but that this was something I had to do on my own and they couldn't protect me from it. Even if they could, it wouldn't be right.

"It's her choice, Rain," Cherise said finally.

"If you say so." Rain dropped her arms and let me pass.

I angled for the door.

"Willa! Are you in there?" It was a male voice, muffled through the heavy wood, calling from the other side.

I'd hoped to turn myself in, to go of my own free will, but now I was probably going to be dragged away in handcuffs.

In the end, it didn't really matter, did it? Either way I was going to jail.

More pounding, and then the voice again. "I can hear you moving around. Open the door!"

Time seemed to slink and slow as I unlocked the dead bolt and slid open the chain. Its links dropped one by one until it was hanging free. My hand was on the knob.

I braced myself for the frozen wind that was about to blow inside Rain's house, and for everything else that would follow. This was it.

I opened the door.

"Willa!" Aidan stepped forward. His cheeks were pink from the cold. Eyes blinking back bits of snow. He was here.

My head snapped back in complete and total shock. As I'd imagined, the cold air whipped around my ankles and fingers and nose. But I hadn't imagined this. Not at all.

"Aidan," I said stupidly. "Where are the cops?"

He looked behind him into the darkness. "Cops?"

"I thought—"

"Are you going to let me in or what?"

Of course I was. I moved out of the way. Body was working. I just couldn't get there mentally. Yet.

He was covered in snow—it coated his legs up to his knees and it was dusted all over his head and jacket. Had he *hiked* here?

When he was fully inside, I reached out to hug him, wrapping my arms around the dense muscles of his shoulders and back.

He'd found me. It didn't feel real, somehow, even as the chill clinging to his body passed into mine. I squeezed my eyes tight, and everything else fell away.

There were other things to think about, I knew— that girl and those text messages, all of his secrets. And yet, now that he was in front of me, the worries and doubts didn't seem as important. We were here. Of all the places in the world we could be, we were both here and that felt like a sign.

He let go first. The world came rushing back into the space between us. I was a little embarrassed at my shameless display of emotion. Also, the goofy pajamas I was wearing.

"I got off the bus and tried to look for you, you know."

"You did?" A smile played at the corners of his lips.

"I thought you were going home," I whispered. "I thought you were finished."

"I couldn't do it," he said, staring at me the whole time. "And we're not finished."

The four of us sat down at the kitchen table, Aidan and me on one side, Cherise on the other, and Tre at the head of the table. Rain hovered around us, throwing down snack packets of cereal and granola bars and mugs of coffee to fuel our brainstorming. Yes, the cops were still out there, but now that Aidan was back everything had changed—I was less sure I wanted to give up. Either way we had to make some decisions, and make them fast.

I spread out the FBI files around the table. Aidan thumbed through them. "Time to bring out the big guns. Can we use your computer, Rain?"

"Sure," Rain said, leaving the room to retrieve it. She

returned with a laptop, which she set down in front of Aidan.

"What are you doing?" I asked him as I watched his fingers dance over the keyboard.

"What I should have done earlier. Hacking into the database."

"Into the *FBI* database?" I repeated.

"Awesome!" Rain said.

"No. Not awesome," Tre said, clapping a hand to his forehead. "Dude, you're insane."

Aidan looked up from the screen. "Look, Tre, we've got to get some information. This is the only way I know."

"And how exactly are you doing this?" Cherise asked, coming behind him to peer at his work.

"Code. It's called an injection. You use log-in strings to manipulate a routine through the front-end form."

Cherise waved a hand. "Ah, forget I asked. You can explain it to me later."

"It's a time-honored technique," Aidan said, typing. "Never mind. Just give me a couple of minutes, okay?"

Cherise came over to me and watched as I thumbed through the photos again. I showed her the mug shot. "That's the guy that's after her."

She hugged herself and drew back. "Willa, this is no joke. What you've gotten into . . ."

"I know. But what would you do? If it were your parents?"

Her eyes misted over and she swallowed hard. "I don't know. Everything I could, I guess."

Aidan slapped his palms on the table. "I'm in."

Maybe I should have been stressed out about the fact that he'd broken into a federal information system, or disturbed by the delight I saw in his face as he was doing it.

But honestly? It was kinda hot.

On the screen was the familiar blue crest with the gold ring that I'd seen on Corbin's business card and documents. Within another few seconds, Aidan brought up my mom's name. Her real name. We read over his shoulder.

"It says here she was born in Wichita, Kansas," Aidan said.

"I knew that. Scroll down."

"And her mother is deceased."

"Right," I said.

"She was murdered."

"What?" My voice broke.

"Brianna Siebert," he read off the screen. "Born 1965. Died 1997. Death ruled a homicide."

I covered my mouth and backed away from the computer.

"Oh my God," Cherise said, grabbing my hand. "I'm so sorry, Willa."

All I could think was, *Murder. Murder. Murder.*

Then the images. I blinked to block them out of my

head. I pulled the necklace out from underneath my pajama top. I ran my fingers over its familiar contours, like it could tell me something.

My grandmother. Killed. What else had my mom lied to me about? For the first time since setting out on this trip, I had to wonder: Did I really even want to know?

"It doesn't look like there were any arrests connected to that case," Aidan said.

"It doesn't matter. It was him." I didn't need forensic evidence, or any other kind of evidence. I knew who the killer was. I was sure of it.

"But what about—" Aidan asked.

"We should keep looking," I said impatiently. "Can you just do that, please?"

Maybe another girl would have been crying or scared, but right then my main response was anger. I was sick of being the last to know everything. We didn't have time for more questions. The only thing we could do was find my mom, and then everything would be explained once and for all.

"What do you want me to look for?" Aidan asked.

"Surveillance," I said, pointing to a link. "Let's see if they've got anything new."

He moused over to a series of photos in thumbnail size and clicked on the first one on the top row, enlarging it. It was her, looming near what looked like a refrigerator stocked with sodas. She was wearing a disguise—big dark glasses, a baseball hat, and a long coat.

"This was from a convenience store in Bend." He pointed to the caption and numbers on the bottom of the page. "You can see the date there. Yesterday morning."

His words stirred a vortex in my chest. Oregon. That's where the Painted Hills were. I turned to Rain. "What do you know about the Painted Hills?"

"Just that they're freaking gorgeous," she said. "I was there last summer with my parents. They've got a friend out there who's an artist."

"An artist?" I asked, locking eyes with Aidan. After all this time on the road together certain things no longer needed to be explained between us.

"Yeah, she says the landscape inspires her. Why?"

I went upstairs into the room where I'd been sleeping, took down the postcard, grabbed the photo of my mom's painting, and dropped them on the table.

Aidan picked up the postcard, waving it in front of his eyes. "It's uncanny, actually."

"That's got to be it," Cherise said.

It clicked. We were on the right track again. "How long do you think it takes to get to Oregon? We need to get there before she leaves again."

"Or before the cops show up," Tre murmured. "So what's our strategy, Willa?"

"I vote for something not involving hiking," Aidan said. He was still shivering, even though Rain had found him a change of clothes.

"Is your name Willa?" Tre was joking, clearly, but underneath the smile I detected the slightest bit of annoyance.

"We need a ride," I said, raising an eyebrow at Tre. "An alternative means of transport, if you will."

"Well, I don't think you guys should be driving anything right now," he said, shaking his head. "It's too easy to spot you on the road. No, that's just asking for trouble."

"So then what?" I folded my arms across my chest, feeling frustrated. Damn Tre and his safety. He always had a way of making everything more complicated. Safer, but more complicated.

"So then Cherise and I need to come with. We can drive you."

"Speak for yourself," Cherise said, frowning. "I don't want to get mixed up with anything illegal."

"News flash. You already are," Tre said.

"What about you?" I asked Tre. "Are you really sure you want to do this? What about your boundaries?"

"Boundaries are made to be jumped over," he said. "I'm in."

We all turned to Cherise, waiting.

"It's your choice," Tre said. "If you want out, you can take the next bus home. We can drop you off."

Cherise looked at me and then back to Tre, and sighed. "No, I can't leave you guys—not now. I just don't want to get in trouble. I already lied and told my parents that Rain and I were going skiing. If her car is spotted in Oregon, we'll both be screwed."

"Nobody will get in trouble if we plan this thing well," Tre said. "I'm not going to take Rain's car. Give me a little credit, okay? Now, does anyone here have access to a tractor-trailer?"

"Actually, I have something we might be able to use," Rain said, a devious smile spreading across her face.

Between the five of us, we came up with something that sounded workable. A plan that would allow Aidan and me to fly under the radar, yet would advance us to our next destination. As the sun rose, we drove fifty miles north to Truckee and followed back roads to a complex of low-lying industrial buildings. Rain pulled the car behind a warehouse where loading docks were lined up like the teeth of a zipper.

She turned around and smiled at us as she put the car in park. "Finally, my nightmare summer stockgirl job can be put to good use," she said. "Do you have a preference?"

"That one," Tre said, pointing to a truck that was white and square, with a giant piece of powdered-sugar-dusted crumb cake painted on the side. Betelman's Baked Goods. One of my favorites. My stomach growled as we staked it out.

Tre stepped out of the car to get a better look, but not before he readjusted his hoodie and sunglasses.

We'd all been careful to disguise ourselves. I felt bad that yet again I was dragging Tre and now Cherise into my criminal plans, but they insisted on coming with us. The truth was, we needed them to pull it off. Because this plan was as outrageous as anything else we'd done— and after the whole FBI/Denny's scam, that was saying a lot.

"And you're sure no one's around?" I asked.

"I'm sure," Rain said. "They don't get here and load up for at least another hour. Just promise to bring it back when you're done."

"Of course. You think we want to keep this thing? I can only imagine how that'd go over back at home, trying to park in the VP lot," Cherise muttered.

"So, does everyone know what to do?" Tre asked, looking at the rest of us. He'd gone through our positions about two hundred times.

We nodded and we gathered our things.

Rain hugged us each good-bye. "I wish I could go with you. Promise me you'll call and give me an update," she said.

"Of course," Cherise said. "Have fun studying bio."

Rain stuck out her tongue.

"Thanks, Rain," I said. "I owe you big-time."

"Just find her," she said, giving me a squeeze. "We can talk paybacks later. It's been great hanging out with you. The real Willa, I mean."

"And you too," I said.

"Enough cornball stuff," Tre said. "Let's move."

At his call, we dashed toward the truck. My skin tingled as we drew nearer. We were really doing this. Aidan had the side door open within seconds. He grinned at me as he pocketed his screwdriver.

"Not bad for a poor little rich boy, huh? I knew this extra screwdriver would come in handy."

"Not the best I've seen, either," Tre said. "You chipped the paint."

We crept up the steps and into the truck, and crouched between stainless-steel shelves of baked goods. Tre was there to close us in.

"You guys gonna be okay back here?"

"Sure," I said, though I suddenly felt a wave of anxiety about being locked in. How long would this take? It was strange to not be in control. "We'll call you if we need to stop."

"All right." He smiled and I caught a little gleam in his eye. Was he enjoying this? "Headed northbound."

The door creaked shut. We were surrounded in the frigid darkness for what felt like hours as Cherise and Tre got into the front and hot-wired the ignition.

Finally, the truck lurched forward. Aidan took my hand in his. We pulled away and out of the parking lot, back onto the road like we'd never left it.

TWENTY

THE TRUCK WAS cold—freezing actually. Aidan and I huddled close together for warmth. After a little while, our eyes adjusted to the lack of light and I could make out Aidan's profile, just a few inches away.

"I feel a little bad," I said, my words echoing in the cavernous metal expanse.

"About what?" Aidan asked.

"About all of this." The truck heist, bringing Cherise and Tre into our maneuvers, the ongoing police chase. I'd never meant for it to happen this way. I just wanted to find my mom. "It's kind of another level of theft now. And, I don't know. I'm scared."

"That doesn't sound like the Sly Fox I know and love. Look, the whole point is that cops are not looking for a Betelman's truck. It's foolproof."

"No plan is foolproof," I said, trying not to think about the fact that he'd just said *love*. Had he really just said that? Despite the cold, my face was suddenly hot.

"Don't worry. Have a donut. And hey, think of it this way: You're eating the evidence." He pressed one into my hand.

I bit into the cinnamon-covered cake and tried to relax. I was stress-eating now. This was my third donut. My mom, the health-food nut, would have been appalled. But what good was hiding out in a Betelman's truck if you didn't partake in the snacks? And, come to think of it, she probably would have been appalled at just about everything that we'd done in the past few days.

In the darkness, with the low rumbling of the engine, I felt a certain amount of safety. "So where were you, when you left?"

"I called my dad."

"And what happened?"

The truck shifted—Tre must have been changing lanes, and we were slung to the right. I grabbed hold of his shoulder for balance.

"Let's just say he wasn't quite as sweet as he seemed on TV. The first thing he said was, 'Do you know how your little stunt is affecting my stock prices?'"

"So what'd you say?"

"I hung up on him," he said bluntly. "But that was my fault. It was stupid to think he would be any different. People don't change."

"It wasn't stupid," I said. "You have to hope sometimes.

Anyway, I'm sorry that you had to go through that."

"It's a good lesson for me to learn. You shouldn't be sorry."

"Well, I pushed you away. I think that makes it my fault."

"I know. I mean, we both made mistakes," he said, his fingers tracing along the inside of my wrist. "But that's not important now, is it?"

God, I had missed him. Those few hours he'd been gone were unbearable. With Aidan next to me, things felt right again.

Then a little doubt crept into the back of my mind. *You still don't know, Willa. You still don't know why he got into trouble or who this other girl is.*

"I just wish we could do this all over," I said out loud. "This hasn't been the best time for us to start something."

"We don't need to. I mean, we're still starting, aren't we?"

The truck shifted the other way and we were thrown together again. I laughed, embarrassed that I was on top of him. Not that I didn't want to be.

The truck straightened itself out, and we fell back into our positions. Before I could answer Aidan or say anything else, our phone buzzed. I rummaged through my bag to bring it up. "Hang on."

It was a text from Tre.

COP ROADBLOCK AHEAD!!!!! GET OUT ASAP.

"Oh my God." So much for our foolproof plan. I didn't need a memo to know that the cops were most likely looking for us. "Cops. He says get out."

"How?" Aidan said.

"Jump, I guess."

"What are they going to do?"

WHAT ABOUT U? I texted.

Tre couldn't afford to get in trouble any more than I could. My pulse tripled its tempo and my thoughts pinged from the police ahead of us to Tre and Cherise, to me and Aidan flinging ourselves onto the road.

GO.

I grabbed my bag and crouched by the door. Every nerve running through my body twanged with fear. We could feel the brakes clamping and the truck decelerating.

The moment was here. We had to go.

Aidan opened up the door. At first all I could see was the light, piercing the blackness in a sharp column. Instinctively, I reached up to shield my eyes.

"I'll go first, okay?" Aidan said.

"Okay."

"Then follow me."

He grabbed my hand and squeezed it. Then, just like that, he was gone.

It was only me now in the gaping opening, air blowing in. I threw my backpack out first. Then I closed my eyes and dove after it. It was like swimming against the current, my head and chest going in one direction, my legs in another. When I finally landed, my feet touched the road. Just as quickly I was tumbling forward with the force of my own weight, down down down into a grassy gully until I finally landed on my back. I opened my eyes and watched the Betelman's truck rev up and drive on, taking Cherise and Tre with it.

Then Aidan was crouching over me. "You all right?"

"I think so." I reached a hand down to my leg and felt the fabric torn, the flesh of my thigh hot and tender to the touch.

"Road rash," he said. "Can you walk?"

I stood up carefully and took a few steps. We were still in the depression on the side of the highway. I turned back to look in the direction of the truck. It was tiny now, receding into the distance. Beyond it I could just make out the black-and-white police cars lined up in a row across the pavement.

"I hope they're going to be okay," I said.

"I hope *we're* going to be okay."

"I just mean Tre. I don't want him to get in trouble again." I limped a little bit.

"Well, he took that chance, didn't he? He knew what he was getting into."

"I guess so." I was surprised at how callous Aidan seemed about the whole thing. They were our friends.

They'd risked their well-being and freedom for us.

"This is survival, Willa. There must be a rest stop somewhere along here," Aidan said. "I suggest we walk that way. We can figure out where the hell we are and go from there."

I hated to backtrack and I was eager to find another ride, to keep going and get as far from the police as possible, but I knew he was right.

We walked, huddled close to the ground, back in the direction we came. The grass was overgrown, strewn with tall flowering weeds, and it was easy to get lost in it. But I still felt like I was wearing a giant target.

TEEN FUGITIVE right here, folks. Step right up and take a shot.

Thankfully, a truck stop wasn't too far off—my leg was throbbing by the time we got there.

We walked inside, stopping at the little store in front to buy a map. Then I went to the bathroom to clean my wound, wrapping toilet paper around it. Probably not the most advanced first-aid technique, but it would have to do. I balled up some extra and stuffed it into the bag. I'd finally gotten rid of my schoolbooks, leaving them at Rain's house, and now it was much lighter with more space for needed supplies. Aidan was carrying the FBI files.

When Aidan went up to the front cashier to get us some snacks, I looked at our map. Judging by the distance we'd already covered that morning, I estimated it would be another hour before we hit Fossil, which was the entry point to the Painted Hills, according to Rain's parents' guidebooks.

I traced the route with my finger, brushing over a town called Azalea, and another called Drain.

Azalea and Drain. That sounded familiar.

I reached into the pocket of the windbreaker for what I'd thought was my mom's shopping list.

Needles, Posts, Crest, Azalea, Drain, 3RS.

Now, looking at the list and back at the map, I realized that those must have been places. Places she was going on her journey.

And Crest was where Corbin had found her car, wasn't it?

Aidan came back to where I was sitting and I showed him what I saw.

"So this was part of her plan all along, too, to throw off anyone on her trail. The car was a decoy." I said it with relief. Now, at least, I had some proof that she knew what she was doing.

"Nice work, Colorado," he said, patting me on the shoulder. "We're nearly there. I can feel it. Are you ready to jet?"

He followed my eyes to where I was looking. At the entrance, where two policemen were shuffling in.

"Yes," I said very quietly, grabbing his arm. "Let's go now."

Aidan and I turned around and walked directly—we

didn't run, though I was tempted to—out through the back entrance. Behind the truck stop was a huge lot. There were a bunch of cars parked there, some tractor-trailers, and a row of motorcycles. Aidan made a beeline for the bikes.

"Are you crazy?" I pictured leather-jacketed gang members coming after us.

"Crazy and stupid," he said. I watched as he sat down on the saddle and used his foot to jar the handlebars loose from their locked position. Then he got out his screwdriver, stuck it in the ignition, and pulled out the key barrel, tossing it on the ground. He jammed the screwdriver back in and started the bike. Aidan, the hot-wirer extraordinaire, revved up the engine, which roared and then dropped to a rumbling sputter. "Get on."

I jumped on the back. Aidan U-turned out of the truck-stop entrance so that we were headed south. Then we picked up another road going west. All I could do was hold on to him, my arms encircling his back, feeling his muscles pulse as he steered and changed lanes. The windbreaker did not exactly live up to its name on a bike. The wind was freezing as it whipped around us, and the warmth of our bodies smashed together was the only thing that was keeping me from going totally numb.

But for a moment it was almost like our first day on the road, that exhilarating feeling of being alone, the two of us, and free, and wild.

I kept looking over my shoulder, expecting cops to

pull up next to us. We just had to get there, I told myself. *Only a bit longer now.*

We continued on the highway up to an area just outside Eugene, and from there headed east on a smaller road, driving deep into the coniferous woods of the Willamette National Forest.

Just when I thought my arms were going to fall off from holding on to Aidan, we started seeing the signs for John Day Fossil Beds National Monument, and the town of Fossil.

We parked the bike at a picnic area. From there we would have to go by foot on into the Painted Hills, a good six-mile hike. I strapped on my schoolbag, which was now stocked with bottles of water and our snacks.

It was late afternoon, on the cusp of evening. There were no other hikers on the trail now—it was too cold and about to be dark within an hour or so. In the distance the mountains rose high and sharp above the flattened-out hills. It was beautiful, one of the most unusual landscapes I'd ever seen, but it was also eerie, too. Vast and dry and moonlike.

Farther down the trail the colors became more vivid; the stripes I'd seen in the photos emerged in the hills, almost like they were streaked with watercolors. The sun was hanging low, illuminating the dusty green sagebrush and the clay reds of the undulating land.

With each turn the view became more and more striking—marked by steeper ridges, stronger colors.

Then the ground started to drop away on either side of us, into deep rocky gulches. The place was foreign and yet also familiar—I thought it must have been from the dream I had the night before.

As we walked, the dream was coming back to me in pieces. I just wished I could remember my mom's face. The more I tried to grab hold of the image, the more it slipped away.

The trail started to fork off into two different directions and as we followed the left branch, we caught a glimpse of a fire pit in the rock basin below. It was the first evidence of human life we'd seen out here.

"That could be it," I said.

We followed the trail down the stony side of the ravine. It was very steep so we inched our way in tentative steps, not wanting to trip or lose our footing. I was so focused on the ground just beneath me that I was nearly to the bottom before I noticed the orange tent.

I broke into a run, and Aidan did, too.

But when we got close we noticed the sleeping bag tossed on the ground beside the tent entrance. It was torn up. The tarp beneath it was kicked into a ball. And then the broken glass, the empty water jug, and plastic wrappers strewn about. It almost looked like it had been ransacked. Like our house.

It was clear, from all the dusty stuff, that it had been a while since anyone was here last. At least a day. Maybe more.

And whoever had been here had left in a hurry. My torso shook as everything in me—my heart, my hopes, my last good plan—crumbled to dust.

We were so close. And yet still not here in time.

"Jesus." Aidan exhaled. "Now what?"

We moved in closer to examine the evidence, to try to piece together what exactly had happened.

Now what, indeed? I reached out and touched the sleeping bag. It was green, like hers, with a plaid interior.

"I don't know," I said, blinking tears, feeling overwhelmed with doubt. This had to be her campsite. There was the sleeping bag. The surveillance pics. The painting. The list. It was too much to be a coincidence. And yet we'd been wrong again.

Maybe it really was too late. Maybe they got to her.

Just then there was a scraping sound behind us.

"Did you hear that?" I asked Aidan.

"Hear what? Must have been an animal."

"No," I said. We hadn't seen many animals on our hike. "I don't think so. Listen."

We were quiet, waiting. There was another sound, like a handful of tiny rocks scattering. Another silence, and then more scraping, in a distinct rhythm. Repeating itself. Like footsteps.

This wasn't an animal.

It was a man. His voice echoed over the desolate crags as he called out to us from a distance. "You guys looking for Leslie?"

TWENTY-ONE

I WHIPPED AROUND. I could see them then, just over the ridge. Two men, thick-bodied, bundled up for the cold. They were running now, coming toward us as they made their way to the campsite. I didn't need to look closely to know that one of them was Chet.

"Don't look so scared," he yelled. "We just want to talk to you."

Aidan gave me a warning look. "Is that—?"

I nodded.

He was here. Right in front of us. A killer.

I was stunned, unable to move. Rooted to the ground in pure terror.

"Look, we know you're looking for her. And we are, too." Now that he was closer I could see his broad chin covered with an auburn-silver scruff, his hazel eyes that were heavy-lidded, and a forehead just slightly lined. The black wings of his bird tattoo curled around his neck.

The other guy stood behind him, silent. He was taller, and wearing a ski cap.

"I just can't seem to track her down." Chet was still panting from his run, but a smile tickled his fleshy face. "You have no idea how frustrating it is to be on the road, looking for someone who keeps slippin' through your fingers."

I did, though. I knew exactly how frustrating it was. On that, at least, Chet and I could agree.

"So why'n't we work together, huh?" He reached out a hand toward me, as if he wanted to shake on the deal.

I glanced down at his thick fingers and took a step backward, finding my voice clumped and rusty in my windpipes. "You ransacked my house." *You murdered my grandmother.*

"Oh, that wasn't personal or nothing, was it, Bailey?" The guy behind him shook his head no.

Bailey. I remembered the name from the rap sheet.

"I'ma be honest with y'all." Chet shrugged, still wearing his stupid, nasty grin. "She's got something of ours. And me and Bailey, we need it back."

My muscles convulsed then locked up. The money. He was looking for the money. "I don't know what you're talking about. I don't know what you're looking for."

He moved in so he was standing squarely in front of me. Now I could see the flat emptiness in his pupils, the spots where his teeth had yellowed at the edges. His voice was still calm. "Sure you do. Don't play dumb now, Willa."

He knew my name. Sickening. Chet was too close, his shoulders hulking over me. I took a few more steps back. I looked at Aidan. His eyes were wild with fear. I looked down again and my eye caught on what was left of the campsite at my feet.

"See? We all want the same thing. So if you can cooperate with us, it'll work out great for everyone."

I saw Bailey reach up under his jacket. I saw a flash of silver. That was enough *cooperation*.

I didn't think. I picked up the tarp at my feet and flung it at them. We broke out into a run, pounding past the tent and aiming for the opposite edge of the campsite.

As we scrambled for the other side we saw it wasn't as simple as just running away. We were surrounded by unforgivingly steep, bare rock walls—and we had to make it back up the basin again, with no trail. In fact, it looked as if no human had ever climbed this way before.

Aidan started to climb. It was like pulling yourself up a ladder without rungs. The rock was smooth in places, making it hard to get a solid grip or foothold. I struggled until I found the necessary movements: hands up first, then feet. Fold in half, like an inchworm. Then repeat. But it was going to take all my strength.

I could hear them behind us, footsteps and shouting. I tried not to listen, tried to focus on my next step.

"Don't be stupid," Chet yelled. "You'll never get up that way. Come back now. We'll forget your stupid tarp trick if you turn around."

They sounded close, maybe fifteen yards away. I was afraid to turn around, to see just how close.

Aidan moved much more quickly, so that now he was closing in on the top. I pushed on anxiously, not wanting to be left behind. Only this time as I felt around with my feet for a crevice, there was no place to put them. They just slipped off. I was left hanging, holding on with my fingers for dear life, about ten feet from the ground.

As my legs dangled beneath me, the pads of my fingers began to slip off the rock.

"Aidan, I can't—"

He turned around just when I lost my grip entirely. I screamed, tumbling backward as I grabbed at the air. He watched me fall, and I watched him watch, terrified, for what felt like minutes.

My body slammed down, back-first on the ground. The wind was knocked out of me, and my thoughts, too. Everything went dark as I gasped for air.

Pain, hot and red, seared through my body.

When I regained my breath I looked around quickly, taking stock. My knee burned. I figured I probably scraped it against the rocks on the way down. Between that and my road rash, my legs were a mess. My pepper spray was on the ground beside me—it must have slipped out of the bag. I grabbed it.

"Willa, are you okay?" Aidan's voice was frantic.

"I think so," I called up to him, feeling around to make sure I hadn't broken anything. I still had the bag. I scrambled to my feet, then limped toward the rock wall.

"Look out!" Aidan called.

A hand closed around my arm and I screamed in surprise.

"You see? People get hurt when they don't listen. Don't be foolish now," Chet said. "Stop and we can still work this out."

I wrenched my arm loose and punched Chet, knocking him backward into Bailey.

I heard a sound like *oof* and then their curses. Furious, I jumped up to grasp whatever part of the rock was graspable and worked to start pulling myself up again. I was pretty sure I'd hit them solidly—I could still get away if I moved quickly. I had to start over, ignoring the sensation in my leg and my hands, trying to stay focused on one step at a time. All I could see was gray stone, and I had no concept of how much farther I had to go. I found one foothold, and then another, inching closer. Pain zipped through my arms and legs. I only had one and a half hands to work with now because I was gripping the pepper spray as I climbed. They were close behind me but I reasoned that they would have to climb to reach me, and it wasn't easy for anyone.

I had to get there. I had to beat them. I looked over my shoulder and saw through my peripheral vision that the two guys were moving in closer, two blurry forms.

"Hurry," Aidan said. "Don't look at them."

No physical thing I had ever done had prepared me for this challenge. If only they set these kinds of goons after you in gym class when you were doing rope climbs. Because I was learning that you could get seriously jocky when your life was threatened.

C'mon, Willa, I coached myself. *You can do this. Keep pushing.*

I was making good progress. Until one of them grabbed my leg.

"I've got you," the voice belonging to the hand said. It was Bailey. "And we're not letting you out of here."

I used all my strength to kick back, slamming my foot into his hand and shaking my leg free. "Let go of me," I gasped. "Don't *touch* me!"

Bailey yelped in pain and fell to the ground. "Stupid bitch!"

It was like waking a sleeping giant. They were really angry now. Now it was outright war. Chet yanked on my knapsack, tried to pull me back down. I held on as tightly as I could—his weight against mine.

"You just don't know when to quit, do you?" Chet snarled. "You're just like her."

I was terrified of losing my grip again—if I fell this time, I probably wouldn't be so lucky—but it wasn't just me now. If I let this guy pull me off the rocks, I was endangering both of us. I just had to focus on that. And if anything happened to Aidan—well, I couldn't bear to think of that.

I still had the pepper spray in my hand. I just needed to . . . reach him. I struggled to twist around while holding on to the rock—one slip, or a few seconds off, and he would have me on the ground. This was risky, but I had to take my chances. I was sick of people telling me I'd made mistakes. I was sick of people telling me what to do.

I let go with my right hand and felt around with my index finger. For a moment I was just hanging there, swinging wildly, the weight of the bag and the man behind it dragging me down. I couldn't look, not without falling. I pressed down on the button, angling it behind me, hoping for the best.

The chemicals misted out like an impatient sigh.

"AAAAAHHHH. What the hell?"

Judging from his response, I'd say the spray hit him in the eye as planned.

I dropped the spray, threw my free arm back up, and grabbed for the rock.

"I *am* just like her," I said, more to myself than anyone else.

I could see Aidan's hand now, outstretched for me at the top. Only a few arm's lengths away. When I got close enough, I grabbed it. He reached down for my armpits and helped me pull myself up onto the edge. I stood up.

"Quickly," he said.

I paused. I looked down to see Chet pointing a gun up at us.

"Another move, we shoot," he yelled from the rock floor.

Aidan yanked my bag off me and lobbed it down at Chet. "C'mon," he said to me.

Chet must have dodged it because there was no cry. Away from the edge we couldn't see them any more, but I didn't know how long that would last.

My heart raced as we broke into a run, beating our feet against the dusty earth. My body wanted to limp, to collapse, but I pushed everything I had into that run.

Chet kept his promise. I could feel the gunshots actually ricocheting off the rock wall, the vibrations ringing through the soles of my shoes. And I knew it was only us and them in this barren, cold stretch of desert. We were just two bodies that could easily be disposed of.

If we died here, no one would ever know. I thought of Corbin, and all his warnings. This is what he'd been talking about. The fear burned in my chest, along with the cold air in my lungs.

The land began to rise up underneath our feet. We were headed straight for the hills. And we soon discovered that climbing the hills was worse than the rock, because there was no traction, just shifting sand slipping beneath us. I thought of all the signs we'd seen warning us to stay on the trails and how we were probably committing a federal crime by even walking on these eroding dunes.

But this was a survival situation. We were just going to have to add it to our growing tab of offenses.

The sun was hanging lower, making our shadows longer. We reached another peak. From here the landscape looked like a wrinkled cloth plastered into stillness. There was no movement of any kind, not even birds flying overhead.

"Are they still there?" Aidan asked.

We listened.

There were footsteps, and then one of the men's voices, shouting out orders. More gunshots. They were shooting at the sand now, just to scare us.

Aidan looked at me wearily. "We better keep going. They're not giving up anytime soon."

We ran down the other side, only to see that the hills kept going like that, up and down, for what looked like miles. We were effectively trapped by the sculpted landscape. Sure, it was beautiful, but right now it looked like death. We were running and it felt like we'd have to run forever.

My lungs stabbed with pain, the cold air constricting my entire respiratory system. I didn't know how much longer we could keep going at this pace. I didn't know how many bullets they had.

As we climbed and crossed another hill, it was getting dark, and the sun slipped behind us, faster all the time. That triggered another wave of worries for me. We had no flashlight or compass. We had no blankets, or any place to camp out if we needed to rest. I'd lost the water and all of our food with the bag. Aidan had his watch that glowed in the dark, and that was it. The bike was miles away. I doubted if we would ever see it again.

Who knew how long we'd be out here? We'd long since lost sight of any kind of trail. We were going deeper and deeper into the wilderness.

"Aidan, I need to stop soon," I wheezed.

We climbed over a ridge, and the rock formations beyond it rose high into the air like turrets on a castle.

"Okay. Maybe there's a cave in here somewhere," Aidan said. He was breathing hard himself. "We could find a place to rest and hide out."

We circled the base of the rock formations for a while until we found a suitable crevice. The area was cold and dank and small. We could only both fit if we balled ourselves up tight, clutching our knees to our chests. But it was its own kind of fortress, and in the thickening night our pursuers would have a hard time spotting us here.

Inside, it was darker than dark. We didn't dare move or talk much. I tried not to think about what kind of animals lived in here and what they might have left behind. We just waited and waited, the sounds of our breathing intermingling.

At some point I must have tipped over on top of Aidan because I woke up to him trying to move my arms.

"Willa, you've crushed my upper torso," he muttered, sliding out from underneath me.

"Sorry," I said, startled. I pulled myself back up into a ball. "What time is it?"

He checked his watch. "Five A.M."

We'd spent the whole night here. I stepped out of the cave and stretched, trying to get some feeling in my cramped-up limbs and back. There were scrapes along my arms, an open cut on my knee from when I'd fallen. This, in addition to the road rash from earlier. That was another thing. I'd lost the dang toilet paper.

Aidan stood up, and ran a hand through his hair. He was bruised, too—I could tell by the way he was limping.

"You're hurt," I said, reaching out to touch him.

He shrugged and looked over his shoulder at the back of his leg. "Just my ankle. Must've twisted it."

"How far do you think we are from the trail?" I asked.

"A couple miles, maybe? We were running for a while. If we head north, we'll hit the river at some point. And if we follow that, we're bound to get to a town or something eventually."

We started walking in our broken way. The coming daylight glowed pink on the horizon, reminding us that we'd made it through the night. I should've felt optimistic, but I didn't.

I was sick with hopelessness. We'd lost her. Again. And now we'd come face-to-face with what she was running from. They wanted to kill us. I was sure now that they would try to kill her, too.

Nothing we'd done had mattered. In fact, we probably made it worse. And in the end, we would go to jail and she would still be out there, somewhere, in danger. Or maybe she would go to jail, too. I felt like a fool for putting us through all of this, for thinking we could actually change things or help. I'd hurt us both.

"I'm sorry, Aidan," I said out loud.

He looked at me with narrowed eyes. "Are you apologizing to me again, Colorado? Because I've had enough of your apologies."

So he was mad.

"It was stupid. I messed up again—"

"If you don't stop, I'm going to give you something you'll really be sorry about." He mock-punched his own hand and I realized he was kidding.

I frowned at him in disbelief. "Okay . . . so I won't apologize for almost getting us shot? Because that's a totally normal thing to do?"

He flicked his hair out of his eyes. "Did I ever say I wanted anything remotely normal? Normal is over-rated."

"What about living? Breathing? Our lives? Are they overrated, too?"

"Probably." He kicked at some pebbles. "What most people consider living really isn't much to write home about. I mean, look at what we've left behind, lifewise.

Just a gossipy town with a bunch of snobby people."

"But we're going to jail. You know that, right?"

"I know," he said quietly. "And it's been worth it. Every second."

He was nuts. I was nuts. Ever since we'd reunited at Rain's house—that moment of him appearing on the doorstep adorably disheveled and snowed-on—I'd felt that old spark flaring again. That intense feeling I'd had back in Paradise Valley, where I could barely bring myself to look away from him, and I could barely stand for him to look at me.

Only it was all a little softer now, more tender, more serious. Maybe because we'd been through so much together. All these days on the road, it was like it was us against the world, like we were the only two people who mattered.

The sun was fully breaking out through the clouds now, and I saw something shiny and sparkly in the distance. "Aidan," I said, grabbing his arm. "Is that the river?"

An hour later, we'd found our way back to the road. We walked along it, silent now, delirious from hunger, thirst, and pain. My feet were covered in blisters and I had wounds on each leg. Aidan limped along, too, with his twisted ankle.

I unhooked my arms out of the armholes and hugged myself under the windbreaker, trying to think warm thoughts. Mittens. Fireplaces. The spicy noodle soup I loved from Valley Prep's lunchroom.

We hadn't talked about what was supposed to happen or where we were going. The only thing we could do was walk. I stared at the ground, looking for the next sign.

About two miles down the road, I saw it. The sign, I mean. It was green, with white lettering.

THREE RIVERS, 25 MILES.

Three Rivers. Three Rivers. 3RS.

The words spun together and formed a shape in my mind.

The final place on the list. It had to be destiny. And our best, last chance.

I showed Aidan the paper again. "I think this could be it. I mean, I know I've said that before."

"Like a million times." He smiled in a pained way. "But I'm willing to try it. Let's find a ride there."

A tanker truck appeared from around the bend and Aidan leapt to his feet, trying to flag it down. It passed us. Ten minutes later, a beat-up Chevy pickup passed us, too.

"Are you sure we're going to be able to get a ride?" I asked Aidan.

"This is hippie central. Of course I'm sure."

"What if those guys come driving by?" I asked, scared

suddenly by the idea that we were out in the open again. Vulnerable.

"Then we make a run for it."

The thought of running again seemed physically impossible, but then I remembered learning in health sciences class that the human body is always more powerful than the mind thinks it is. Meaning, if we had to, and our survival depended on it, then we would probably find a way to haul ass.

Four cars later, a Honda Element slowed down to Aidan's dramatic waving. The driver rolled down his window. He had gray curly hair and sunglasses and he was listening to jazz. "You guys want a ride somewhere?"

"Three Rivers," I said.

"I'm headed that way. Get in," he said, unlocking the doors.

Aidan got in the front seat and I sat in the back. The interior of the car was neat and orderly and smelled like sandalwood oil. The sounds of trumpets and cymbals were a comforting halo. I wasn't a big jazz fan myself but I figured you had to trust a guy who listened to jazz in his car. He probably listened to NPR, too. Which made him about as safe as strangers went.

He didn't offer his name, thankfully, and so we didn't have to offer ours. He definitely didn't appear to recognize us. Maybe our story hadn't been on NPR yet. But he seemed thoroughly comfortable with the idea of carting around two filthy, injured teenagers. Perhaps Aidan was right about the hippie thing.

He did, at one point, look up at me in the rearview mirror. "So what are you guys doing in Three Rivers, if you don't mind me asking?"

"Just—checking it out," I said, feeling the force of my hopes swelling and pressing against my rib cage.

"Ever been there?"

"No," Aidan said.

"It's not much of a place for kids. Off-the-grid community. Nothing to do, really. A lot of retirees and old people."

Off-the-grid. Just like Corbin said. I almost couldn't breathe.

"That's okay," I said, trying to sound more casual than I felt. "I'm really interested in learning about that kind of stuff."

The driver shrugged. "Three Rivers it is, then. I can't promise you it's going to be all that exciting."

He signaled a turn onto a smaller road. I chewed on my thumb anxiously, hoping against hope that he was wrong.

TWENTY-TWO

THE DRIVER LET us off at the end of a dirt lane in front of a small wooden sign. "This is Three Rivers," he said. "Like I said, not much to look at, is it?"

We thanked him and assured him it was fine. Then we got out of the car, and he drove on.

We were both still sore and hobbled by injuries but as the road unfurled in front of us and another sign pointed to the "recreation area," I had a sudden burst of energy and I walked faster, kicking up puffs of dust. It was like I was being pulled by a magnetic field or other invisible force.

"Hey, wait up," Aidan called. "I can't exactly race right now."

"Sorry," I mumbled. But I couldn't slow down, either.

We rounded a bend and the first things I noticed were the shiny black solar panels emerging from behind the tops of evergreen trees. Arranged here and there, the wooden frame houses were simple and cabinlike, with big plate windows. Some had outhouses set behind them. A few had hot tubs—nothing like the kind I'd seen in Paradise Valley, of course.

No, everything here looked like it was made from and belonged to the wilderness. But it was also dry, and except for the ponderosa pine trees, all of the green vegetation had gone to yellow straw in the winter cold. In the distance, I could hear the sound of running water—one of the three rivers, I assumed.

"I think I've read about this place in *Wired* magazine. A lot of Silicon Valley types have vacation houses here," Aidan said. "There's no electricity or telephone lines, did you notice that? The perfect place to hide. It's brilliant, really."

I couldn't say anything. My throat was tight. My mouth was dry. I peered inside the windows as we passed more houses, examining them as if we were casing another place for a break-in. Some were totally empty, and some looked too settled—with dish towels, plastic children's trucks, and pet beds strewn around. Clues that told me exactly where we wouldn't find her.

On the right, the path forked off into a dirt lane called Leisure Road. Lined up along it was a row of trailers and RVs, capped with their own solar panels and satellites.

A chipmunk scurried across our path. At every tiny sound I wanted to jump out of my skin. My senses were lit up and flaring. It was like I could hear everything: a wind turbine whirring. The thwacking of laundry flopping in the breeze. My own blood beating through my head and chest.

Then, the question-mark creak of a door opening, and the soft crush of feet on the ground.

I saw her before she saw me. She was standing outside one of the trailers, gathering wood.

A hoodie and jeans dwarfed her petite frame. I don't know what I'd been expecting but she looked the same, more or less, as the last time I'd seen her. Same blond hair, same tiny nose, same peachy-colored skin. Same birthmark on her right cheek.

She was here. Alive.

Relief swelled and poured into every space of my body like water.

As I stepped closer, I imagined the tight clutch of her hug, the warmth of her breath as she whispered into my hair. How happy she was to see us. How she'd missed me. How everything was going to be okay from here on out. Because here we were. We'd made it. We'd actually found her!

I broke into a run.

She turned around and dropped the armful of logs, and they scattered on the ground, splintering. Her arms appeared to be frozen in midair, her fingers splayed out like she was grasping for something.

"Mom," I called, now inches away.

"Willa?" Her face was drained of color. Her voice was hoarse. "Oh my God."

I sucked in a breath. It wasn't the reaction I'd hoped for. Not by a long shot. Not after everything we'd gone through to get to this place.

"You—you shouldn't be here."

"I know," I said quietly, trying to choke down the mixture of disappointment at her scolding and the plain, dumb happiness that she was still alive.

"Dammit, Willa." She gritted her teeth. "Well, come inside before someone sees you."

We followed her up the side steps and in through the trailer's small entrance. I was surprised to see that it was as nice as some of the apartments where we'd lived, with wall-to-wall carpeting, wood-paneled walls, and plush armchairs. I noticed a pair of her sneakers on the floor by the door. Just the way she kept them at home.

I was hit again with longing—was it possible to be homesick for a person when they were standing right in front of you?

Once inside, with the door shut behind us, she finally hugged me, but it was not the embrace I had imagined. It was rough and quick and I felt her huffing a sigh over my shoulder. Almost like she was impatient. Or angry. Why was she so angry?

"This is Aidan," I said, introducing them.

"Hello," she said. "I hope you understand that this isn't really the best time and place to be meeting a friend of Willa's."

He nodded, and shoved his hands into his pockets. "I figured."

She closed the shades on the few unconcealed windows before she went to put the kettle on. "So do you mind telling me what you two are doing here?"

Wasn't it obvious? "We were worried. We wanted to make sure you were okay. . . . *I* was worried."

She took this explanation in with a stiff smile and turned around. "I'll make some tea."

"What's wrong?" I prompted, following her.

She hunched over the stove, looking broken. "I'm glad to see you. But I really wish you hadn't come. In fact, I was hoping you were going to turn yourself in. I saw you on the news, you know. And you're in big trouble, breaking your probation."

That was enough. All the days of endless dead ends and exasperation exploded in fury. "Yeah, I *know*. But what was I going to do? You just take off and leave me and I'm supposed to go to school and hang out with friends like nothing's the matter?"

"You should've listened—"

"No. I shouldn't have. I'm sorry but it just doesn't work that way. And you're insane if you think it does." I'd never been so blunt or disrespectful to her before. But then, it was an extreme situation.

She pointed at me with a shaking index finger. "You're too young to understand. You have no idea what you've just walked into."

"Actually, I have a pretty good idea," I said, cutting her off. "I know those guys are after you. And I think it's time you stopped treating me like a baby and just tell me what's going on here, *Leslie*."

The name dropped into the room like an explosive device. I actually saw her shrink back.

My heart whirred in anticipation of what I knew was coming. It was time to get some answers—time to finally find out the truth.

"You really want to know, huh?" Her voice quivered. "Fine. Sit down. I'll tell you."

Then the kettle went, screaming out in steam. She poured us our tea and brought the mugs over to us.

We sank into the chairs at her little kitchenette table. My hands curled into tight balls around my cup. I felt Aidan's stare on me, but I didn't dare turn around to look. I was pretty sure I knew what she was going to say, but I needed to hear her say it.

Except nothing could have prepared me for what she said next.

"There's no good way to do this, so I just have to come out with it." She closed her eyes and pressed her lips together as if squeezing the words out of her mind. Then she opened her eyes. "Willa, I'm not your mother."

Everything just stopped. Everything cracked open.

I dropped my mug on the table, the hot liquid leaping everywhere. I was too shocked to notice that it had splashed my arm and stained my shirt.

Not my mother? The words hung and swayed over me like a guillotine.

"You're burning yourself," she said, and got up for a damp cloth. She came back to the table and started mopping it up.

Then she tried to wipe my sleeve, but I recoiled from her touch. I gathered my arms across my chest.

"Who are you?" I asked slowly, my voice gravelly and ragged.

Her eyes met mine, the same eyes I'd been looking at all my life. "I'm your sister," she said, letting out a heavy breath. "And technically your name is Maggie Siebert. I renamed you Willa Fox, though. Officially, I mean."

I looked at Aidan's puzzled face and then back at her—Leslie, my sister—with growing agitation. My real name. None of this was making any sense. "What are you *talking* about?"

She wrung her hands together, and her face crumpled. "You were a baby. We were living in St. Louis then. With our real mother—her name was Brianna."

Instinctively, I grabbed at the bird necklace. So the woman I'd thought of as my grandmother was actually my real mother? "And she was killed," I said, thinking back to the FBI file.

"Yes." Her eyes welled up at the memory and she flicked her head as if she were trying to shake it loose. "One day after school, I picked you up from day care, like always, and we came home to see Mom. That's when I found her body. She'd been shot. The house was trashed. I was only sixteen years old but I knew something was wrong. She'd done something. I knew that they were going to take us away, maybe separate us, if social services or the police found out what was going on."

"I don't . . . understand," I said. But it wasn't even like I was actually sitting there and asking the question. I no longer felt like I was inside my own body.

She reached across the table and put her hand on top of mine. "You were so cute. I'd practically been raising you myself since Mom worked so much. I couldn't bear the thought of you going to a foster home. So I grabbed you and a duffel bag with our stuff and took the first Greyhound bus out of town."

She paused, looking down. I could hear a clock ticking somewhere, and the sound of the breeze rattling against the window, and someone's radio humming a few trailers away. The quiet of this place.

"So this other woman—Brianna—was my mother. But then who's my father?"

"I don't know. That part is true—what I've always told you. He took off before you were born and he's never been around."

Great. Another big family mystery. "But is he—do we have the same?"

"I don't think so, Willa. I never knew my dad, either. At least, no one ever told me who he was. That part, about me having you at sixteen, that was Mom's story. She was kicked out when she had me. Do you want me to continue with what I do know?"

I nodded with a sour, pinching face. "No point in stopping now. Have any more bombshells about our screwed-up family? Because I'm all ears."

She withdrew her hand and let out a sob. "This isn't easy for me, either, okay? You don't know what I've been through, what I've given up, how hard it was to leave you. You don't have to be sarcastic."

I did, though. Couldn't she see that? I needed to grasp on to anything I had left and hold on tight. Even if it was my own bad attitude.

"Just tell me, okay?" I spat, surprising myself with the force of the outburst. "I'm sick of these secrets."

She raised her palms in defense. "Okay. Fine. When we got on the road, and I went to change you at one of the rest stops, I noticed that there was something sewn into the lining of the duffel bag. I ripped it open and found the money. It was a lot of money, Willa. Five million dollars."

"The money from your paintings?" I asked. But I wasn't really asking. "You had it all along."

"It was an accident that we even found it. Mom had hidden it away. She'd been acting weird—she moved us, and she was using a new name, though she'd let us keep ours. I realized that's what they were looking for, those guys. And now *we* had it. I was scared. That's when I decided to change our names, too."

"And Joanne Fox?" Aidan asked. "Was that just a name you saw in the paper?"

She turned to him. "She was the same age as me."

"She was a runaway," he said, thinking out loud. "So you could assume her identity and no one would notice."

She nodded. "I even took on her social security number. It gave us a fresh start."

I bit my lip. "And my name?"

"And Willa, well, I just always liked the sound of it. I had a doll named Willa when I was a kid."

The fury boiled up inside me again, breaking through the haze of confusion. She named me after a freaking doll? She wasn't even my real mother. Who gave her the right to do that?

"It actually worked for a long time. I mean, I would move us every now and then—that was just to keep us safe," she said.

"And you told me it was because you were 'inspired,'" I said bitterly. "I can't believe I fell for that."

"I was trying to protect you! Do you think I was ready to be a parent? All I ever wanted was to give you the best opportunities. And I think I managed to give you a pretty normal upbringing despite it all."

Normal? Nothing she was saying was normal in the slightest. In fact, it all added up to the most deranged childhood I'd ever heard of. I couldn't help looking at her differently. Even if she was still related to me, this woman was a liar. And a thief.

Then, a voice in my head: *Maybe you come by it honestly after all.*

She kept on talking, even though I was no longer making eye contact. "I finally thought it was safe, that I could use the money to give you all you deserved. It was great for a while, wasn't it? I mean, we loved Paradise Valley, didn't we?" Her voice was almost pleading.

I didn't answer. Just let her question trail off and hang. There was no more "we" as far as I was concerned. Her despair—that was something I just couldn't deal with. Not right now.

I pulled my chair away from the table, and its legs dragged noisily on the floor.

Her lashes were wet with tears. "Willa, please believe me—"

"I've gotta go," I said.

She was on her feet, reaching for me. "Don't go—they could be out there!"

I didn't care. She couldn't control me anymore. As if pushed, I flung myself out through the screen door, banging it behind me, ignoring her calls.

It was cold outside and there was nowhere for me to go, really, but I felt like if I stood still I would vomit. Before I knew what I was doing, I broke into a run.

The rhythm of my feet and my breathing pulsed between my fevered thoughts. In all the time we'd been on the road trying to find her, I'd never once imagined this possibility. Of course it was one of those things that, once imagined, couldn't be unimagined.

My feet kicked up the dirt as I ran past the trailers.

It was too overwhelming. I'd come all this way only to find out that she wasn't who I thought she was. *I* wasn't who I thought I was.

Nothing would ever be the same for me—five minutes into this new reality, I knew that already.

I ran until I hit water. A river. I stopped, huddled over my knees, trying to catch my breath through sobs.

"Willa! Wait!" Aidan's voice carried behind me.

I turned around and he was there. Right there. I fell into his arms and sobbed. "I'm done, Aidan. It's over."

"No." He patted my hair. "We've come so far. Don't say that."

"I don't understand how this could be happening," I said through my crying. "You were in there, right? You heard it."

I wanted him to tell me I'd made a mistake, or that this was just a dream. I wanted an escape hatch.

"I know. I heard. And I can't imagine how you must be feeling right now."

"Well, I'm pissed," I said. "I mean, how could she do that to me?"

"Willa, I don't think she had anything but good intentions. Look, I'm sure if we go back in there, she can explain what was happening—"

"I can't go back in there," I said. "I just want to go home."

But even as I said it, I knew that home didn't really exist for me anymore. Not without her.

I didn't realize I was swaying until Aidan steadied me by putting his hands on my shoulders.

"Look," he said. "You have every reason to be upset right now. I mean, she basically just pulled the rug out from under you. But let's not do anything rash, okay? Let's not throw it all away. She needs you. They're still after her. We have to help her."

I gasped for air. "I can't, Aidan. How am I supposed to want to help her after all of that? She lied to me my whole life."

And then, I remembered. My mom—Leslie—wasn't the only one. I pulled away from him. "And what about you? You've lied to me, too."

His face didn't change exactly, but I saw his jaw tighten. "Never. I've never lied. Whatever you think about me, you need to believe that."

"But you haven't told me the truth. Isn't that the same thing?"

"No," he said. "I'm trying to protect you. That should count for something."

And that's what she was doing, wasn't it? Protecting me. *Look how that turned out*, I thought. "How can I trust you, or anyone else?"

Aidan shook his head. "You wanna know the best thing about trust? Either it's there or it isn't. That simple. It's not a partial sort of deal. You have to go with your gut."

I thought about this for a moment. In my gut, if I was

being honest with myself, I did trust Aidan.

But maybe my gut was twisted and confused. My gut didn't even know its own mother.

A chill ran through my body as it all hit me again. "My whole life is a lie."

"It's not, though," he said. "How she feels about you? That's real. I can see it in the way she looks at you. She might not be your real mother, but she is your parent, for all intents and purposes. She raised you, and she protected you. That's what good parents do."

I shook my head, and felt hot tears drop on my face as I looked out at the vast body of water in front of us. "She changed my name. She made me into someone I'm not."

"Do you really think that? It's just a name. Willa, you are who you are. And I don't think having your real name or even growing up with your real mother if you'd had the chance to would have changed any of that. At least, I hope it wouldn't have. I wouldn't want to see you be anyone else."

His green eyes cut into me, so that they were all I could see clearly beyond the clouding of my tears. He traced a small circle on my cheek with his finger.

Then he smiled. "Besides, Willa Fox is way cooler than Maggie Siebert. Especially for a butt-kicking criminal like yourself. I mean, she pretty much nailed it with the name choice."

I fixed my hair and wiped at my face, sniffing. "You think so?"

"Totally. Sly Siebert just doesn't have the same ring to it."

I laughed, despite myself.

"Should we see her now?" He took a step away and cocked his head in the direction of the trailer. "She's probably losing her mind in there, worrying."

I wanted to be suspicious. I wanted to protect myself. And yet his smile was so sweet and so convincing that I couldn't possibly turn away from it. I'd planned a lot of escapes by now, but this wasn't one I was prepared to make.

"Okay," I said. I took his hand and we walked back together.

TWENTY-THREE

LESLIE WAS WAITING for us in the doorway, arms crossed in front of her, gnawing on a knuckle. It reminded me of the first time I biked to school on my own, back when we lived in Washington State. I was twelve, the school was three miles away, and she had the same look on her face when I got home.

But if she or Aidan thought I was just going to forgive her and be all sweet and cuddly now, they were delusional.

"Thank goodness," she said. Her face was still lined with worry, but it was softer than it had been before. "Did anyone see you out there?"

"You mean your buddy Chet?" I said cruelly. "I don't think so."

She grimaced. "How do you know his name?"

"We've met him," I said. I wanted her to know that we'd done okay without her. And okay, maybe I wanted to shock her now, too. "Twice, actually. You're right, though. They're in the area. He and his right-hand man."

She reached over and took ahold of my shoulders. "Oh my God. Are you okay? Did he threaten you?"

I ducked away from her. "You left me. How could you leave me behind when that guy was after us, when he knew where we lived?"

"He was after me, though. Or so I thought." She threw up her hands. "I didn't know what to do, without turning myself in, and I had to think on my feet. I figured if I left, I'd draw all the trouble away from you, and let you have your new start without me, living with Cherise. I mean, it was all my fault I got us into this mess, so I thought with me gone—anyway, that was poor judgment. I realize it now. I was putting you at risk."

"Better late than never, right?" My eyes flashed at her. "Anyway, we're fine. We're here, aren't we?"

I knew I was being bitchy. Maybe Aidan was right. Maybe I needed to focus on what was real, not on what wasn't. Still, I couldn't help but feel distant from her, even as she acted momish. Or maybe because she was trying to. I couldn't help feeling betrayed.

"You're not fine. You're bleeding," she said, pointing to the leg of my jeans.

I shrugged. "It's probably dry by now. But Aidan's ankle is hurt."

"Let's fix you guys up."

She stepped away and brought back a first-aid kit.

We sat back down at the table and I washed off my cuts with an alcohol swab. She handed Aidan an Ace bandage and some ice. Then she gave me some Band-Aids. In the old days, she would've unwrapped them and stuck them on for me. Now I wouldn't let her get that close. I just took them out of her hand and put them on myself.

Things were going to be different for us from now on. She wasn't my mother. She could no longer tell me what to do. But I also couldn't take her for granted in quite the same way.

"How did you end up here, Leslie?" Aidan asked, breaking the silence. "You didn't tell us that part of the story."

"Back in Arizona, Agent Corbin started calling me— he was working on Mom's case and he'd tracked me down after I started spending that damn money. I didn't want to have anything to do with him—I was afraid. I thought he would take me in. But he wouldn't leave me alone. He wanted me to cooperate." She worriedly picked at her shirt. "I mean, I know he was trying to help. And then, with the whole Sly Fox thing, our house was on the news. I started getting calls from Chet, and I had to run."

"So Chet killed our mother," I said finally. "Is this whole thing all about the money?"

She nodded, pursing her lips together. "Yes, but it's personal, too. I think Mom and Chet had a thing, back in the day."

I shuddered. "That guy? He's so gross."

"I remember seeing him around the house some-times, before we moved. There was another guy, too. I really don't know a lot of the details, but I do know that the money is probably his."

Suddenly I had a million questions. "But how did you end up here?" I asked. "What was your plan?"

"I keep these lists of places, all the time. It's a habit, I guess, from all the years of moving. When I knew I had to leave Paradise Valley I tried to get you settled and then I took the money and hit the road. My strategy was to jump around. If you look on a map, it's not a straight line between stops—it's more like a knot."

Aidan and I knew this, of course, because we'd traced her route at least part of the way.

"So I started in California, but I always knew I was going to make my way up here. We visited the Painted Hills when you were really little, Willa. Do you remember?" She looked at me expectantly.

"I didn't," I said. "At least not until we went there yesterday. We saw your campsite."

"I figured I could camp there for a couple of nights and no one would bother me. No one's around much this time of year. Something spooked me, though—the other night I woke up in a sweat, sure that Chet was lurking around somewhere. I can't explain it. It was like an extrasensory thing. But I was freaked out."

I thought of my own nightmare, the millions of ways

we were still connected. "They were there. You were right. And this place was on the list, too, wasn't it?"

She nodded. "I always try to have a backup plan. So I just abandoned my tent and hiked back up to the road and caught a ride here. I'd seen a trailer for rent online. The woman is letting me pay cash on a day-to-day basis. It's been a good setup. But I obviously can't stay here—not after they've seen you." She ran a hand through her hair. "Look, we don't have much time. Those bastards won't give up until they get what they want. You guys need to turn yourselves in, and I need to get on the road again."

I crumpled up my bandage wrappers. "You can't keep running and hiding like this."

"Neither can you," she said, looking me in the eye.

"It's different," I said. "Our situation is different."

"How so? You're all over the news. Do you mean to tell me there *aren't* cops in four states looking for you right now? Don't think I haven't noticed. I've been in hiding but I can't escape seeing your face on every newspaper. I mean, leaving notes, Willa? That was insanely risky." Her voice had gone scolding again.

"We've got it under control," I muttered.

"Do you, though?"

We paused and stared at each other for a moment. Did I? I honestly had no idea.

Aidan broke the silence. "Leslie, you should know that we've talked to Agent Corbin. And he's looking for you, too."

"That guy. He just can't mind his own business, can he?" she said, allowing herself a little smile. Did she *like* him? "But it's not really him I'm worried about. It's Chet and that other guy."

"So *you* should turn yourself in," I said. "Then at least you'd be hidden away."

She waved away that suggestion. "It's not so easy. I committed a federal crime, impersonating a dead girl. There are major penalties for ghosting, not to mention the fact that I've been carrying around stolen money for all these years. Millions of dollars. Technically, that makes me a thief."

"But if a jury heard your story, they might sympathize with your situation. You weren't stealing; you were just trying to survive," Aidan reasoned. "And you were trying to protect your sister. That makes you likable."

Leslie clasped her hands in front of her as if in prayer. "Remember that we don't even really know where the money came from in the first place—it could be laundered. Mob money. Drug money. Whatever. It's definitely shady."

"But you didn't know that at the time," I insisted.

"It doesn't matter. I don't think a jury is going to understand why I held on to it. I'd be sent to prison for a decade at least. And those guys would wait for me. I mean, they've waited for me for fifteen years. No, it's run or nothing. It's run or die."

I had no doubt that the danger was as bad as she

imagined. I'd seen those guys up close, after all.

But a life of perpetual hiding sounded awful and lonely, not to mention difficult. I tried one last time. "I really think we should call the police—if we explain the situation . . ."

"Please don't, Willa," Leslie pleaded. "I beg you. I have this under control. I know how to stay underground. Look, it's not easy, but I've long ago given up on the idea that I will ever have a normal life or get married or settle down or anything like that. Don't feel sorry for me. I've come to terms with it. It was a sacrifice I made willingly."

I sank back into my seat, feeling truly exhausted by the situation. This was not how it was all supposed to go. We were supposed to find her and bring her back home with us. Go back to life the way it was before. And now it had gotten so much bigger, so much more complicated than I'd ever imagined.

"What are *we* supposed to do, then?" I asked. "Just let you disappear into the wilderness? We can't do that, Leslie." Saying her name still felt weird, too conspicuous to be normal.

"I have no choice. But just because I'm caught up in all of this doesn't mean you have to be." She turned to me and her eyes were glittering.

I felt my throat tighten. "We've skipped out on probation, stolen multiple vehicles, broken into places, trespassed. We both have records. They're going to lock us up."

"But you're young," she said. "Your sentence would be light—maybe a few months for each of you."

"And then what?" I couldn't imagine there being much of a life for me after that. "I couldn't go back to Prep. I'd have nowhere to live."

"You could go live with Cherise's family for a while, maybe start at the public school there. This is your chance, Willa. Don't you see? If you go back to Paradise Valley now, you could still have the life I dreamed for you. You could still go to college. Forget about me now." Her voice broke again.

She cared about me. I had to admit it. And she probably did just want the best for me, as I did for her.

I looked into her face. So familiar, and yet, different now. Or maybe it was just me that had changed. Maybe it had happened before today and I'd just never noticed.

No, I couldn't keep acting like I was her child. It was time for me to take control of the situation.

"Aidan," I asked. "Where's our phone?"

We were expecting the knock on the trailer door—just not so soon. Somehow, Corbin made it to us from his L.A. office in two hours. I guess FBI folks have their own special ways of avoiding traffic.

There he stood on the doorstep, in a black jacket over jeans. Plainclothes style. The last time I'd seen him was back in Tahoe, and that was when I nicked his files.

I'd never seen him this close up before. His face was

scruffy, like he hadn't shaven in days. He was definitely nice-looking, for a bothersome authority-figure type of person.

"Willa," he said, narrowing his eyes at me. "Long time no see."

I shook his hand. "Hello, Agent Corbin."

"Can I come in? You're not going to break into my car, are you?" He gave me a wry sort of smile.

"Be my guest," I said, a little freaked out that I was inviting the FBI in past the threshold. It was like asking a vampire inside—anything could happen and once it did, it could not be undone. "And no. You're safe."

"Leslie," he said, making a beeline for her. "You're okay?"

And then he *hugged* her.

Aidan and I exchanged looks. My suspicions had proven correct. Corbin had more than a passing professional interest in my sister. And that could only be useful for all of us.

"The last time I saw you . . ."

". . . was in that restaurant in Phoenix. I know. I blew you off. I'm sorry. I knew they were closing in. I was afraid, Jeremy." She looked up at him in a way I never saw her look at anybody. "I'm glad you're here. But we don't have much time."

"Right," he said. And to me, "You said something on the phone about an arrangement?"

"We need your help," I said. "We need to kill her off."

"I can assist you with that," he said, interlacing his

309

fingers and then pointing the steeple at me and Aidan. "As long as you promise that you two will come back to L.A. with me and turn yourselves in. Like we discussed a few days ago, yeah?"

I looked at Aidan and he heaved his shoulders, signaling that he understood. That we were out of options. That we would rather do anything but that, but he had us cornered. That this was our best hope of helping Leslie and getting home in one piece.

"Deal," I said, shaking his hand.

And so we set about killing Joanne Fox. For the second time.

Late at night, when the work was almost done, Leslie and Aidan went to lie down for a couple of hours—Leslie on the bed, and Aidan on the floor. Corbin and I were standing guard, sitting at the trailer's little table, drinking coffee.

We sat in silence mostly, which was interrupted every so often by the sound of sipping.

Finally I spoke up. "So you knew all along that she was my sister?"

He nodded.

"Is that why you didn't tell me what was really going on? You wanted her to be the one to tell me?"

"Yes and no. I didn't want to be the one to break the news, no. But I was also trying to protect you both, and I still am."

"Why are you helping us?"

"Why?" He looked at me, his blue eyes surprisingly clear and bright under his heavy eyebrows and lined forehead. "Because I got this case my first day on the job and I was always haunted by the murdered woman and her missing children. And because people make mistakes, Willa. You know that as well as anyone. She was sixteen years old. She didn't know what she was getting herself into—she didn't know that it would have all of these repercussions. No matter what they tell you, it's not always black and white. I'm a cop but it doesn't mean I don't recognize that. Most of all, though, because I care, okay? I want her to have another chance to find happiness, and until we set her free from all of this, I don't think there's any way for that to happen."

He stared at me, challenging, and I could read a hundred different feelings in his face, a hundred different scenarios he'd seen, and a hundred different choices he'd made in his career in law enforcement—disappointments, errors, lost causes. And yet, about this decision, he seemed absolutely sure.

"So does that answer your question?"

I set down my mug. "Yes."

TWENTY-FOUR

IT WASN'T QUITE morning when we stood at the doorway, all four of us. Corbin hugged Leslie good-bye. "This is going to be fine," he said.

"I hope so," she said, under the press of his shoulder.

"You know where to find me if you need me," he said. He kissed her on the top of her head.

I could have sworn I saw her blush.

It was all arranged. The only thing left to do now was for us to say good-bye, too, like we'd planned.

Leslie clasped her hands in front of her. "Well, this is it, right?"

"Yeah. Are you ready?"

"I think so." She heaved a sigh. "It might be a long time before I see you next."

"I know." I swallowed hard. There would be no contact and no visits, not now and maybe not ever.

"Willa, these past few months have been really hard.

For both of us. We've both made decisions we probably regret, but I know we were both just trying to do what we thought was best. Just don't ever, ever forget that I love you."

I stared at her and felt the full weight of all she had done, all this time, to take care of me. And in her unflinching hazel eyes, I saw what I knew was recognition: She understood that by skipping town, risking my life, I had done the same for her. We had both made sacrifices. Willingly. For each other. We had both done the wrong thing in order to do what we thought was right.

And then, for a moment, I could see a flash of the woman I thought I knew. The woman I'd always thought of as my mom.

Mom. The word was still in the back of my throat.

"I—" A sob engulfed me, sending tremors through my lips and cheeks.

"It's okay. Just be careful. Just promise me that."

We embraced. Her hair brushed against my cheek, her tears dropped on my shoulder, and I could feel her tiny bones compressed against muscle.

How could I let her go? After all this time looking for her, how could I just walk away?

There were so many things I wanted to say, but I would have had to learn a new language to say them. And of course, there wasn't time.

I gave her back the windbreaker and then took a mental picture of her standing there, wearing it, smiling at me through her tears. Joanne, Leslie.

We gathered what was left of our things and stepped further out into what remained of the night. A bit of light was rippling through the sky now, tracing the water's surface with brassy filaments.

The cab we called pulled up. The driver was waiting.

She got into the backseat, waving. Then the car pulled away and she disappeared into the bleached darkness, the car trailing blurry lights as it scrawled a path on the unpaved road.

"You two wait for me in there," Corbin said, motioning to his Nissan.

We did as he asked, sliding into our respective positions, me on the driver's side, Aidan on the passenger side. My body was tensed up, coiled with energy, and he noticed. . . .

"We're not really doing this, are we?" Aidan whispered, casting me a glance.

By now he had to have known that I wasn't the type of person to let things lie. I needed more answers. Leslie's words still reverberated in my head. I wanted to do what was right. I really did. In this case, though, the right thing meant accepting never knowing, and that wasn't something I could ever do. "No," I whispered back.

I watched from the side mirrors as Corbin slipped inside the trailer. He was lighting the match to the wick we'd taped to the floor. This was it.

Aidan and I looked at each other again, the

understanding of all that was about to happen passing silently between us, and in a flash we were out of the car, dashing into the woods. By the time we were at the river's edge, the flame had reached the kerosene heater.

When it went, the blast was like nothing I'd ever heard. The sheer force of the sound rattled in my chest. I couldn't help but look behind us.

The fire rose up in the sky, raging orange and black.

And then I saw something small and white flying through the air. Leslie's sneaker. The one I'd seen by the door.

I covered my mouth as the bile rose in my throat.

"She's okay," Aidan assured me, hurrying me into the boat. "She got out of there, Willa. We saw her go."

I knew this to be true logically. But it didn't make it any easier. I just couldn't shake the feeling that we'd made a terrible mistake.

I could hear Corbin yelling after us, too, but his voice was barely audible over the roar of the fire.

"C'mon. We have to move."

We dipped the paddles in the water in a steady rhythm, propelling the boat forward as we made our way south. The river twisted and turned, the scenery changed, but I was stuck in my own head. I couldn't stop thinking about it. About what we'd done. About this new gamble we were taking. About all that I had just lost.

• • •

It took most of the day to row down the river and hitch another ride to Bend.

The bus depot was nothing more than a small waiting room connected to a bowling alley. Aidan and I walked in and stood in front of the ticket counter, which was a desk. Even though it was separated by a wall, we could hear the thunderous rumbling of balls spinning down the lanes. Then, the clattering of falling pins, echoing.

Aidan grabbed some schedules and I sat down on a slatted bench. I unrolled the cuffs of my jeans, which were still damp from the boat. As were my socks and shoes. I was probably going to get pneumonia. Today felt like a new low. We'd really scraped the bottom of the barrel as far as fugitive life went.

But we are here, I had to remind myself. We'd pulled off the plan. Yet another plan. We'd dodged jail. At the moment, it felt like a hollow sort of victory.

There were only a handful of other travelers in there with us: an older woman with a backpack; a twenty-something guy with a suitcase; and a mother with two young kids. I didn't know any of their stories, but none of them, I was willing to bet, had traveled as far as we had.

Aidan came back to where I was sitting and studied the pamphlets. "The bus to St. Louis takes about two days. If you're sure that's what you want."

"I am sure. I need to know what happened. What really happened. To my real mother."

He still looked skeptical. "So now what? You'll just stay in hiding?"

I nodded. "I know it sounds crazy."

"Yeah, it does." He sat down next to me on the bench. "Dude, you're probably the craziest person I've ever met. And that's including me."

I tried to explain myself, my line of thinking. "I know it's risky. I figure this is my only hope of doing this, if I leave now, while we're already on the run."

He stared at me, hard. "You're really pushing your luck, Willa."

"Maybe so," I said. It didn't exactly feel like luck anymore. I'd just lost my entire family—what little I'd had in the first place.

His brow was furrowed, as if he was still mulling it over. I'd pretty much prepared myself for the possibility that I would be making this journey alone. Aidan didn't want to go to jail, I knew that. He would probably just stay on the run, go somewhere far away.

I was already feeling anxious about him leaving, about being away from him for any amount of time, but I knew there was no way I could expect him to put himself on the line. Again.

"You do understand the danger you're in, right? Those two dudes are still out there looking for you, and that's a whole hornet's nest you'd be stirring, trying to bring up the past. You know that they're not going to be happy about that."

"Screw those guys," I said. "They're thugs. I'm not afraid of them." This, of course, was a gigantic lie. They were killers and they freaking terrified me.

"Fine. But you're also crossing the FBI, the only guy who has really helped us."

"I know," I said. And I thought of Corbin. Sure, he was annoying but he'd come through in the end. He could've just taken us in right then and there. He should have. But he'd done us a favor. And we'd taken advantage of him.

It bugged me. Other than Leslie, there had been so few adults in my life who took an interest, who really tried to protect me. I was an orphan, after all. And now doubly so, if you counted the fake death of a fake mother. Corbin deserved better.

"I think he's going to start playing hardball."

"True." But Corbin had been the one to say it, hadn't he? That it wasn't just a matter of black and white. "He should've known I had another score to settle. That his plan would never be my plan."

"Make that *our*," Aidan said.

"Excuse me?"

"Our plan."

I eyed him sidelong and gave him a hesitant smile. "Does this mean what I think it means?"

"That I'm getting sucked into yet another one of your outlandish adventures?" He closed his eyes and nodded. "That I'm in it to win it? Yes. Yes, it does."

"Are you sure?" I held up a hand. "Don't just do this

because you feel pressure to stay and help me. Because I'd totally understand if you wanted to go your own way."

"Don't give me that understanding crap. You couldn't get rid of me if you tried."

Relief settled over me, cool and soothing. I realized that there was nothing I wanted more than for Aidan to stay with me.

We sat there, on the bench in the middle of the depot, smiling at each other like two fools. Two fools about to do something really, really stupid.

Oh well. At least we'd be together.

He raised an invisible roof. "St. Louis, here we come. It's going to be a long-ass bus ride."

"Better than boat travel," I said, thinking of the pitiful canoe.

He leaned over and picked up an abandoned newspaper next to him. "I guess I'll take along some reading." His eyes caught on something and a smile broke out over his face. "No way."

"What?" I asked.

He held up the cover for me to see. It was a *National Enquirer*. There was a picture of Sam Beasley on the cover. Wearing a Sly Fox Rules T-shirt and holding up a piece of paper. My note.

The headline: *Actor Sam Beasley Visited by Teen Outlaws*.

Holy freaking crap.

"We've got friends in high places now." He winked. "Well, I guess I'll go buy our tickets."

When he got up I dug out our temporary cell phone and called Tre's number. I hadn't spoken to him since the truck incident and I was worried he was in jail or worse.

"Willa!" he said, picking it up after the second ring. "Where are you?"

"I'm at the bus depot in Bend, Oregon. Where are you?"

"Home."

"You made it past the roadblock? How'd you do it?"

He sighed. "That's a long story."

"So you're okay? Is Cherise okay?"

"Yeah, yeah. We're fine. Free as birds. What are you doing? Did you find your mom yet?"

"Yes," I said, taking a deep breath and feeling my chest sink as I let it go. "We found her. But she's not actually my mom. I can explain it more when I see you."

"Whoa," he said. "That sounds deep. How are you?"

"Honestly? My world is pretty much exploding, but I'm hanging in there."

"So are you coming home? Do you want us to meet you anywhere?"

"We're going to stay on the road a little bit longer. There's some other information I need to find out. About my real family."

I could practically hear him shaking his head. "You just don't know when to quit, do you?"

"Look, I need a couple more weeks. A month, tops.

Do you think you can help us with the page and everything? And with some cash? We're going to St. Louis next."

"I really wish you wouldn't. This is getting crazy now. And I'm worried." He paused, and I hung on, waiting for the comforting sound of his voice again. He sighed. "But I know I can't stop you. And you know I'll do whatever I can to help you out."

"You're the best, Tre. I'll call you when we get there."

"Okay. But, Willa—one more thing. I forgot to mention it the other day. We found your bike."

My bike! It survived! I went giddy at the thought of it. "You found it? Where was it? How is it?"

"It was left on the side of the road. I was driving by the other day and I saw it there." He laughed. "Couldn't really mistake it. No other bike like it. It's a little mangled and dirty, but I think I can get it cleaned up for you."

I was floored with gratitude.

So I hadn't lost everything after all. I had my bike, and I had my friends. And Aidan, too. I could see him sliding money across the ticket desk. Preparing us for the next leg of our journey.

"You know what this means, right?"

"What?" he asked.

I smiled. "I'm coming back to Paradise Valley. It might not be for a while but just you wait."

"Don't worry," Tre said. "We'll be ready for you."

EPILOGUE

"WILLA."

Nudge.

"Willa, are you awake?"

I felt Aidan's elbow on my ribs and I opened my eyes. It was almost fully dark inside the bus from our seats on up to the driver. All was quiet except for the vague sound of music muffled by headphones, some soft snoring here and there, and the steady scrape of the wheels on the road.

I wasn't, in fact, awake at all. I'd fallen into some weird style of sleeping, my knees crunched up against my chest, my head resting on the cool, fogged-over window. But it was unconsciousness nonetheless.

"What is it?" I rasped, rubbing at my face. "Did we miss our stop?"

"No," Aidan said. "I can't sleep."

"What's wrong?" I asked.

"Just, I realized something."

"About . . . ?" I was still groggy, my brain smudged in dreams.

"About us. I'm taking a risk by coming with you. Probably a bigger one than before, even."

I sat up in my seat, straightening my limbs, a little alarmed now and unsure what he was getting at. Was he changing his mind? Was he going to get off at the next stop?

"And?"

"And, so, I hope you can do the same thing—I mean, go with it. We only have each other out here."

This again. "What you're saying is that you still can't tell me what happened."

"I don't want you to think it's anything personal. It's just . . . complicated."

"You're asking me to take a leap of faith."

"That's what trust is, right? Sometimes people just need their space. Sometimes people have their reasons."

"Yeah," I said, thinking of Leslie. Of Tre and what he'd told me about Aidan's legal agreement. Of all of our own deceptions. We hadn't meant to hurt anyone. "Maybe so. The truth is rarely pure and never simple. Isn't that what you said?"

"I didn't say it. Oscar Wilde did." He grinned. "But very good, Willa-san."

"If anything, I should be Miyagi-ing you right now. After all that stuff I taught you?"

"True. You did teach me well. The motorcycle was pretty good, wasn't it?"

"Your finest work." I reached into my pocket, remembering, and pulled out the caramel he'd given me. "It's a little smashed up, but do you want to split it?"

I broke it in half. He took his part and popped it into his mouth. I ate mine, savoring its deliciousness. Sweet and salty—Aidan was definitely on to something.

We were quiet for a moment, chewing.

"Tomorrow's Thanksgiving, you know," he said. "We should celebrate."

"How?" I asked.

He looked at me, open and questioning, like he was searching my face for an answer. Like he was waiting for some kind of invitation.

This time I wasn't going to wait for him. It was all me. I angled my head and leaned across the seat toward him. He met me halfway and our lips pressed together. The skin on my neck tingled as he traced his fingers along the back of my head and behind my ears. I felt myself melt into him and the kiss grew more forceful, more feverish.

It was like we'd been looking at a painting from a distance and now we were right up against it, seeing every last detail in a new way. It was stunning, and breathtaking. And a little scary, too.

After a few moments we pulled away but we were still locked in each other's arms. I felt the warmth of him, the specific imprint of his breath and touch on my skin.

And then my picture grew wider. I thought of Leslie, who was hopefully closing in on Mexico by now. And beyond her, the family that I knew nothing about. The stark, frightening emptiness of my own canvas, which had just been wiped clean.

I rested my head against Aidan's chest. Directly in front of us, the road stretched out, long and straight, illuminated only by the headlights as they swept over it. We, in the back, were pressed together as the bus hurtled forward into the darkness.

ACKNOWLEDGMENTS

SOME NOT-SO-SLY THANK-YOUS: First and foremost, Willa Fox would not have gotten off the couch, much less across state lines, were it not for Claudia Gabel's brilliance, patience, and encouragement; Melissa Miller's savvy edits and eye for detail; and Katherine Tegen's vision and loveliness. I'm so proud to be part of your fine imprint.

Thank you to my agent, Leigh Feldman, whose constant, fierce support has become a pillar in my life. Big thanks to the rest of the team at HarperCollins, including editorial assistant Katie Bignell, marketing mavens Megan Sugrue and Lauren Flowers, and publicist Casey McIntyre—clever and delightful collaborators, one and all—plus Joel Tippie, Amy Ryan, Howard Huang, Tom Forget, Laura Lyn DiSiena, Cara Petrus, and Barb Fitzsimmons for delivering a cover that once again stuns with its fabulosity.

Huge love to The Apocalypsies, my fellow 2012 debut authors, for their kindness, counsel, Thursday-night chats, and tweetage. A secret writers' handshake and a hug to the Philly chapter: K. M. Walton, Eve Marie Mont, Tiffany Schmidt, and E. C. Myers. And another big squeeze to Diana Renn, Laura White Handy, Kristen Kittscher, Talia Vance, W. H. Beck, Trisha Wolfe, Cole Gibsen, Lynne Kelly, Karen Abbott, and the KidLit Authors Club—wonderful writers, wonderful people. Could I take a moment, too, to thank the blogosphere? Because the amazing dedication of book bloggers has blown me away time and time again.

I'm so very lucky to have a family whose loyalty is very nearly biker gang–ish, minus the blood oaths and tats. Thank you to my father, Stephen, for loving Willa and offering ingenious plot twists and marketing ideas, and to my mother, Zella, for keeping me calm, offering daily reinforcement, and bravely approaching teens in B&N to pimp my books. To my sister Aubrey and her husband, Jared, for reading this book in small, stolen snatches of office paper (Willa would totally appreciate this) and for being awesome in general. To my sister Susannah, for her creative intuition, professional experience, and always-right gut instincts. To the love of my life, Jesse, who keeps me grounded, reminds me what matters, and makes me swoon daily. Finally, a pâté-flavored thank-you to my late cat, Beau, for his snuggles.

Willa Fox promised to turn herself in.
But you can't take a thief at her word . . .

Turn the page for a sneak peek at how
her exciting adventure concludes in

PROLOGUE

"RUN!"

Aidan and I darted through the maze of bleeping machines, dodging the mindless drone-type people attached to them. Our mirrored selves moved in my peripheral vision, silver flashes amid the blinking lights and too-bright colors. To anyone else, maybe, we were just part of the shiny casino décor.

We followed the patterned carpet out into the hallway where it seemed to stretch out into infinity. Past the dimly lit bar area, smelling of ancient smoke. Past the gift shop with its decks of souvenir cards and ashtrays and fuzzy dice. Past the change station with its yellow plastic buckets of tokens.

My heartbeat egged me on, a steady drumming. Legs, arms, lungs moving together in an orchestra of fear and adrenaline.

And my brain, churning. I thought of all we had

learned so far, and what we still needed to find out. There were some clues by now, but too many unanswered questions. That was what kept me going. No matter how hard things got, I couldn't forget what I'd come here for—to uncover the truth.

"Look out! Heads up!" Aidan called out as a man wheeled a metal cart in front of him. Aidan's reflexes were quicker than mine as he lurched to the right and re-upped his speed. But I paused, feet jamming on the floor.

Big mistake.

A hand grabbed my shoulder.

I shuddered as I turned around, expecting to come face-to-face with the man who'd tried to kill us.

But when I looked up, I saw that the hand belonged to a security guard, a tall acne-faced guy in a pale blue uniform.

"Miss, can I see some ID?"

Bailey was after us. So were the police and an angry FBI agent in California, not to mention the general public, who'd seen our police sketches on the evening news. Now was not the time to stop.

"Sorry," I called back over my shoulder, ducking out of the way.

He shouted something but I hurled myself onward, ignoring him, and followed Aidan through the entrance to the Rock 'n' Steaks restaurant.

We tore past the hostess stand and the people waiting

in line. Then the waiters and tables, the giant guitars. An Elvis statue and a mannequin dressed like Katy Perry and a buffet spread of green things and brown things.

"Excuse me," I called out repeatedly to the customers, not wanting to be rude. Sure, we were interrupting their prime rib platters like the two derelicts on the lam that we were but at least we could be, you know, polite about it.

The side exit dumped us onto the dock in the middle of the river. The sky was darkening now, and I was trying to get a hold on where we were, where we would go. We had to get back on solid ground, back to where the road was.

"This way," I called to Aidan, angling us around the outside of the boat toward the front entrance.

Our feet pounded the wooden boards and we flew down the ramp toward the parking lot. I had a stitch in my side and my head throbbed, but there wasn't a fragment of a second to lose now, certainly not enough time to get our stolen car back from the valet. We'd abandon the wheels and go by foot.

The lights of the city were just flicking on, cars turning on their headlamps to forge through the purple dusk. I could make out Aidan ahead of me as we scrambled up the steps to the pedestrian walkway of an old railroad bridge. There was still shouting, sounds of running behind us. I couldn't say how close.

We kept on running while two lanes of traffic rushed

by in each direction, the Mississippi seething brown and frothy far below our feet. We were crossing back into Missouri and the Gateway Arch loomed ahead of us, lit up by strategic spotlights. Like a reassuring smile. Or a mocking one, depending on your frame of mind. Mine was, needless to say, a little bit bugged out.

I'd made mistakes. I'd taken chances. But I'd done it out of love, and that had to count for something, right? I only knew one thing and it was this fact that kept me going: We had to get there, before he got to us.

ONE

AS WE ROLLED forward, I flitted in and out of the dream. Me and Leslie, racing our bikes. In this imaginary world we were the same age—maybe eight or nine—going around and around a dead end in a suburban neighborhood. New Mexico, maybe? Or Washington State? I couldn't place it. All I could see was the pavement, sparkling through the spokes of my wheels, and Leslie's blond head bobbing in front of me. We were singing a child's taunt: *They can't catch us. They can't catch us.*

Then she stopped short.

Mom's calling, Leslie said.

I looked up and saw what could only be a bullet, metal glinting against the white sky, the body of it twisting in excruciatingly slow motion, coming for me.

Look out!

I startled awake, gasping. A scream caught in my throat.

"Willa? Are you okay?"

I nodded. It was a dream, I knew that. Yet the pain on my brow was real. The driver must have hit a bump; my head must have hit the window.

"Damn," I said, rubbing it. Sensation flooded my body as the reality came back in bits and pieces. The bus. Aidan next to me.

"You had a nasty bang-up there."

"Yeah. I startled myself," I said. What I didn't say was that the dream was worse than the hit. The dream chilled me to my bones, and I wanted it gone from my mind. "Where are we?"

"Almost to St. Louis. We just crossed the Missouri," he said.

Sure enough, the brown-and-green strips of farms had given way to office buildings and shopping centers. A little later, the city skyline appeared on the horizon, silvery and ghostlike, the famous Arch cupping it protectively. It was a welcome vision, a relief. We were here, finally.

We limped out into the fluorescent light of the Greyhound station on a Monday afternoon, the noisy, low-ceilinged den filled with people and their sprawled baggage. It was a thirty-six-hour bus ride from Bend, Oregon, or it would have been except that we got off at Boise, Idaho, and spent a few days lying low, waiting for the media firestorm to die down. This included Thanksgiving in a diner, eating open-faced turkey sandwiches.

Which, believe it or not, was not as depressing as it sounds.

Thanksgiving was rolling into Christmas as it's wont to do, and the new holiday was already here, it seemed, hanging from the green boughs strung up all over the depot. There were also cardboard strings of dreidels, even red, green, and black flags that said HAPPY KWAN-ZAA. It was time for inflatable, lawn-sized snow globes, peppermint everything, sugar binges, and forgetting grudges.

I welcomed the cheery atmosphere, especially after this last leg of the journey, a full seventeen hours. My knees had forgotten how to straighten, and my whole body felt sore and battered. That wasn't even counting the bruises and aches we'd both acquired while running away from the cops and the thugs that were trying to kill the woman I'd always thought was my mother but who, as it turned out, was actually my sister.

Let's put it this way: It had been a rough few days. Add to that my constant fear that everyone we saw was looking at us funny, and I was in quite the jacked-up state.

Still, I couldn't help but feel a little more hopeful in a new place. On the way out, I grabbed a city map from the tourism and information desk. Neither of us had been to this city before and that added to the sense of possibility and excitement.

Then we put on our sunglasses, adjusted our hats—all

part of the disguises we'd picked up at the last stop in Denver—and stepped out into the cold air. I was already rocking the hideous dye job I'd given myself at Sam Beasley's house in Santa Barbara, California, a few days back. (Yes, *the* Hollywood star Sam Beasley, and no, we did not get to meet him, because, well, we'd broken into his house and squatted there overnight.)

Aidan pinched the thrifted, baggy, boy jeans that were hanging off my hip bones. "Anyone ever tell you that you look sexy when you're undercover?"

My heart lifted and shimmied, like one of those inflatable men outside of a car dealership. No, nobody had ever said that to me. Sure, I'd never been on the run before, but I'd also never really had a boyfriend, either.

"You don't look so bad yourself," I said, appraising his hunter-green down vest, the now-shaggy blond hair falling across the broad planes of his face and some newly acquired stubble. Even thirty-six hours on a bus and countless days on the road before that could not diminish his charms. He was a hottie. It was his essential nature, like birds and flying, or the sun and rising. Just something he did very, very well without trying.

Aidan held up a plastic-wrapped wedge we'd picked up somewhere along the way. Boise? Laramie? "We've got half a roast beef left. Want some?"

He took a few bites and handed the sandwich to me, which I gobbled gratefully as we walked, even though it was soggy and the bread was now infused with the chemical flavor of its packaging. "Can I just say that you're awesome?"

He put his arm around me. "You don't have to say it."

"I do, though. How many guys would put up with this?" By "this," I meant the life on the run, the danger, the crappy food, the questionable fashion.

His green eyes locked on mine. "Since you come along with it, I'd say it's a pretty good deal. Besides, I kind of like the excitement." That part I already knew. He outperformed everyone, even me, in the danger junkie Olympics.

I melted into the crook of his elbow. At least I had Aidan. After she'd disappeared, we'd spent days searching for my sister, Leslie—it was still weird to even think of her as my sister and to call her "Leslie" when I'd always known her as Joanne/Mom. It was when we'd finally found her that she'd dropped the bomb about who she really was. She was on the run, too, and now, with the help of FBI Agent Jeremy Corbin, we'd "killed" her off and she was on her way to Mexico. I'd probably never see her again.

I'd lost everything—I had no structure, no semblance of real life, nothing else to keep me tethered to any kind of sanity, but I had Aidan. We'd gone through some rough patches, and he still harbored secrets—namely why he'd gotten kicked out of school and why some skank named Sheila was sexting him. I'd chosen to look beyond that, though, because I couldn't have done any of this without him. And because I had a major case of the lovins.

We were salty and sweet—together a perfect combination, like a caramel, which was our inside joke. If he was still a mystery to me in some ways, well, that made him all the more alluring.

"Think Corbin knows where we are yet?"

I shrugged. Corbin was supposed to take us into FBI custody, and we should have been back in Paradise Valley awaiting trial. But we'd skipped out on him. "Maybe. I hope not."

Not that it mattered. We were going to have to proceed with our plan either way. I knew I couldn't keep running forever, but I was going to do this thing, find out who my real mom was, while I still could.

We crossed the street and a man in a knockoff Burberry overcoat passed us, holding my gaze for what felt like a long time. Panic shot through me like an electric shock. Did he see us? Did he recognize us? Was he a cop? Or was he working for Chet and Bailey?

No, I told myself. He was just some guy. Maybe he was admiring Aidan's vest or he recognized someone behind us. There was careful, and there was complete paranoia. *Get a grip, Willa.*

Besides, we were better off here than we'd been in all those small towns in California. In a big city, we could find resources more easily and duck into a crowd if we needed to. Surely, the people of St. Louis weren't looking for us when they had their own criminals to worry about. This was one of the murder capitals of the United States, wasn't it? I smiled to myself, mostly at the twisted fact that being in a murder capital could be so comforting.

Then I remembered that my real mom had been murdered. She was one of those statistics. The smile was replaced by a sudden bout of nausea.

"I see coffee," Aidan rasped, extending his arms out like a caffeine-deprived zombie in the direction of the nearest green sign.

"That's a Starbucks," I said, trying to shake off the icky feelings. "Out of our budget."

Our cash was limited—we had three hundred dollars our friend Tre and a network of supporters had given us. We'd used most of it on the bus tickets and we couldn't use credit cards, not unless we wanted to be traced. (We also had our phones from home, but we couldn't use them, either; they were secured in a GPS-free off position while we relied on a temp phone I'd bought in Tahoe.) I was pretty sure that Aidan, son of a high-tech CEO, had never heard the word *budget* in his life, let alone observed one. So it was up to me to be the guardian of spendage.

"You're killing me, Colorado," Aidan said, using the pet name he'd given me when we met at the beginning of the school year, because I'd moved to Paradise Valley from Castle Pines.

That was all before my life had spun out of control.

Where my mom was my mom, where there were no secrets (that I knew of), where I was a regular teenager without so much as a mailbox-whacking on my record.

Aidan was still looking at me like my pupils were double espressos. He showed me his shaky hands. "C'mon. Help a brother out."

What could I say? A four-dollar latte was out of the question. I scanned the blocks ahead for other options. "There's a 7-Eleven across the street. Go in there. I'll wait out here and look at the map."

He disappeared through the hot dog–decaled doors, leaving me outside as I tried to orient us to our new surroundings. I could see where we were. Olive Street. I just needed to figure out where we were going.

As I trailed over the page, scanning landmarks and unfamiliar names, a moving smear of white and blue caught in the corner of my eye. I looked up.

Cops.

My pulse skipped over itself.

Two cop cars, actually. City police. Now in the parking lot. A few feet away from where I stood.

They were probably here for donuts, right?

Except, I remembered, it was late afternoon.

I cast a tentative glance over and saw an officer sitting in the front seat of the car closest to me, talking into a radio. Looking actively involved in police business of some kind. Like he could be reporting something suspicious. Me?

No. No way. No.

When Aidan emerged, carrying a brown paper bag and two cups of coffee, I grabbed his elbow and steered him away from the store parking lot.

"We need to move," I said through gritted teeth.

"Five-oh at four o'clock," he said.

"Right."

We walked a few paces hurriedly. Then I saw a third police car, coming toward us in the opposite direction. It seemed to slow down as it neared.

Oh shiz. I was tempted to break into a run.

"Act natural," Aidan said, holding me back with his firm tone. "We're just walking."

There was nothing natural about it. We were wanted. I'd imagined the scenario too many times to count, when and how I'd be dragged back to juvie. The place I swore I'd never end up again. The place where everything seemed to veer offtrack.

If I hadn't been caught stealing stuff and trying to help the kids in my school, I wouldn't have been on TV. And if I'd never been on TV, those guys would never have found Leslie and gone after her. She and I would still be together. But then, I never would've learned about my real mom, either.

The police car was almost in line with us. We had only a minute, a minute and a half, maybe, before they caught up and dragged us away. My heartbeat raged through every artery and vein. My eyes darted around, looking for an escape hatch. On our right was a big granite building fronted with marble-relief panels, the bulk of the thing taking up most of a block. On our left was just a park. No cover at all.

Think, Willa.

If I didn't find something quick, I'd never find out who my mother was. If I couldn't figure this out, it was all over, before it had even begun.

BONNIE and CLYDE?
Try WILLA and AIDAN.

"A pretty twisted, modern-day Robin Hood story."
—Melissa de la Cruz, *New York Times* bestselling author

JOIN THE
Epic Reads
COMMUNITY

THE ULTIMATE YA DESTINATION

◄ DISCOVER ►
your next favorite read

◄ FIND ►
new authors to love

◄ WIN ►
free books

◄ SHARE ►
infographics, playlists, quizzes, and more

◄ WATCH ►
the latest videos

◄ TUNE IN ►
to Tea Time with Team Epic Reads

   Find us at **www.epicreads.com**
and **@epicreads**